The Dirt Chronicles

ARSENAL PULP PRESS | VANCOUVER

Kristyn Dunnion

ARSENAL PULP PRESS
#101-211 East Georgia St.
Vancouver, BC
Canada V6A 1Z6
arsenalpulp.com

The publisher gratefully acknowledges the support of the Canada Council for the Arts and the British Columbia Arts Council for its publishing program, and the Government of Canada through the Canada Book Fund and the Government of British Columbia through the Book Publishing Tax Credit Program for its publishing activities.

Efforts have been made to locate copyright holders of source material wherever possible. The publisher welcomes hearing from any copyright holders of material used in this book who have not been contacted.

Lyrics reprinted with permission:
"Black Iron Heart" written and composed by A Storm of Light. "Object, Refuse, Reject Abuse" and "Deaf, Dumb and Male" written and composed by DIRT.

"In The Air Tonight," Words & Music by Phil Collins, © Copyright 1981 Philip Collins Limited. Imagem Music. All Rights Reserved. International Copyright Secured. Used by permission of Music Sales Limited.

An earlier draft of "Stargazing at Eddie's" was published by *Fab* 310, December 2006. An excerpt from "Ferret Hunt" was published in *Winterplay! Pinkplaymags*, December 2009.

This is a work of fiction. Any resemblance of characters to persons either living or deceased is purely coincidental.

Book design by Shyla Seller
Editing by Susan Safyan
Author photograph by Jamie Carlisle
Cover photography by Lachlan Black, *www.flickr.com/photos/thebadseed/*

Printed and bound in Canada

Library and Archives Canada Cataloguing in Publication:

Dunnion, Kristyn, 1969-
    The dirt chronicles / Kristyn Dunnion.

Issued also in electronic format.
ISBN 978-1-55152-426-9

    I. Title.

PS8557.U552D57 2011   C813'.6   C2011-903323-2

MIX
Paper from
responsible sources
FSC® C103214

ACKNOWLEDGMENTS

This book is dedicated to the kids.

In loving memory of Will Munro (1975–2010), pied punk piper who brought us all together, and Elizabeth "Luscious" Baxter (1978–2010), who fed us her generous, incomparable love.

Thank you to Carolyn Beck, Anne Laurel Carter, Anna Kerz, Shannon Quinn, and Cheryl Rainfield, who gave tremendous encouragement and critiqued earlier drafts. Thank you to Greg Hawkes, Annie Ouellette, and Annetta and Patrick Dunnion for consultation on vital matters. To Cherish Violet Blood and Tammy Manitowabe who first brought me to Wiky on the Red Pepper Arts Spectacle bus. To John MacDonald, for keeping it real.

The author gratefully acknowledges the Toronto Arts Council and the Ontario Arts Council for financial support.

CONTENTS

Migrant

(for Patrick)

You can blame me for coming up with the plan. But it wasn't so much *forcible confinement* or *abduction* like the papers said. Hell, I rescued this kid from a life of hard labour and petty disappointment. He was born in the wrong place at the wrong time and, frankly, I consider it an act of man-love solidarity, like assisted suicide.

I'd nursed a wicked hangover all day and was finally heading home in the Coupe, sipping a premixed Caesar I kept tucked between my legs. Folks out to see the lake on a Sunday drive, maybe get an ice cream down at the docks, they'd seen my hand-painted sign: Larry's Putt Putt Mini-golf come to slap down their money, have a game with the kids. Sadists, if they knew how little I wanted their business that day with my headache, my dry mouth and withered ego. They were flies buzzing. Their shrieking kids fought over the clubs. Worn out, sweaty and bickering, they were now going home, just like me, east or west on the two-lane highway that followed the Lake Erie shoreline, County Road 20. The sun burned its way to the horizon, overheating the car. Heading west, I had to squint behind the steering wheel, having lost my sunglasses during last night's debauchery. The windows were all the way down, but driving sixty clicks was not making much breeze.

I cranked the radio—"101 FM, the home of rock and roll, baby!" The steady drum intro, the opening discord, the distorted voice: "Iron Man," off Black Sabbath's genius second album. I air-drummed on the wheel, banged my soon-to-be-long-again hair to the beat. I croaked along with Ozzy. The bass line thumped through my dashboard; it jangled the keys that hung by my knee. I wanted to gun it, travel at light speed, and sail in time with the music.

But right ahead of me about a dozen men rode their bicycles in a line at the very edge of the asphalt. A dozen buttoned-up, long-sleeved, cotton-polyester white shirts, all in a row. They wore deep-billed baseball caps—ones with John Deere or Del Monte logos—low over their shining jet hair, shade for the setting sun. They were going home too, back to the shacks they lived in during the months they worked in Ontario. There wasn't enough room to really pass them safely, and the east-bound cars were not budging. Bikes often got bullied into the gravel shoulder on this stretch of road, even beyond it, sometimes landing in the deep ditches that collect run-off rain water from the fields. Probably because of that, no one other than migrant workers ever rode along here. Christ, they had no other way to get around. I may be a First Class Ass, as Sharon liked to say, but I'm not a road hog.

I was at the tail end of their parade, debating whether or not to pass them all. That's when I first noticed the kid, one dark rebel in the line of white-and-beige clothes. I thought I was hallucinating. I leaned into the glare. I took my foot off the gunner, let the engine purr down. *No.* It just so happened he was wearing a Sabbath 1978 World Tour T-shirt, faded black. I used to have the same one. His black hat was swivelled sideways and his red bandanna was tied around his face like a bank robber's, I guess to keep out field dust, whipped up by the cars.

I kept pace with the kid and watched out the side window. He immediately turned toward the music. He tugged the bandanna down and grinned, his dazzling smile a lightning bolt that split his handsome brown face almost in two. A balloon expanded inside my chest, making it tight and hot in there. Devil horns up, the kid shook his hand at me. I shook mine back. The kid belted out the chorus and I joined in. We were heavy metal brothers, separated at birth.

Behind me some jackass honked. I gave the one-finger salute out my window. Can't even have a quality rock-and-roll moment with a stranger, for Chrissakes. The driver shook his hands from behind the wheel of his Honda Civic. Times have changed when you can drive foreign around here and *not* be worried about a slit tire or a fist fight. Mostly we got Chryslers and GM trucks, even though the auto industry pretty much laid off every other uncle. Someone else honked farther back in the line of cars forming behind me, our procession dragging into the sunset ahead. Honda Civic jackass behind me edged into the oncoming lane. He wanted to pass on a solid with hardly a breath before the oncoming car. I rode the line to block him, tell him what's what.

Sharon always called me a stubborn man. *Maybe*. But the hell I was heaving off for some 'tard in an import. I drained my Caesar and lobbed the empty bottle into the back seat. I was beginning to consider myself the kid's bodyguard, a dark green 1969 Impala patrolling beside his bike, like we were in a gang. I waited for the instrumental part of the song, where the drums go crazy and your blood runs faster. I revved my engine. Giving the cyclists a wide berth, I gunned it, scaring the east-bound cars. I peeled away, the kid still rocking it old-school, thumbs up. I laid some fast tracks. About a quarter mile up, I cut a sharp right onto a side road, fishtailing into the dirt, sending a spray of small stones and dust onto that twat Honda that was trying to keep up with me.

Ah, did that kid ever make my day.

But seriously, you got to know those shirts aren't easy to come by. Not even here in Ass Crack, Ontario, where the mullet never left and acid-wash jeans are still raring to go. Later that night, I decimated the neighbours with *The Number of the Beast*, my nearly forgotten Iron Maiden record. I downed a quart of rye and ginger ale. I dug through my drawers, the hall closet, the now empty second bedroom (Sharon's World), and even the mildewy boxes in the garage. I was searching for lost treasure—ripped posters I once worshipped on my bedroom walls, concert shirts I'd long since outgrown, my vinyl collection, my most sacred teenaged belongings. Underneath a box of *Star Wars* action figures was the dispossessed electric guitar and amp of my youth. I'd forgotten all about it. *Poor baby*. I opened the dusty case. The sunburst Fender glared. I lifted it. "Shh, shh," I slurred. I dragged the amp into the living room and cleared out a corner.

After Sharon moved in, I'd packed my crap up, bit by

bit. She complained she had no space for her shit. *Sharon*. What the hell had I been thinking? Clearly I would've been a famous musician by now, if I hadn't let that woman run my life. I left my rediscovered things strewn about the bungalow and in piles on the lawn. The mess announced my triumphant return to bachelorhood. Maybe I'd even get a roommate, a partner in crime! Still, no matter how many cupboards I rifled through, how much crap I dumped on the floor, I couldn't find that one missing box. *Where was the damn shirt?*

I stumbled through the living room, tripped on an open suitcase and landed on the worn out couch. I decided to stay there. I was hammered again. My last thought, before passing out, was highly unoriginal and not worth repeating.

I woke with a pain between my eyes. My mossy tongue rotted in my foul mouth. Sunlight from the living room window burned a thin strip across the couch, across my face. My pits reeked. My skin was clammy. No surprise, really. In Ass Crack, summers are hot, humid. By mid-morning your clothes stick to you, your hair goes frizzy and awful. Noon, it's unbearable. You wouldn't know that unless you're from here or you been here.

I thought about the hot drive to work. About sitting in that stifling shack where I rented out the clubs. Who would choose to do this today? I was my own boss. Then I thought about my Visa bill, cable, alimony—to make any money, I'd have to deal with people. I'd have to sit there and smile and try not to let my ghastly beer farts scare them off. *Groan*. I rolled over, blocking the hot sun strip with my shoulder.

I faced the back of the ratty couch. It was the Summer of Suck.

When you're a kid, you live for it. No school, no job. You bust out in all your heated glory like a feral Tom running the neighbourhood, all day long and half the night, too. When you get sick of the heat or if you have cousins visiting, you go down to Lake Erie. There's always someone there. You go west to Cedar Beach; there's the broken pier you dive off, the best spot being right by the warning sign about rocks. Or off the bridge, where you find one or two old men trolling for catfish. There's Ken's Variety and Bait Shoppe, where you get candy and ice cream and worms for your line. The actual beach has usually got dead fish on the sand, clumps of stinking seaweed, tampon applicators, and broken glass. But the water is not too deep and the waves are nice and big.

When you're a teenager, you get the beach bonfires going at night. You steal booze from your parents' stash or you pay that old wino in town an extra dollar to buy a bottle at the liquor store. You get kids to bring their teenaged cousins so you can all check each other out. You roast marshmallows, you try to make out. Someone always drinks too much and then they puke.

When you're an adult, though, you mostly just stay in town or out on the concession roads, wherever you live, and suffer the heat. You get up and go to work and earn your shit pay. You come home, eat too much, and sweat in front of the television. You drink yourself to sleep. You dream of an air conditioner on sale at the Walmart.

Yes, sir. Ass Crack is hot and flat and the fields run for

miles, except where the roads cut through. Nowadays the fields are almost all covered by aluminum-framed plastic greenhouses, hundreds of them everywhere, unending. Fields or greenhouses, you still need hard workers to turn and plant and tend and pick food from dirt. To lug those heavy tomato crates, those fruit baskets, those apples and cherries, peppers and squash. I did it myself for a few years: detassling corn with the other pot-smoking burn-outs when I was sixteen, finally tall enough. Nearly broke my back picking beans and strawberries, too. Nowadays, kids don't do that. They got machines for the corn, and foreigners for the picking.

"Seems to me our only real shortage is hard-working Canadians." I drained more of my beer and belched. "'Spite of all those layoffs." I looked around the pub for a response. A circle of large, balding men glared. One particularly neckless dude wearing a Windsor Spitfires jersey growled.

"You're too good for fieldwork?" I said. "You got something better to do?"

The beer-bellied dude at the next barstool told me to shut up. He was solid, like a Kenmore fridge. His nostrils flared.

The bartender slapped my bill on the bar. "I'd pay that before Donny here kicks your teeth in," he said.

"My point," I continued, "is nobody here wants to break their back in the heat for shit money. Cushy union brats."

Donny stood up. "Get your ass out of here, goof." He pushed me hard in the chest.

No one had touched me in a long time.

The bartender tapped the circled total on my bill. I pulled out my wallet.

"Used to be Frenchies, come pick the fruit," I mumbled. "Then Haitians. Now it's Mexicans. Salvadorans." My chest glowed where Donny's meaty hand had been. In my confused state, it felt a bit like love.

The bartender did not give me my change.

"Ah, fuck it," I said. I walked towards the door. "You'd think there'd be open minds in a big city like Windsor. Can't even talk to some people."

I left, but not before urinating on the front stoop.

Take that, assholes.

The other thing about Windsor, any city really, is you can't see a thing in the night sky, all those buildings, that electric light. But out in the country, now that's darkness. Sky so black you can taste it. And the stars—it's like God puked up a glow stick. Barns as large as ships: invisible in the night, unless they're splattered with oncoming headlights. The horses, the pigs are all tucked into their stalls. Hens curled up quiet as cats around the yard. No cows here, no rolling hills for grazing, nothing like that. It's dead flat.

Cops just sit out at the Fifth Concession, that notorious country road, and turn out their lights. They see everyone coming down from the bypass, coming back from Windsor like me, or from the bush parties or whatnot, and they clock you without batting a lash. Unless you're in the habit of driving blind, like I am, when you outsmart those fucks at their own game and shut off *your* headlights. Which reminded me to roll up the window—didn't need to tip them off with my favourite station filling the air with power chords: Steppenwolf, Rush, April Wine. Driving blind, I didn't even need to stop at the signs. I'd just plow straight home fast as I liked, tight as I was. I could always see some joker coming at me, right, cuz he'd have *his* lights on. I sang out loud when they cued up Led Zeppelin: "Been a long lonely, lonely, lonely, lonely time."

I was thumping the steering wheel, keeping the beat. I'd already forgotten those knobs at the bar. I was remembering being sixteen, getting my licence, shitting myself, and driving for the first time on this very road in broad daylight. I had reached over to change the radio station and ended up in a twelve-foot ditch—true story. Right about here. Driving just ain't right without music. Around here, folks got a healthy respect for country classics, a mild curiosity about the blues—what started it all—but mostly, a god-sworn allegiance to classic rock.

That got me thinking. A guy doesn't just give away his concert shirts. No, sir. That's unheard of. I was wondering about that rebel Mexican, working the fields and wearing the Sabbath. How the hell did *he* get a hold of that shirt? Maybe that makes me a jerk, but honestly. And why couldn't I find mine? I used to wear it every day of the week. Obviously, I was not at that show; it was given to me on my thirteenth birthday by a favourite uncle when he found out I loved metal. He'd *been there*, in person. It was a rite of passage, getting that holy relic. I'd give my left nut to teleport back in time and tailgate party my way around, worshipping at the band's platform heels.

Who am I kidding? I'd give them both.

I woke with a start. It was this side of dawn; I could tell by the strange light that stole through the window where my bedroom curtains did not quite meet in the middle. I looked out of habit, but of course, Sharon wasn't on her side. I blinked.

It was obvious. Some dude, possibly even a buddy of mine I hadn't seen in years, probably keeled over and died. His mother or worse, his wife or live-in girlfriend, probably packed up those hallowed shirts and dropped them down at the charity Goodwill. *The nerve.* That Mexican kid might have scored an entire lifetime supply of rock and metal paraphernalia for a few bucks.

And why shouldn't he?

That was Sharon's voice haunting me from beyond divorce court.

Is he less deserving than you and your fat, balding friends?

That'd be just like her, take the side of a kid from a place she'd never even been, over her own husband.

I have so been there. On our goddamned honeymoon, you prick.

Ah, Sharon. You got me there.

The following Sunday, also hungover, I decided to close the shop early. In fact, I couldn't wait for this one family to finish their game. The parents looked vaguely familiar and were probably dweebs I'd hated in high school. They wore matching polo shirts, like from some depressing Sears Catalogue photo shoot. The kids fought. They were a whole new brand of ugly, a screeching, snotting ad for birth control. Watching them made me hate the world a little bit more than I already had when I'd got up that morning. Made me want to lock up this stupid shop and burn it to the ground. I reimbursed them half, since they played half the course, and kicked them the hell out.

"Now you look here," said the father.

"Look at my dick," I replied. The eyebrows, the open mouths.

I slammed the door of the Coupe and cracked a luke-warm beer. I drove straight ahead into the heart of Leamington, where our town's tomatoes get turned into ketchup in their big Heinz factory. I drove deep into the relaxed pulse of the town's innards. It was full of farm workers on their day off. They were everywhere. They ran errands, phoned home, wired money. They sat on the town benches that were usually just real estate agent ads. Workers leaned against the giant photos of those smiling phonies in their beige suits. Canadians, I realized, don't enjoy ourselves. We go about our uptight business all day and relax, or not, when we get home. Mexicans seemed to know how to use public space, how to spend time together. I decided to park the car and join them.

I walked up and down the main drag, looked into windows, nodded and smiled at people. They nodded back. I followed one group of workers who headed toward the information centre in town, an enormous all-weather tomato where some kid sat all day, bored as a stick, reading Harry Potter, in case anyone stopped and asked for directions or wanted tourist brochures. *As if.* The men turned onto a path I'd never noticed. It was hidden by the giant tomato and a line of large thorny bushes, Ash no doubt. I hesitated briefly. That path led into what used to be an old parking lot. Smells found me almost immediately—smoke and meat, spices, and roasting corn. I could hear Spanish voices laughing and singing. The lot had been transformed into some kind of square.

I felt like Alice in goddamned Wonderland.

About fifty men were hanging out in this alternate universe. Some drank from small dark bottles of beer, others from round flasks they kept at their sides. They were having a good time, nothing rowdy, just relaxing. There were a few benches, all taken, and in one corner there was an old metal container being used as a giant barbecue. Meat sizzled on a makeshift grill, corn in the husk smoked along the edges. Two men worked the grill and filled plates for the others. Nearby was a second smaller grill with a flat sheet on top. A dark-haired woman was forming patties from pale dough, tortillas maybe; she slapped them into shape with expert hands and placed them on the hot metal sheet. She laughed as she worked, her voice drawing the shy men closer, waiting for the food to be ready.

My stomach rumbled. Eating had not interested me lately, but these were some pretty good smells.

A large-bottomed guitar was brought out, and a man began to play. It had a deep bass sound. He played a simple tune the others seemed to know. It was a bit rollicking, but as the other instruments joined in—an accordion, a regular guitar, a horn—it had an altogether different effect. Men began to sing. Larger bottles made their way around. I could have used a belt, whatever it was. This strange music drew me in. It was like country, but slower and more halting. Like a slightly drunken waltz. I liked it and didn't like it at the same time. There was something about the plaintive calling in the voices that popped up from the small knots of men in the yard that tugged at my insides and threatened to let loose some uncontrollable emotion.

I panicked. I looked around and noticed several of the other men's eyes darting away. I was the only white Canadian here. Those around me were silent, even when I said hello. They kept their eyes on the ground and did not reply. The nearest ones had stopped joking around, too. I was spoiling the party. Fun crusher, me? I stumbled backwards, and blundered my way toward the path. The hush spread around me like a pox, and I felt every pair of shining dark eyes upon my back. I hurried, fatally, and twisted my weak ankle, an old hockey injury. I thrashed about in the Prickly Ash before falling heavily to the ground.

The silence was remarkable. Even the music stopped. I could see the path from down there and decided to crawl onto it, thinking it was less conspicuous than standing back up to announce my situation. I hoped no one noticed. As if on cue, there was a resounding burst of laughter; chuckling baritones, a giggling alto choir, and several higher-pitched hilarious sopranos, who succeeded only in provoking the whole square into louder fits of hysteria.

Humiliated, I lurched forward on my hands and knees, still tangled in the bush. Thorns tore at my flesh. A pair of Converse knock-offs blocked my way. I looked up. It was the kid again, wearing that same shirt. The kid's black hair was longer than the other men's, about my own length. His eyes were two black stones that shone wetly: pupils indistinguishable from iris, they were so dark. He reached out a calloused hand. He was muscular from working the fields and pulled me up easily. His skin was surprisingly soft to touch. He smelled of earth and Sunlight detergent and of a faint manly sweat that was not bad.

"Thanks, man," I said awkwardly. I was several inches taller than him. I stared at the shirt which fit him very well. There was a familiar tear on the left sleeve. I rubbed the matching scar on my arm—skateboarding wipe-out. A splotch of white paint along the shirt hem was a ghost from grade ten art class. This *was* my bloody shirt!

He shrugged. "You got the nice car, right? The Coupe?"

He had an accent, but his English was better than I expected. I nodded.

"Bet it's a fun ride." He spoke softly.

My cheeks burned. Blood and sweat trickled down my neck. I pulled a thorn from my scratched hand. I needed to get the hell out of there. I wanted my shirt back. I jangled the keys. "Want to find out?"

There was that jigsaw smile again, lighting up his face.

"You like Sid Vicious?"

"What? That punk?" I sneered. I had regained my confidence and cynicism by then, zipping along the main drag.

"You don't like punk rock?" Geraldo said this with total disbelief.

I refused to reply.

We were cruising the strip, the Leamington "L," the way it was done back when I was in school. You went from the McDonald's drive-through to the town centre just past the giant tomato, took a right, and rode the strip right to the very end of the dock, slammed on your brakes, then turned around and did the whole thing over again only in reverse. Most of the action used to be either down at the docks or up in the McDonald's parking lot—girls smoking and tossing their bleached hair, dudes looking to fight, couples making out. In grade eleven I'd hooked up with Sharon on this very piece of real estate.

"Seriously?" Geraldo sniffed his Big Mac. He took a bite. "More than anything," he said, his mouth full, "I want to be in a punk band."

Well, I nearly pulled over and made him give me the shirt off his narrow back. I was speechless. I opened an emergency beer that he passed me from the glove compartment.

"No, but why can't you like metal and also like punk? That's silly. It's all rock and roll, man."

I choked on the warm beer. It sprayed from my mouth, hit the windshield, dribbled down my chin, wetting the collar of my shirt. I coughed and breathed deeply. Those heretic words from Geraldo's mouth washed over me as my chest relaxed and I wiped the set line from around my mouth, loosening the tension in my jaw. For the first time in my life, I heard some truth in that statement. Geraldo sounded almost reasonable.

Later, I let him take the wheel. "You know how to drive, right?

"Oh yeah," he said. "I been driving since I was nine years old."

It was some time before Geraldo elaborated. He meant

he'd been driving the village *tractor* since he was nine, which is a very different thing. He drove slowly, carefully, right down the middle of the road. The tip of his tongue stuck out at one corner from concentrating. He had a glazed smile plastered on his stunned face. He did okay, considering he freaked if I urged him beyond thirty-five kilometres an hour. We kept to the back roads, and any company we met simply passed us, leaving the Coupe covered in fine dust.

"Take a left and park." I had to draw the line somewhere. Even combines were booting past.

We sat at the top of the ridge, closest thing to a hill in these parts. There was a nice view of the farmland below that stretched a mile or two down to the shore. Sharon and I used to come here to neck in the old days. Before she moved in, of course. Before my parents died, leaving the bungalow to me, suddenly making me the most popular guy at school. *Larry, party at your house, right?* Right.

"This used to be lake." I pointed to the farm land below us.

"Heh?" His eyebrows arched. I noticed they were graceful like a woman's: not too hairy.

"A-gwa," I said loudly. "A long time ago all that was water. Now it's soil. Dirt."

"Oh." He nodded gravely. "My grandmother's village had that, only the opposite. It got covered up. Disappeared." He gripped the steering wheel. I watched the muscles move up his forearm, along his bicep.

"Oh." I inhaled. The smell of him filled me. I opened the passenger window the rest of the way. "What's it like in Mexico?"

"Very different. You never been?" He leaned toward me when he asked that.

I felt stuck in this seat, bare without the steering wheel in front of me, like the car wasn't mine anymore. I cleared my throat. "Just on my honeymoon. Some beach resort."

"Where is your wife?" Geraldo's eyes glittered from his soft face.

"Where'd you get that shirt?"

"Some lady was selling her ex-husband's stuff at a yard sale." He laughed. "Like, she was really mad at him. I paid only fifty cents."

I drained the can and crushed it, one-handed, and tossed it out the window. "Geraldo, let me tell you something. Don't ever get married. It'll ruin your life."

"I am already. I had to marry, to come to Canada."

I looked at him blankly.

"Your government said this. We must be married and go to church if we want to work. So we won't stay here and get Canadian girlfriends. Make Mexi-Can babies." He laughed.

Was this true? That shut me right up.

"We make a deal. We have a little room, but she do what she wants, and me too."

"Huh."

"She is pretty, but she don't like men. Now the others leave her alone. And me, I want—"

"To be in a punk rock band," I said.

He nodded vigorously.

"Well, Geraldo. You sure got your shit together, don't you?" It was about then that I decided to let him keep the fucking shirt. Suddenly, I didn't care if I never saw it again.

After I dropped Geraldo at the laneway to his farm, I headed home. I needed an actual cold beer and a talk with Jack Daniels. I poured the amber liquid over a big chunk of ice. *I'll sip it*, I thought. *Just a little*. I wondered what Sharon was doing tonight, wherever she was. Sunday nights we used to go bowling, back in the day. Or down to Cedar Beach. In winter we'd rent movies and pile quilts around us on the couch to stay warm. We're talking about ten years ago, before I got the heaters fixed.

Try fifteen, jerk.

I poured a second helping.

Sharon used to say she loved that I could crush a beer can in one hand. She loved to fiddle with my long hair. Then suddenly it bugged her. She wanted it cut off.

And grow up while you're at it, Larry.

Fuck ice cubes. I pulled straight from the bottle.

"Arrgh!" I yelled at the large amp. I plugged in, turned that bad boy on. The guitar was seriously out of tune. It needed new strings. I managed to blast a few notes into the dark bungalow. My hands were stiff, too clumsy to do anything right. I gulped more whiskey. The burn comforted my throat.

Why did broads fall for you the way you were—holding your liquor, cracking your jokes, feathering your hair while the rest of those turds from your class went bald—then demand you change? As soon as they owned your space, they wanted you to turn the music down, stop watching the playoffs. They cried if you didn't do the dishes or if you didn't do them *right*; when you didn't notice their new hairdo; when you told them to lay off the chips or they'd never fit into their skinny jeans again. What is life for, anyway? You head off to that shit job she found (minigolf, seriously?), wearing a phony shirt with a clip-on tie that *she* bought. You come home for a crap dinner and lite beer, and find her banging some dude who looks a bit the way you *used to*, before she cut off your balls and zipped them into her purse, forever.

Ah, Sharon.

That Geraldo had the right fucking idea.

All summer long, it was green and black and gold and red: walks in the fields, Sunday drives along the lakeshore in the Coupe. There was beer and whiskey. There were awkward moments, standing too close or bumping against him or stumbling together across the lawn, loaded. A buzz ran through me, electric, that zapped whenever Geraldo's skin brushed mine. I'd shake it off and drink more. There was music, lots of it, blasted from my stereo and from my amp. Geraldo had a gift. He could play that guitar, make it sing like I never could. His face shone with joy when he wailed on it, chugging steadily and ripping off some scorching solo. I stared at him outright then. I felt like some groupie creep, a pre-teen girl with my very own private boy band in the living room.

Late August was yellow and fiery orange. Geraldo grew slightly stooped from bending and picking, from the even longer days of heavy lifting and lugging that was harvest. His eyes sparkled less; he had little energy for playing guitar or anything else. By then I had stopped opening the shop during the week. Instead, I would drive out to the fields at first light and work alongside the men, all the burning hours of the day and into the cooler night. My body ached from it, my hands were ruined, but it made me feel real to sweat and bend and dig and haul. I'd bring something for lunch, something for me and Geraldo. In the shade of a leafy tree, we'd eat these lousy sandwiches and shoot the shit. He'd try out lyrics for his imaginary band, Migrant, but mostly we'd just sit in our hot stink and chug water before going back to work.

Unbelievably, some fields remained untouched other than by feasting birds if it cost more to pick and transport the produce than the owners would be paid for it. Instead, the food was left to rot. Neighbours would come after dark to fill their quiet baskets—midnight picking. Eventually, the soil would be turned over, tomatoes and all. Explosive harvest reds drained into mid-fall grey-browns. The air grew crisp. The nights got cold. Every year at this time, the workers were rounded up and sent home, back to Mexico, and our world returned to its usual cold, white winter.

Migrant workers were not eligible for E.I. even though they paid Canadian taxes. I roared when I first heard that, but Geraldo quietly said, "We signed English papers." Like that explained it all. When I trumpeted something about workers' rights, he smiled cynically. His dark eyes pierced me. "We have the right to remain silent," he said, and opened a fresh beer. "You complain, and they take you off the list. You can't come back next year. Then your whole family goes hungry and ashamed." The guilt was almost unbearable. It occurred to me for the first time that he might *never* come back.

We were sitting in the Coupe on the ridge one night

when I finally asked about that. He was too tired to go all the way to my place and come back for daybreak together. He smiled sadly. "Maria warned me on the phone," he said. "The village thinks you're a *chupacabra*, a goatsucker."

I knew the other workers didn't even talk to him, if they could help it. But it never occurred that they'd blame *me*, the strange gringo, for poisoning him. I was stunned. Geraldo didn't know if they'd asked the farmer to take his name off the return list, or if the boss man himself had decided.

"Either way," he said, "I'm different. They don't like that."

Guilt ate at me. That's when the plan started simmering. Years ago, driving home from the bar, I'd seen farm hands lined up along the side of the road. Boss man was handing back their special work permits as each man stepped onto the bus—a shitty loaner school bus. They were packed up and driven straight to Toronto Pearson airport in the middle of the night. *Do not pass go, do not collect two hundred dollars.* It reminded me of an old photo I'd seen at school, an American plantation owner leading a chain gang of slaves to market. Don't get me wrong, not all farmers are racist a-holes, far from it. They're working harder than you or I to make a living so the rest of us can eat. Frankly, if we ungrateful fucks paid more attention to how food got onto our dinner plates, we'd know how hard it is for farmers to break even.

Still, I felt no regret chugging northeast on the 401 on that particular pre-dawn day, keeping pace with Geraldo's crew bus, none whatsoever. What I couldn't believe was that the thing didn't stop, not even once, on the four-and-a-half hour drive. I had to pull over to take a leak and get a jumbo coffee to keep my eyes open, which meant another pit stop in twenty minutes. I lost track of the bus, but finally caught up with it as it choked and shuddered curbside, in front of Terminal Three.

The men wore their hats low, as usual. They shivered in sweaters. Our fall was cold for them. It crept in and chilled their inside parts. I think it scared them. Might have felt like death. They shuffled from foot to foot, holding their bags and souvenirs—toys for the children they'd been missing, gifts for their wives. Boss man hadn't seen me yet, but the rest sure had. Blame radiated from their turned backs. I felt dirty, old, *wrong* in ways I never had before. For a minute I wondered if I should really go ahead with the plan. Maybe Geraldo's life would not be ruined after all. Maybe they would forgive him back in their land, in their own language, far from North America and its rampant diseases: greed, sloth, lust, pride. If so, Geraldo and his pretty fake wife might just work things out.

Shit. I drummed my fingers on the steering wheel. It was now or never.

The idea was simple. Create a diversion, stuff him in the trunk, get the hell out of there. The tricky part was the distraction. None of the workers would risk helping. Geraldo had fretted about how it would all come to pass. "Details, details," I'd said, and changed the subject, thinking I could wing it. Be truly *in the moment*. In fact, I was starting to panic, not seeing Geraldo in the crowd of men, not knowing if he'd noticed my car sitting about thirty feet behind the bus. I bit my knuckle worrying. I turned off the engine.

Then a taxi van pulled up behind the bus and in front of me. Crying, shouting family members with oversized luggage spilled out. There was a colossal intergenerational argument; a dog yapped from underneath a large woman's arm. A second cab arrived with the rest of their group. It was a travelling carnival of chaos—weeping in-laws, couples struggling with all their crap, several nose-picking, stumbling children.

God help them all.

I turned the engine back on and slowly inched up beside the taxis, blocking them in. I parked, got out, and nonchalantly opened the huge trunk. I scanned the line of workers. I whistled to myself. Suddenly, there he was. Geraldo slipped past the other men, weaving amongst the hysterical family members. Geraldo chucked his bag into the huge open trunk. He almost didn't notice the guitar case and amp in there.

"It's yours," I said, and blushed uncontrollably.

"No way!" His eyes sparkled. His smile brightened the early morning haze. "Thanks, man."

He hugged me hard to his chest. His hot breath singed my neck, my left ear. Wherever his body touched mine— hands on my back, torso against my own, thighs burning against my jeans—those parts melted away, hot and strange. I'd never own them in the same way again.

Then he was curled inside the trunk, an arm around the case, one thumb up, still smiling. I whistled some more, slammed down the lid. I slid behind the wheel. I turned the engine over, changed gear, and chugged away, past the arguing, weeping family, past the school bus and driver, past the line of men who now stared at me openly, in shock. In disgust. One pointed an accusing finger. I can feel it to this day.

I turned the radio up so Geraldo could hear it, too. Pink Floyd was ending, thankfully, and Judas Priest was singing "Breaking the Law." I nosed the Coupe back onto the highway and we headed south, into the deep belly of sin city, down to Torannah. If ever there was a place for a Mexican runaway who dreamed of starting a punk band, I guessed this'd be it. He had an address, a phone number, one name in a city of five million. Most important, he had a backup if he needed it. As I had already told him, the second room in my bungalow was totally clear now. It was his for the taking. He could do what he wanted, and me, too.

Two Ton: An Opera in Three Acts

ACT ONE: SOFT ROCK

Him: flying down Yonge Street, ripping past lanes of stalled traffic, weaving between all those cars. Him: zigzagging the wrong way through intersections, his delivery satchel strapped around his barrel chest, a two-way radio squawking at his shoulder. I noticed that particular bike courier in the downtown core more than all the others. It was his bright blond hair that got my attention, and the bigness of him. He was a gladiator, an urban warrior and, most notably, I never saw him without a wide, gleaming smile.

We couldn't have been less alike. I was his shadow: thin, dark-haired, introverted. I hated drawing attention to myself and was afraid of trying new things. I followed rules, not even jaywalking with the rushing hordes each morning. Not even when he and the other couriers blocked the honking cars with their insolent dawdling, completely immobilizing the street with their bike tricks and general disregard for traffic bylaws.

I worked in the tallest, blackest tower, forty-seven floors up. I scratched out a meagre salary in an office of overworked accountants. This was thanks to the charity of one of my father's former schoolmates who gave me the job. I was the whipping boy of two aging receptionists, Gladys and Helen. Each morning Gladys turned on the adult contemporary radio station while Helen made my To Do list. I filed and fetched, took messages, made the tea, all while Phil Collins bleated mercilessly in the background. "I can feel it coming in the air tonight, oh Lord." I did everything Gladys and Helen did not want to do, but never exactly the way they preferred. I was of no real significance, except perhaps as an object of their daily contempt. They often smiled while sounding sharp, which confused me. They were like two birds of prey—one taller and beakier, the other shorter and more feathered. Both perched at the edge of their seats expectantly, knitted sweaters ruffled around their bony shoulders. They exhibited a maternal shrewdness that frightened me, and I often hid in the hall closet when I heard them calling my name.

With Gladys and Helen, my gender imposed a certain further expectation, a specific skill set. When things got jammed, when things ran out, they called on me. I could usually refill paper and ink without total mishap, but what to do when the machines went on the fritz? Let me be very clear. I was not, *am* not, a man of handy abilities. I can't hammer or saw or drill to save my life. It was luck, surely, or a wave of total synchronicity that somehow coincided with me placing my bewildered hands on one noncompliant machine and its subsequently choking itself back to life.

Gladys and Helen clapped. They looked at me in a new light, like I wasn't *completely* useless after all. Satisfied that I had a knack for fixing things, they continued to call on me whenever the equipment failed. That spark of curious surprise returned whenever I performed the ritual and it resulted in some unlikely degree of success. Each time I wondered—had I some paranormal ability like the comic book characters I'd worshipped as a child? Wariness and skepticism crept into those silly ideas, those blossoms of hope, and killed them. Surely I was an imposter. It would only be a matter of time before the ugly truth was exposed.

Gradually, I spent more time in the copier room, the sectioned-off pen with the machines, the electronic animals that *seemed* to thrive under my quiet murmurings and casual pats. I hid in the mysterious folds of this new persona, however false it may have been. I was Mister Fix-It to the old birds. *Machine Man*, I silently corrected. I daydreamed a spandex suit for myself, a cape, a more muscular body, and perfect vision. From my new post behind the copy room door, I could see out to reception as all sorts of well-dressed peons minced past. They rarely noticed me, but I started to recognize everyone who came and went.

Gladys and Helen were forever gossiping about the other staff when they weren't clucking over the sales pullout in the daily paper. Randolph had gout, likely due to his drinking. Penny cheated on her husband and was seeing a dapper accountant down the hall. The new manager had a gambling problem, and Sylvia next door was bulimic; they'd heard her ritually cleansing after a carrot cake had gone missing from the lunch room. Gladys and Helen were equally relentless in documenting their own mundane affairs: I heard all about their bone spurs, their parking tickets, their irritated bowels. All this with Celine Dion screeching on the radio—honestly, it was too much to bear.

Surely this was some social science experiment. *It had*

to be! I had less in common with other people than I'd ever imagined. Hall & Oates sang "Private Eyes." I despised everyone, I realized, the two receptionists most ardently. I fantasized about their sudden injury: elevator accidents, lunch-room poisonings, a tainted water cooler. I was living inside my own detached brain almost exclusively.

Perhaps they noticed. When either Gladys or Helen had to enter the copier room alone to send or collect faxes, each would give nervous sidelong glances at me and leave as quickly as possible. More than once I'd heard them talking. "There's something wrong with that boy," Helen said. "He's not all there," Gladys agreed, and I snorted with delight. Then Helen said, "Can you imagine his poor girlfriend?" and Gladys clucked her tongue savagely. "What we women have to put up with." That froze me, and I thought of Linda.

Linda was a friendly girl from my college chemistry class who'd Facebooked me out of the blue, almost a year after graduation. She had asked me to the movies week after week without incident. Then about a month ago, she had insisted I come to her place for a drink. She'd left me in the living room, presumably to get our beers, and returned from the kitchen fully naked. Certain that my mediocrity and inexperience would prevail, I nevertheless tried to oblige her, however she instructed. The sex was not all I'd hoped it would be. No doubt Linda was even more disappointed. In the ensuing weeks, more half-hearted attempts brought similar results. At times I climaxed almost immediately, more out of stress and surprise than pleasure. Other times I could not find release no matter what ingenious tricks *Cosmo* suggested she attempt. It was not the love affair of the century, of this I was certain. Somehow I hadn't expected sex to be so mechanical and awkward. But I continued to try my best, so to hear the old biddies taking Linda's part without knowing us at all, well, that pushed a limit.

It was in my new station, the copier room, that I caught regular glimpses of the blond courier as he breezed in and out. Two Ton was his name. "How are my girls?" he'd ask in his faint Eastern European accent. My enthralled supervisors cackled. When the sounds of Air Supply filled the office, he sang loudly to "Every voman in the vorld!" The old broads would bat their lashes and cross their ankles. He left pink cheeks and giddy smiles in his wake. Gladys and Helen would inevitably spend the next forty-five minutes recalling his jokes, his various attributes, his astounding physique. For once I yearned to hear them as they listed his superior qualities. I hummed along with Lionel Richie. Two Ton was so refreshing compared to the other people in my office. He was so much of what I longed to be, so much that I never *could* be. I began making excuses to follow him.

The first time it was quite by accident. I had taken a late lunch break and, on my way back up the tower, I alone shared an elevator with him. The small space closed in around us. His scent filled it; the heat from his body charged the air. I felt faint from all the pheromones, the testosterone flooding from him. I couldn't think of anything to say. He, for once, was silent. I felt him looking at me, and I could hardly breathe. An instrumental version of Led Zeppelin's "Black Dog" was piped into the airless chamber. The elevator chimed as we sped upward. When the doors opened on my floor, I had to hide in the men's room for several minutes just to compose myself.

From then on, whenever Gladys or Helen had errands, I would gallantly offer my assistance. I'd even go so far as to pay for their diet colas or low-fat cappuccinos, just so I might catch a glimpse of him elsewhere in the building, striding past tinted doors, spreading his charm along with the padded envelopes, packages, and waybills he delivered. Sometimes he took unmarked staircases and narrow corridors for short cuts. He made long-distance calls on unattended phone lines. He drank free espressos, ate food from catered lunch trays when no one else was looking. Some days he took smoke breaks in hidden garden squares with incredible statues or in elite balconies decorated by gorgeous planters bursting with colour. Two Ton worked the building like it was a hive and he the one autonomous bee who evaded the unrewarding menial chores that the rest of us drones were genetically predisposed to accept.

One summer afternoon I followed him into an unmarked room. It was a swanky CEO's private washroom and classical music was playing. The room had beautifully tiled floors, large clean mirrors, granite counters. There were cloth towels and fragrant soaps. To the left was an area that included a shower and sauna. I walked quickly into the first available stall and sat on a designer toilet seat. I could hear him urinating in the stall next to me. Even Two Ton's piss had a heady, masculine aroma to it, and it disabled me in some strange way. He didn't flush, I noted with delight. I took it as an act of defiance; it was synonymous with spraying a hydrant in this elite world of powerful men. I listened as he washed his hands carefully, whistling along with the sonata, and didn't dare open my door until the main door had clicked shut behind him.

I gasped. Two Ton was still standing inside the men's room, blocking the exit. His eyes followed me as I limped toward the nearest sink. I kept my head down while the water ran hot over my soapy hands. Violins sawed away, building to a frenzy; minor chords crashed loudly.

"Vat is this?" he said.

I made eye contact with him using the mirror. "W-what is what?"

He stepped towards me. "This." He nodded toward the speakers. "The music. If you know vat the name is." He twirled his bike-lock key on a string around and around his large index finger.

"Uh, sure." I was transfixed by the little silver thing.

He smiled. "So you gonna tell me?"

"Oh. Debussy. Claude Debussy."

"Huh. I think I hear it in a movie or something."

"Probably." My hands were red from the scalding water.

"Like, scary movie, maybe. Sound like something bad might happen. You know?"

I swallowed. The steam from the taps was starting to obliterate my reflection in the mirror.

"Be careful. You gonna burn yourself," he said.

It was as if he broke the spell with those words. I pulled my hands away—they were throbbing. I couldn't turn off the tap.

Two Ton was beside me then. I felt the fabric of his shirt against my bare forearm. He turned off the faucet and rested one big hand on my shoulder. He squeezed my flesh and patted it lightly. "Debussy. Thanks."

Then he was gone for real. The door swung shut. I stood fumbling with the second sink, trying to turn on the cold tap to soak my injured fingers.

After that, I began thinking about Two Ton even more. At the end of each day, I crawled out of the tall, black beast of an office tower and showed my paleness to the fading sun, among hundreds of other beetles, pouring from the nest. I looked for him in the streets as I trudged along in second-hand dress shoes that pinched my toes, spectacles sliding down the bridge of my nose. From streetcar windows I'd scan for a glimpse of his big, blond head. Sometimes I'd spot him in a tight knot of smaller couriers, laughing and smoking a joint right on the marbled front steps of some upscale hotel. I found myself retelling his jokes, relating anecdotes about him to Linda during our increasingly pained silences. She thought he was my friend and wanted to invite him for dinner. I said he was married and needed to be home with his wife. I stopped saying his name out loud, but even Linda had become fascinated with him. Why this bothered me, I wasn't sure. I only became certain that I did not want to share him anymore, that I did not want her taking him away from me, from my imaginary companionship. She was like all the other women he encountered—easily smitten. Her face lit up when she asked about him, so much that I lied again, saying he had switched companies and no longer came to my building.

Then I began to dream about him. He figured even more

prominently in that nether world of image and nuance. He rescued me from drowning, he taught me how to snare forest animals, he reset my broken bones in an alpine climbing disaster, and carried me to safety. Once, his bike refused to work and only I could telepathically correct the problem. He beamed graciously and was forever indebted to me. Sometimes I awoke feverish, nausea and guilt souring my mouth.

In our office, all the ladies were dressing more provocatively, even Gladys and Helen. They wore higher heels and more lipstick, did strange things to their hair and faces. Whitney Houston sang "You Give Good Love" as they cantered through the office. Then they gathered mid-morning, expectantly. When Two Ton arrived, lightly glistening with sweat, carrying a stack of mail, each one tried to steal more of his attentions. They baked loaves for him, offered coffee, water, juice. He flirted with them equally, leaving each one even more hopeful for his next visit.

Men liked him, too, I noticed, albeit grudgingly. You couldn't *not* like him; he was so capable and athletic. He had an easy way about him that made other guys, suits or not, want to measure up. One morning I actually overheard our Big Boss, who rarely even *made appearances* in this department, exchange pleasantries, shake hands, and chat him up about a possible career change, perhaps an interview in sales where his networking could really pay off. I held my breath. Two Ton turned down the offer so gently that neither the boss nor I realized it until a moment after he was gone. I exhaled.

At lunch I couldn't eat my sandwich. Karen Carpenter

crooned "Rainy days and Mondays get me down." I felt a sharp pain lodge in my throat. When I opened my mouth, a sob broke from it. Something was dreadfully wrong.

ACT TWO: WHITE NOISE

"We never go anywhere." Linda pouted just a bit.

I couldn't argue. It was true. So, in an attempt to seem normal, I agreed to go camping with her during the long weekend in July. I hadn't used a sleeping bag since I was ten. I hadn't started a fire since I burned my diary in junior high. I hated insects and was desperately afraid of drowning. I knew this was a bad idea. Linda did, too, deep down. We both suspected she really wanted to break up with me. It was a doomed journey, but she'd already rented a car. At the last minute, no doubt terrified at the prospect of spending all that time alone in the woods with me, she'd invited a couple of girlfriends along.

Karen and Brittany were vacuous and had an irritating habit of singing out loud with the radio commercials. "You deserve a break today!" "Why buy a mattress anywhere else?" One would finish the other's sentences, an eerie echo of their mediocre mind-meld. Linda was more at home with their inane banter than she had been with me in all our dating history. *Who is this strange woman?* I thought, as she drove and tossed her ponytail over the headrest so that the Siamese twins, joined at the IQ, could play with her bleached-out hair. She laughed as I'd never heard before. She burped loudly, competitively, and sang along with

Kylie Minogue to the radio edit version of "Red-blooded Woman."

I coughed. Had I really imposed my sweaty incompetent self into her private life? I was incredulous. I fiddled with the radio, leaving it between stations so static hissed in their ears and they could no longer sing their three-part harmony. The white noise also set me on edge. *When will we get to the campsite? Might I stab these girls with a marshmallow roaster? Couldn't I take some pills and just die?*

I tried to tune them out and watched the drama in the BMW ahead of us. Some alpha male was arguing with his wife, gesticulating wildly. I watched him ream out his better half, the kids, even the dog, all the way down Spadina Avenue. What a shitty way to start their weekend. Suddenly there was a crash. The next thing you know, his SUV was wrapped around the guardrail and our car was rammed up his bumpered ass. There were the stuttered thuds of all those other miserable carloads slamming into us. It was quiet. Doors opened and shut, faces got red. Mouths opened. There was yelling. Finger pointing. Cell phones popping open. Sirens started up in the distance, and cars honked loudly.

We were all fine. *Physically*.

"Wow," I said after a long pause. I undid my seat belt. My ears were ringing. I found my crumpled glasses on the dashboard. I put them back on. Linda looked at me as though I was a stranger. Her blonde hair was lopsided, the derelict ponytail askew. "Are you all right?" I asked. She blinked. The other girls were just as silent. I peered into the backseat; Karen had lipstick smeared across her face. A broken chunk of it was mashed against her cheek. The girls were in shock, maybe. Brittany sniffled. I felt as though I should do something, anything, but I had no idea what that might be. I got out of the car. I closed the door. The three girls looked like those dogs at the pound, their big eyes welling up inside the smeary glass partition.

What did they want from me? I hated this, the whole mess. People began to crowd around, their voices raised and their arms waving, pointing.

Just then, who came chugging around the bend, no-handed on his gorgeous, custom-built bike, but Two Ton. His T-shirt was wrapped around his head like a turban, and his skin warmed to the open sky. His wide chest and abs were clearly defined. I felt a strangeness in my belly. Blood pumped through me. His heavy bike lock chain hung around his neck so that he looked like some Eastern European gangster. He guffawed at the wreck, at our bad luck, and at the joke of his self-powered thin metal frame coasting past us. He was an evolved creature pedalling away from this ecological disaster. We all stood silent, watching him glide past into a sleek future without us. He was so cheerful, so free, as he sped toward the next exit that led down to the waterfront trails.

My bike was on the roof rack, heating in the sun. I didn't think twice. I unfastened it, flipped it down to the hot asphalt, and opened the back seat door. My backpack was there, wedged in between the girls. I grabbed it, hopped on my bike, and raced to catch up. I left behind my percentage of the groceries, a prepaid gas card, and a wicked stash of premium weed, scored from my roommate at Linda's request. It was wonderfully liberating, the best ride of my life. Those hundreds of metres along the highway, uninterrupted asphalt all my own: Two Ton a small blip on the road ahead of me, the girls, the cars, the chaos and conflict left far behind. I beamed like some demented kid, catching fruit flies in my teeth. I choked them down when I laughed out loud. I hooted, tried standing on my pedals to really catch the wind. It billowed up my shirt and made the fabric flap with joy.

Two Ton was down at the water skipping stones and drinking beer from a can when I caught up. I stood awkwardly, waiting. Again, I had nothing to say to him, nothing to offer. I spat out some mashed bugs. Not too far away seagulls shrieked and fought over a bag of potato chips. Two Ton looked at me carefully, not smiling.

"Hi," I said. I coughed and spat out another batch of bug saliva.

He nodded, seemed to make a decision, and tossed me a beer from his pack. His hands hung long at his sides, swinging beside his ham-hock thighs that poured from ripped jean shorts. I sat down and opened the can. Beer foamed up over my fingers as I slurped it.

"You're the black tower guy," he said.

"Uh ..." I wasn't sure what he meant.

"The photocopy dude."

I shrugged. "Mister Machine," I said quietly and licked my foam moustache nervously.

"Mister Machine, hmm?" He said it evenly. Not especially friendly. Not how he usually sounded at work. "You follow me around?"

I started to think this was a terrible idea. "Uh ..." I swallowed the beer. I wondered if he was going to beat the crap out of me and spoil all those Golden Boy fantasies I'd been having—the ones where we saved each others' lives and hung out doing guy things, like playing squash and fishing off the end of some lonely pier.

"You gay?" The way he said that word made it seem bolder and a bit uglier than I had recently come to think of it. It shocked me that he'd say the word aloud, that *I'd* be suspected of such a thing, that he'd reduced it all down to something so base, so pedestrian.

"I have a girlfriend," I said, in a warbling voice. It sounded phony, even to me.

"I don't," he said. And that was it.

In an instant, everything changed. My growing obsession with him, the dreams I'd had, the roiling heat in my belly, the fact that I'd deserted my girlfriend in a crisis to follow his godlike body to the beach. This clearly was something quite different from a regular fraternal overture. In that flash I realized how transparent my own undiagnosed longing must be. I blinked, stupidly.

Gay.

He turned away from me and tossed one more flat stone so that it skipped in a graceful curve leading away from us five, six times, before settling to the sandy bottom. He was just that kind of guy. I watched him differently now, up close, without the affable weekday veneer that I supposed was his armour in the corporate world. Then he turned suddenly, held a hand up to shade his eyes from the bright sun. He was looking right at me.

"You coming?" he said. It wasn't a question. Not really.

He hopped on his bike and I followed. I don't know how I managed to ride all the way across town to his warehouse loft. The traffic sounds merged with heavy construction machinery as we passed road crews and skeleton sites of future condos. Drills blasted through cement, trucks beeped in reverse and dumped their loads onto the dry ground. I couldn't breathe—from the dust and physical exertions and from the strangeness of it all, the day, the turn of events, my good fortune. "Red-blooded woman!"

At the warehouse, he hoisted his bike on his shoulder and took the stairs two at a time, up to the fourth floor. I was sweating, shaking with fatigue. My nose ran from the effort, and I was terrified that I might faint, might fall backwards and be crushed under the weight of my rusting bicycle. Somehow I willed myself up those same stairs. The hallway was deserted when I got there. I stood still, trying to catch my breath. I wondered if this still might end badly. He might leap out at me, for instance, and his courier friends could lynch me, or worse, mock my apparent desire.

"Hello?" I called. "Two Ton?" And then the door ahead on my left swung open. Two Ton stood in the doorway wearing nothing but his chain lock draped across his perfect chest. I dropped my bike.

He smiled lazily and leaned deeper into the wooden frame. He chugged from a new can of beer and watched me carefully. He was built, as they say, like a brick shit house. Like he hadn't been born so much as unloaded from a refrigerator box, already assembled. Tall, yes, but with large, square shoulders that his massive arms dropped from. A

nipple on one of his smooth pecs winked at me from behind the thick chain. Hints of his ribs framed his muscled
belly. I looked to the hard flat area below his navel. He had
those shelf-like muscles above his hips that male models
and athletes get. His thighs, as I already knew, were perfectly formed. I stared at his overdeveloped calves, down
to his bare feet. Two Ton cleared his throat loudly. I looked
back up at his wide grin, his beaming face, but not before
noting his ample and aroused genitals.

"Coming?" He was enjoying my obvious distress. He
raised his hands playfully, like he was under casual arrest,
and turned slowly. His back was a wide muscled expanse,
his buttocks perfectly toned. I had never seen such beauty,
never in my life. *What could he possibly want with me?* Bubbles of feeling choked me. I thought I might weep, he was
so perfect. Two Ton glanced over his shoulder and winked.
"I promise I von't hurt you," he said. "Much."

I left my bike on the hallway floor and stepped forward.

ACT THREE: BLACKENED METAL

I spent Labour Day weekend in the strange kingdom of
Two Ton's loft. He talked easily and brought me out of
my shell. He was naked most of the time, but I never tired
of looking at him. He was comfortable in his body as he
moved around the space, pointing out his various treasures.
Two Ton didn't have a television. There were books, a record player, some albums, little carvings he made with a
knife, some cracked dishes. He had extension cords strung

up, power bars taped to the walls, old lamps stuck haphazardly on tiny shelves he had nailed erratically to the wooden support beams. Whatever he possessed, he said proudly, he had mostly pulled from other people's trash.

"Hey, look," he said. He waved a CD at me. Claude Debussy. "I listened after that time, you know. It reminds me of black metal. So intense."

I had no idea what he meant, but I was thrilled that he remembered our encounter in the men's room. That he cared enough about that sonata to locate a copy, and that I had been the one to tell him the composer's name.

We drank endless beers from his old fridge and crushed the empty cans dramatically, then tossed them into a growing pile in the corner. There was a hot plate and a plug-in kettle, but we ate spaghetti cold, right out of the can. He juggled tennis balls. We pelted them against the bare wall until a neighbour pounded loudly and swore at us in French. We smoked joint after joint; time stopped altogether. He played Black Sabbath, Iron Maiden, Slayer. We sang with Rob Halford to "Living After Midnight," Two Ton in his marvellous baritone, me an alto who attempted falsetto now and again, which brought us to fits of laughter. My life, whatever it had been, no longer existed. My name no longer mattered. He called me *Mister* or sometimes *Machine*, which made me smile. I was in that perfect moment, and though I could scarcely believe it, Two Ton seemed to like me.

We worked our way through his music collection, a great deal of which included black metal bands, Norwegian and otherwise. The drumming was intense—long repetitive instrumental passages with shrieking, grunting vocals and fast tremolo picking on distorted guitars. Some songs were slower with atmospheric wailing and foreboding gloom. I'd never heard most of it before: Bathory, Venom, Darkthrone. Two Ton gave a lecture on the history of the first and second waves of black metal, talked about Swedish and Norwegian rivalry, and described the battles of various metal subcultures: death, doom, gothic, glam, industrial, sludge, speed, stoner—the list was endless. His detailed knowledge impressed me. He was an open encyclopedia to a world I knew nothing about. The music loosed a primitive urge in me that grew the more I drank and smoked. I collapsed on his torn couch and closed my eyes. I imagined wolves, priestesses, medieval weapons, revenge. "Feed on my black iron heart!"

When I opened my eyes, Two Ton was kneeling on the floor in front of me. He placed his warm hands on my thighs and looked at me intently. I felt the stirrings almost immediately. It seemed to be what he was waiting for. Two Ton effortlessly peeled off my shirt. He undid my jeans, yanked them down around my ankles. He massaged my astonished flesh as I struggled to tug the pants over my large feet. I was naked. I tried to hide myself from him, kept my arms folded over my thin chest, but he pulled those back too, like they were just another layer of clothing. He stared into my nervous face and told me exactly what he would do, and then he did each purposeful thing. At some point we were on the floor rolling, kissing. Then we were half on his old futon mattress. He held me, sometimes stroked my face, talked quietly to me, and watched me closely, as though to gauge meaning from every surprised little sound I made. I didn't know my own skin until he brought heat to it. I was as cherished as any bride, blank as any slate. I grew bold touching him, trying to learn what he liked, what I liked.

In between exertions, we lay in tangled sheets on his bed. He slept soundly, curled into me, his even breath warming my neck. He was a boy then, perfect and passive, and that's when I stared outright: his chiselled profile, the cleft chin, those pale lashes. I traced his smooth flesh with my fingers. I was perplexed by his beauty and bruised by his attentions. I felt profoundly alive, I realized. As though my whole life had been a series of bumbling missteps that had eventually lead right to this perfect moment in time.

Two Ton would wake suddenly from these naps and begin speaking of his old life, the one he had before coming to Canada. He was from some country in the eastern end of Europe that nobody ever pronounced properly. "Anyvay," he said, "my village changed names so much—every time some army march through it—even *I* don't know vat to call it now."

"Plus," he said to my undoubtedly uncomprehending face, "every time they march, they destroy more of the crops me and my father plant. Hard to be a farmer ven there's nothing to farm." Then he playfully decked me with a pillow.

I threw myself and the pillow on top of him, tried to tackle him, but he crushed me in a suffocating embrace. He squeezed the air from my lungs. My eyes bulging, face reddening, he kissed me tenderly. It was gentle torture, but torture nonetheless. This time when we did it, he paired every sensual gesture with an uncomfortable one. He'd move his wet mouth along me slowly, but only while I was pinned in a half nelson. He'd tease my nipples, but choke me simultaneously. I hated and loved it. At first I struggled, but there was no point. He knew what he wanted. He knew what I wanted too, and that was the miracle. That he could see me for what I had always been when nobody else bothered to wonder. Not even me. "Black Metal ist Krieg!"

Later he elaborated about that land of his. He said, "Those hungry soldiers take everything. The best food, even the good soil, goes avay vith them." It got sucked into the soles of their battered army boots, leaving angry sand behind. Dirt, unable or unwilling to support the potatoes and sugar beets, cabbage and onions. Dirt that one year finally gave up, even on itself, and let the wind send it stinging into the drying river beds. While he spoke, I tugged on his fingers, thick like sausage and always slightly curled from use, from gripping handlebars and hoisting heavy bags. And before that, from lifting machinery, cleaning stalls, and roping calves.

"But how did you end up here?" I asked again. I wanted to know exactly how fate had delivered this gift to me, what stars had aligned for this unexpected purpose. How could he come from some mud-entrenched village on the other side of the world and end up in Toronto, racing through the business district delivering packages for a pittance? Better yet, how had I ended up *here*, crushed in his embrace, sweated upon, kissed and cursed so equally?

Two Ton lit a cigarette. He exhaled and, after a bit,

passed it to me. He said, "My father, he vas old and sick. He had nothing. He couldn't pay his loans for seed and equipment. He vould not even pay one cent to that bank. It humiliated him."

I passed the smoke back and he took hits off it, staring into space. Two Ton swigged the last of his beer, then dropped the end of the cigarette into the can. He swished it around, and I heard the faint hiss as it extinguished itself.

"All the men in my family—father, grandfather, great-grandfather, uncles—ve have this same farm. Grow the same food every year. The village eats our food—some others, too, but mostly ours. This is vat ve do." He told this part like it was a story from an old book, familiar and comforting.

I thought of my own father then. I had no idea if he had such a legacy, if he was shouldering some masculine code handed down to him by his father, and so on. I scarcely remembered my grandfather. My father was a stooped, mild man of medium build, who quietly left for work each morning. He quietly returned around six o'clock each night and ate my mother's meals while listening to her chatter, always seeming vaguely removed from it all. He'd relax in front of the television. He sometimes read a newspaper or a mystery novel, until he'd stand up and say goodnight to all present, then quietly go down the hallway to bed. Like clockwork. Who knew what the man actually thought about anything?

Two Ton said that, to deepen the frown between his brows, all his father had to do was look up the road at dust blowing from the empty field, or out back at the dull brown land, or to the empty barn where the animals had once been, or at the flat-tired truck he'd driven to market twice every week since he was eleven years old. "This vent on for a long time," he said. He leapt over to the fridge and grabbed another can of beer, opened it, and slurped at the foam. "Until von day." Two Ton's eyes glittered. "My father got out of his creaky chair; he make a pile of all the coins he finds in the house. He writes a letter to me. All his thoughts, you know?" He walked back and sat on the edge of the mattress with me.

I leaned closer. I lay my warm hands on either side of his spine, flattened them against the places where his lungs would be. I could feel his heart pumping inside there, strong and regular.

"He smokes. He cleans the ash. Then he picks up his coat, his hat, and his gun and valks in straight line past the fields, into the bush." Two Ton turned and stared right through me. "He use his last bullet."

We were quiet for a while. I had no idea what to say, but my hands smoothed his skin, like he was one of the broken copiers at work. Two Ton seemed distant, aloof. He was perhaps tired of me being there. It had been two or three days and, after all, we were virtual strangers. I had never spent such a long uninterrupted period of time with anyone. I'd never heard anything so personal.

"What did the note say?" I finally asked.

Two Ton reached over to the orange crate he used as a nightstand and pulled out a small painted box. Inside was a piece of folded paper, thick and cream-coloured, but smudged from being handled. He tossed it to me. His father's handwriting was careful: squared off at the top and bottom loops, like he'd used a ruler almost, and the letters, so many consonants, slanted sharply to the right, like they were marching headlong into the far side of the paper, in danger of falling off the edge if they arrived too soon. I had no idea what they spelled out, or even what language it was.

I waited for Two Ton to translate those life-altering phrases. What damning insights had his father inked? What great-grandmother's recipe, what bastard child or torrid love affair, what ugly family secrets might be revealed in such a letter? I found myself wondering what my own father might attempt to share in such a profound moment. Two Ton scratched at the light hairs on his chest. He leaned toward me and drank another long gulp. His eyes bore through me; they shone and provoked a shiver from me. I struggled to comprehend all he was not saying. I didn't know how to comfort him or if he even wanted that.

"What did you do next?"

"Easy," he said. He spoke quietly. "I drink the last beer. Then I cut up the last bread and eat it, sitting in my father's chair. Later, when the moon comes out, I lay down on the bed and cry. Finally, I sleep. In the morning, I pack a few things in a bag and just leave. I travelled. I did some crazy things, you know," he said, his voice catching. "Some time, I just heard about coming to Canada, and so I did that. And now, you see, here I am."

I smiled when he said that. But I noticed he didn't. His face was impassive. Like the flat, smooth stones he had skipped at the lakefront.

On Monday morning, I woke with a furry tongue, my head

in a vice. I stank. Two Ton was not in bed. He was standing by the large open window in an antique wash basin, an
oversized tin bucket with edges that reached just below his
knees. He had rigged a garden hose to the sink faucet and
had duct-taped a shower head on the end of the hose. He
showered in cold water, lathered up with soap stolen from
one of the office washrooms, and then rinsed again. It occurred to me that this was slightly more barbaric than the
amenities offered at the campground Linda had booked.

Linda. That poor girl.

"You're avake," he said loudly. "Good." He stepped out
of the basin, turned off the tap, and towelled himself off,
all in the same movement. "I have to do some things today.
Not vork, but, you know."

I looked around the room. My knapsack was on the
floor in one corner, my things vomited up from it, strewn
the length of the room. I moved slowly, collecting familiar
items as I went. A sock. My damp shorts. A box of condoms meant for the terrible sex with Linda, emptied now,
with torn wrappers scattered around the room. It hurt
when I bent to pick them up. The long bike ride, the stairs,
the beer, the sweaty wrestles—it was all much more than
I was accustomed to. I dressed myself. I washed my face
and rinsed my mouth but couldn't spit out the dread that
burned at the back. I could hardly look at him, certainly not
in the eyes.

"You're like a voman," he guffawed. "You should eat a
sandwich." He was slapping peanut butter onto slices of
bread and dropping large dollops of jam on top. He handed me a folded-over piece and thumped my shoulder blade

in some kind of manly gesture. I winced. He ate several sandwiches just like this while I choked through that single one. The peanut butter stuck in my throat. I could hardly swallow, even though I kept sipping from a large glass of water.

He was dressing quickly, moving purposefully around the room. He gathered his wallet, bike lock, keys, cap. He was oppressively cheerful. He was putting on other layers, too, the invisible ones that bricked him far away from me, hundreds of ocean miles between us, and I simply could not stay the maudlin waves from flooding. *This*—whatever had happened here in his room, whatever affection and intimacy he had poured over me the past few days—this was all gone. The air was changed. Two Ton smelled different. I was his shadow once more, and I could hardly bear it. The thought of seeing him at the office, me on a stool in the copier room, him captivating the maven gatekeepers out front, it sickened me.

"Ve had good times," he said at last, jingling his keys by the door. I was tying my shoelace, peering at him through my dark bangs. "Don't pout," he said. "I don't like that."

Of course it only made things worse.

Out in the hallway the remains of my bicycle glared at me. It was my fault. I had abandoned it, not thought of it once the whole time I was inside Two Ton's loft. The front wheel was missing, the gears were stripped. My pedals were gone. The seat-less post glared obscenely at me. Two Ton swore. "I forgot to varn you about my neighbours," he said. He looked sad. To see a bike desecrated, well, that truly hurt him, I could tell.

"I'll take the bus," I said. I couldn't begin to carry the thing home. Not now.

"Hey," he said, and it was more the conspiratorial sound of his indoor voice, the intimate one I had heard all weekend. "I fix it. I bring it to the black tower ven it's ready." He stood in the cavernous hallway, dust sifting through the beams of light that filtered down from high windows of the warehouse. Sunlight played on his face and his large form; shadows crept over unexpected places. He was still the unapproachable guy I saw downtown, but the other one, the gentle-rough one I'd just come to know, that part of him was visible once again, too.

"Okay." I stammered. "If you want."

"Yeah," he said. He stepped toward me. "I bring it and ve ride. See that lake again or some place."

I would collapse, surely, or so I thought.

Two Ton came closer still, and put his warm hand on my neck. "Maybe come here, too. Mister." His lips brushed mine. Then he was off, riding down the hallway, wheels thumping down the stairs. He was whistling, and the mournful tune echoed in the empty stairwell. Downstairs, the main door squeaked open, then slammed shut behind him. When I stood on my toes and peered out the window, I could just make out his blond head, the bigness of him, the grace of his figure, as he sped down the alley away from me.

Stargazing at Eddie's

"I'd-a never tapped that if I'd a known she was such a ho. How 'bout it? You ride that?"

I say, "A-a-as if," and Eddie chuckles, long and low. I hate when he girl talks.

Eddie passes a wee pinner of a joint, really just the filter. I suck 'til my mouth burns.

"Sh-shit." I toss the thing somewhere and pour Pabst Blue Ribbon on my sore lip. I crank back the smoke, try to keep it all in longer. I cough. Smoke and air and beer snort out my nose, even though I'm used to this stinkweed. A burn bubble grows where the ember touched my mouth.

Eddie says, "Easy, Ray-Ray. Where'd you throw that roach?"

I shrug.

Eddie feels around for it with his big hands. I keep coughing, crapping my lungs out. Eddie and me are on his roof smoking, drinking, and bullshitting. His white mom sticks her head out the bedroom window and yells, "Get down here, you're gonna break the bloody ruff," but we don't.

Eddie yells, "Get your fat ass up here and make me!" and she goes, "Fuck, you're like your dad," and slams the window, and that's that for a while. Which is good, cuz even though I know she can't climb up and get us, she creeps me right out.

Eddie rips off his studded cap and roughs up his hair. In grade school he wanted to feather it like all the other toughs, but he couldn't. Not with his dad's nappy hair. Now he's punk. He shaves the sides and his tufty baby dreads stick up on top and all down the back, too. Like a Mohawk warrior. He plops the cap back on, sideways.

He says, "Okay. Who's the hottest chick in our school?"

I spark up another joint so I don't have to answer.

He pokes me. "Well?"

I roll my eyes. "They're all d-d-dogs."

Eddie laughs and slaps the roof. "You're funny, Ray-Ray. They're no porn queens, you're frigging right. Except maybe Mary Lou."

I don't say anything and neither does he. I guess he's thinking about Mary Lou, who is ugly and boring and has really big boobs. We drink more beer. Eddie starts talking his usual crap about running away, about going to the big smoke, and us getting factory jobs and making lots of cash.

"We'll score hot babes," he says.

"Humph."

"They'll like me tall and dark, and you all tiny and white. We'll tag team."

But we both know that women don't like me. They think I'm too soft.

"We'll burn that city down, be so hot," he says. "We'll start a band."

Thing is, Eddie never fills in the details. Like, how the hell would we even *get* to the city, let alone start a band? "W-w-we don't have no b-bus money," I say.

Eddie sucks his teeth. "We won't take an old bus. We'll drive."

"Without a c-c-car?" On a beginner's licence?

"Always poking holes in my ideas, Ray-Ray." Eddie sounds annoyed, like I'm the only thing stopping him from being a rich city millionaire, right this very minute.

After a bit I say, "We c-could hitch. On a t-t-truck."

"You're right," he says, happy again. "That's how I snuck out of Bluewater—in the back of a bread truck, got the hell right out of there. Didn't go hungry, neither. Not 'til they brought me back, anyways."

Eddie tells me that story over again, how he was stuck with some dirt bag trying to finish him off at the boys' detention centre. That *plus* a white power gang jumping him every time he turned a corner. "Brown boys got to stick together in juvie. But we all different kinds of brown—Native, Latino, Asian. One brother blacker than me, that's it."

Eddie almost never made it out, except in a box.

"Wouldn't want to go back, neither. You would not believe the shit you have to do to get by, Ray-Ray."

His voice is thick with bad memories. I wonder what exactly happened to him there. There and all those other places he's been sent. It always takes him a while to settle when he comes back. Then, living with his Monster Mom, he goes bonkers, fucks shit up, and gets hauled off all over again. It's always a circle with him.

Eddie says, "In fact, you and me probably couldn't even be friends there, what with the way they stack it up colourwise. We'd get the beat down."

I've heard all these stories before, but I don't care. I like the sound of his deep voice. Eddie's musky scent fills my nose—that and the smell of the night air, and Old Red's garbage sweetly stewing down the lane, and the white to-bacco flowers from the fields even farther away.

"It's not t-t-too bad here," I say, when he stops talking to light another smoke. I look up at the stars. Look over to the transformer behind Old Red's place. Hear it humming. Look down at the other trailers, the bungalows. Hear Eddie's Tom, Big Fat Rat Catcher, yowl as he slinks out from under a parked car. He's hunting a skunk that crosses the dirt road, then stops right in the middle. I drain my beer and lob the empty King can in a beauty arc, over the crab-grass past Old Red's garbage, so it lands in the dirt like a bomb. The skunk freaks. It flips around, tail up, legs spread, and its head sways back and forth, back and forth, sniffing the night air. A dog starts barking, down aways. Big Fat Rat Catcher stares right at me, like I wrecked his routine.

"Hole!" Eddie knuckle punches the back of my head.

"Ow, feh-fuck."

"You want it to stink up the whole place?"

"N-no," I says, "But you di-didn't have to h-h-hit me." I blink.

"Goof."

The skunk prances away and doesn't spray, after all. I watch the white tip of its tail disappear into the dark bushes. Big Fat Rat Catcher blinks and is gone too.

Eddie burps loud and long. It bounces off Old Red's siding, and we laugh at the echo. In the background, we can hear his mom's TV. She must have opened the window again. She's chain-smoking in bed, probably wearing her lacy see-through pyjamas, watching the late-late show and the even later commercials. The ones that go on forever, selling shit you don't need—no money down, don't pay 'til next year—mattresses, couches, kitchen crap, cars. A zombie studio audience claps and cheers.

Eddie pulls the tab on another Pabst Blue Ribbon. Foam covers his fingers. He slurps it up quick. Beer dribbles off his wide lips, down his chin. Beer glistens on his thick fingers.

I lick my sore lip.

He shakes his hand, shakes the beer drops that land on the shingled roof between us. Eddie leans back on his elbows, looks up at the sky. He's right good-looking, especially now, in spite of his buck teeth. Like a movie man with the light on him in all the right parts. I look away. Bend my knee to block my sudden boner.

"Want more?" he says, so I reach for it, but he pulls the can away.

I say, "G-give me some," and he says, "M-m-make me," and laughs again.

He rolls away and chugs the beer. He keeps rolling along the flat roof, holding the can up, not spilling much. Finally I stand up and lunge, but he scoots away quick. He's still laughing. I'm lopsided from the beers and the weed.

"Whoa."

"Easy there, Ray-Ray." Then he kicks me in the back of my knee and I fall, plop, beside him. Practically on him and such.

"Sh-shit."

"Don't spill it, goof."

"Cut it out, Eddie," yells his mom. "What are ya, goddamn bowling?!" She's got the window open again. She's probably leaning her head out, stretching her neck in a crick, trying to figure out what all's going on.

We crack up. I'm still laughing, and he pokes my ribs. I block. He fakes. He pokes again, and his big hands are faster than mine. He lands them almost every time. Those hard fingers jab my arm pit, stomach, ribs, whoops, my crotch, my armpit. I twist away. He pinches my nipple hard.

"Ow, feh-fuck's sake," I say, and he turns up the volume on my knob.

"Ow, m-mother f-f-fuck," I yell and elbow him. He's still kneeling on top of me, tweaking my nip. He drips beer on me.

"Open your mouth, whore," he says, dead serious.

"Ark." The warm beer pees right on my face. Beer bounces off my shut mouth, splashes my eyes, and pools below my neck, soaks my long hair and the top of my T-shirt.

"Look at me," he says.

I look at him, and he looks good. Streetlight falls on his cheek, his lip; it outlines the tufts of his hair when his cap falls off. His arm muscles flex from holding me and hurting me and measuring out the beer. The lettering on his Ramones shirt glows white against his darker skin.

"Open your twat mouth."

So I do. I open it, right, and catch the stream. And what do you know; I pop wood again, right under him. He's leaning right on it and staring back at me. *He might punch me*, I think. *Or throw me off the roof.* But he don't. He moves around a little, holds the can near his belt buckle, and still pours it into my mouth. I trance out, let the beer pour right in me and through me until it is all gone. And when Eddie unzips, when he slowly pulls it out, I almost lose it right then.

I don't move a muscle, though. I don't even breathe.

His is nice, alright. I already seen it dozens of times. Eddie's always whipping it around in gym class, or when we're loaded, pissing in a ditch somewhere. Other times, too. I usually look away; don't want nobody thinking I'm a Gaylord. But now it's all I can see; the fat head of it sticking out a bit, the rest filling his hand.

"What are you waiting for?" he says.

I don't want to talk and ruin everything.

"Get it out, Ray-Ray," and I don't miss a heartbeat. I want to grind against him but he says, "Easy, Ray-Ray. Don't be no fag."

I'm pinned under him, confused. I don't know the rules, don't even know what game we're playing. So I follow his lead. His hand moves slowly. He says, "Why don't you like talking about girls, Ray-Ray?"

"Huh?" I stroke, light as I can.

"Don't you like them?"

"I d-don't know."

When he speeds up, I do too. When he spits in his hand to work that in, so do I. Eddie leans closer, still above me, and says, "Well? Who do you like?"

I hold myself in a tight fist, count to five, and breathe.

Don't make me talk, I think.

"Say it," he hisses.

"O-okay. I like you, Eddie."

"Thought so." His eyes don't leave mine, not once. "How long you been liking me, huh?"

I shrug. How long is forever?

"Guess."

"Since that time you was tuh-tuh-trashed a-at Junior's b-bush party." That night Eddie got loaded and picked a fight with some out-of-town boys. Then he disappeared.

"You were looking for me?" His whisper is hoarse.

"Uh huh." I lick my lip. I couldn't find him at the fire, in the back lot, or with the other kids down at the pits. I thought those guys were maybe finishing him off, for good.

"You came here?" His hand moves up and down.

I nod. I hate what else happened that night. Don't want to ruin everything. *Why'd I start talking about this stupid night?*

"Tell me." Eddie breathes hard, his mouth hangs open, his eyes are fixed, just like a humping dog.

"She would-wouldn't leave me alone." I hold myself tight, trying not to go limp. There's a roaring in my ears, my head rattles. I squeeze my eyes shut.

When I open them, Eddie's face is even closer. His lips are right near mine. They brush my cheekbone. "Hey. Ray-Ray." He's not touching himself now; he's touching my hair instead. "You okay?"

I nod.

"I did come home that night." He licks his lips. His beer breath heats up my skin. I wish he would kiss me, but I'm not stupid. "I was watching you. Right through the window. Watching her suck that pretty thing of yours."

He was watching me. I gulp. He thinks mine is pretty.

Eddie whispers, "Did you wish it was me instead?"

I nod.

His hand goes back down but he keeps his face right beside mine.

"Me too," he says.

Holy shit, I think. I'm burning from the belly, hot in the balls, and my face cripples up. A vein explodes in my brain. Eddie thrusts once, twice. He groans in my ear, and we shoot onto each other, onto the roof, into the night.

He relaxes beside me. We're panting. Blood thumps in my ears, my chest. His skin is hot, his breath ruffles my hair and tickles my ear. His pulse, his heart beat, bangs in time with mine.

I love you, I want to say. I'm yours. I am nothing without you.

Eddie sits up.

I wonder if he'll kiss me now. I lick my lips, in case. But he don't.

Eddie clears his throat. I wait for what he is about to say. I wonder if this means he's my boyfriend. If this is how it'll be from now on with us. But Eddie doesn't say a thing. Eddie doesn't even look at me.

Cool air blows between us. I poke my tongue out and touch the tiny balloon, the blister on my lip. Eddie opens a new can of beer. He does up his pants, uses the bottom of his shirt to mop the sweat off his face. He drinks. He's all put together. He looks the same as before, softer in the face, but he's far away again, like nothing happened. For all I know, he's thinking about Mary Lou.

I'm still hanging out, shrivelled, pruney. The wet spots could be snot drying on my skin, pulling it tighter. My stomach weeps.

"Eddie, get your ass down here and bring your pretty faggot afore I kick you right off that ruff, ya hear me?" She's as loud as an eighteen-wheeler still, but the harsh edge is rubbed down some. It's warmed up, and there's a catch in her voice. We look at each other and we look away quick, cuz we both know what that means.

"Hope you're good to go," says Eddie and slaps me on the back.

That's when I start to close in on myself. That's when I want to cry or scream or punch something. Jump off this low roof. Run away. Hitch to some ugly, scary city. Throw myself to the wolves, to the wind. But I don't. I bite my sore lip and pull up my jeans. I tuck it away and zip up, button. Jiggle and shake into place. Stand up. Wobble. I follow Eddie across the roof slow, and over the edge slower, and swing myself down through her window, last.

She looks pretty good, in all. A bit like Eddie, only with big soft tits, frosted hair, nail polish, a hairy bush. Like Eddie with an even dirtier mouth, an even harder hit. Why, when that one winds up, you knock yourself. You see stars, alright.

Seven-Dollar Blow

"That guy's got the ugliest dick I ever sucked."

Darcy doesn't say a thing, just keeps rocking back and forth, heel toe, heel toe. He's biting the skin of one itchy arm, peering through his greasy red bangs. He's wearing his huge "Psychiatric Help 5¢, the Doctor is in!" T-shirt. Fucking Charlie Brown. Makes him look pre-teeny, younger than he really is, which is good for business.

"Plus he tried to rip me off."

I lean on the brick wall in the alley, right beside him, and adjust my balls. I bought them at a sex store in the joke section. Pant stuffers. But they've saved my ass more than a few times, let me tell you. I tuck the soft silicone thing into my Y-fronts, average sized dick and balls, and it works. The lump looks pretty good, especially in my ripped-up jeans, though I wouldn't want to be caught pants-down, if you get me. Dudes are always peeking, too. Always trying to get more than what they paid for. Anyways, it feels good having my dick lump, my crotch bump. Definitely better than *not* having it. Sometimes I find myself hanging around, hands down the front of my pants, just mindlessly massaging those soft greying parts. Calms me right down.

I tap a Marlboro out of my pack, put it in my mouth. I feel around for my new lighter. Darcy grabs the smoke out of my mouth and puts it in his own. I tap out another and light them both with a flourish.

Darcy nods at the lighter. His eyebrow arches.

"Oh, yeah. Got this from that American dude last night. The New Yorker." I hold the smoke in my lungs as long as I can, then blow it all out noisily. A piece of tobacco sticks to the tip of my tongue.

"Mister white pants?" says Darcy in his strange scratchy voice.

I say, "Ha ha. Yep, Mister white pants." I spit the tobacco piece onto the sidewalk. *Mister talked too much, took too long, and had a fat, dirty wiener.* "You'd think anyone who'd wear such clean pants would at least wash the cheese off their dick, right?"

Darcy shakes his head. We smoke for a bit. Cars zip by and some drivers slow down and check us out, but they keep going.

After a bit Darcy says, "So what were you saying?"

"Nothing, man." I shrug. "I'm just standing here. I'm not saying nothing."

"No," he says. "Before. You were saying you got ripped off."

"Did I?" I take one last drag, then flick the butt in a tall arc, right into the gutter. "Oh yeah," I say. "Yeah, that guy just now *totally* tried to rip me off. Slips me a bill all rolled up tight and tries to book it, right, but he's not all zipped yet, so I grab what's still poking outta his fly, right? I got his thing in one hand and unroll the money with the other: a fuckin' fiver! So I says, 'It's ten.' And he whines, 'You said seven.' And I go, 'It *was* seven, now it's ten.' He's bugging me so I give him a bit of a twist, and he jumps and is all,

'You said it would be the best seven-dollar blow job I ever had,' and I'm like 'It *would* have been, but now it's the best *ten*-dollar blow job you ever had cuz you tried to rip me off, and also cuz you have the ugliest dick I ever put in my mouth.' Ha ha."

Darcy laughs too.

"And I'm leavin,' right, and he goes, he goes, 'By the way, my sister gives way better head … for free!'"

"No way, dude," says Darcy. He laughs so hard he starts coughing.

"Way. But that's the biz for you, right? You never fucking know."

Darcy's still laughing when I flag my next trick. A middle-aged dude with glasses and a receding hairline, driving an old Tercel. He's wearing a rumpled button-down shirt that's grey around the collar. Probably got his work tie in the glove compartment. He looks like my math teacher from grade nine—pasty skin, dandruff flakes on his shoulders. His wife—I have no doubt at all that he's married—probably hates him. Probably hasn't given him head in years. *I'm charging double*. Darcy waves me off, still chuckling. He's never gonna make any cash tonight.

Later, I find Darcy back in our spot. He's twitched, freaking. I hate him like this.

"Sly," he whines. "Come on, man."

I say, "Jeez." He's green in the face. Those pain pills his gay doctor slipped him are finally all gone. *Party's over*. Now he's jonesing, scratching at the invisible wrigglies under the skin of his arms, bringing up blood with his sharp, dirty nails.

"Please?" He screws up his lips, and I see the tremor ripping right through him.

I grunt. "Fine. But you already owe me twenty. I want it back. Tonight."

"Sure, yeah. Thanks, man."

He lunges down the alley with me. Usually we go behind the can or down the street a ways, but he can't wait. That's obvious. We just fully fire up that nice rock I got after my last guy, and get a fast buzz going. I don't need it yet, but why not? It sure perks Darcy up. Getting high takes his mind off the gut rot and the three-day migraine and the sub-skin crawlers. Getting high helps him forget about his itchy arms so maybe they might even start to scab over proper for once. Getting high helps me forget how much I hate doing this shit for money. So it's totally worth it, right?

"Hey," I say.

Darcy looks at me, right in the eyes, like he hasn't done in a long while. I know he sees me, right? He sees what I really am and not what I'm stuck with, this pathetic half-formed body. I smile and maybe I laugh a bit; I get nervous when people look at me too long. He zooms in real close 'til his sour breath warms my face and bits of his ginger hair poke me. He's calmer now. He's focussed and quiet while the chemicals shoot through him. Darcy kisses me. Kisses me warm and soft and a bit wet, just the tip of his shy tongue touching my own, creeping over into my mouth quietly. His lips move slow and sometimes suck and sometimes slide over mine, that tip of his tongue still there reminding me of what it can do. What it would like to do. And all I feel is my mouth and his mouth and the heat spreading in my crotch, the blood rushing away from my brain.

The sky gets dark and streetlights blink on. The pigs are cracking down tonight. Some nosy neighbours are complaining about the action again. Don't like the boys hanging around, playing with our own titties on the sidewalk. Don't like us swinging around the bus-stop pole, smoking on the corner. Don't like the tires screeching and car doors slamming and stereo music getting loud then quiet when the cars peel off into the night. Don't like their husbands sneaking out for a beer at the corner bar and spending grocery money on a hand job in Kiddie Porn Park. Don't like finding used condoms on the ground the next morning, either, but then, where are we supposed to put them? Don't want their husbands fucking with no latex, right? They just can't win, those broads.

Darcy paces up and down our corner. He's wearing a new shirt with wide stripes, long sleeves. It has a white collar with a few snaps at the top, like some frat guy shirt. Some kind of university shirt. He wipes his nose on the too-long sleeve of one arm. He looks relieved to see me. "The King cruised by with a wagon. He picked up Lil' Brat." He spits.

"Shit." You don't want the King to catch you, that's for sure—meanest cop in town, obsessed with hunting street kids. He calls it pest control, like we're rats or some kind of bug. The nervous twitch under my eye starts up.

"Where were you?"

Darcy's eyes shift one way, then the other. He's sketched. "Fuck it," I say. "I can't get busted. Let's jet." Darcy knows I'm already on probation. Not to mention the complications of getting thrown in the slammer when I'm obviously a boy except for the few inches between my legs. The shit I *should* have been born with, but *wasn't*. Then, if I don't get murdered in the clink, it's off to the shrink factory for me, suits and nurses trying to brainwash me into being a proper biological girl specimen.

"Where to?" says Darcy. He's bugging.

"I don't know. You got that twenty you owe me?"

He blushes. "I did. But, well, now I don't."

I finger the designer name on his chest pocket. "Nice shirt."

He cracks a smile. "That big courier gave it to me." He blushes again.

"Which one?" But I already know the answer. I can even see him wearing the shirt, filling it all out perfectly, whizzing past us on his skinny tires, that satchel strapped around him. That blond one, the big beautiful one, the one we all love. He spins around on one wheel doing bike tricks on our corner, smoking spliffs between calls.

I smell Darcy's betrayal. The wall of secrecy he slapped up when I wasn't looking, when I was out working and he was lounging around, available. There's a small stab in my belly, the jealous knife. I try to bury it. Can't have any of that, right? I don't even know who I'm jealous for: Darcy or that other boy.

Darcy shrugs. His long-sleeved arms swing wildly, like some cartoon guy. Then he starts pacing again. We're broke. It's not the warmest night. The sky might open up and dump rain all over us, any minute. I have one small rock left. Four cigarettes—three, cuz now Darcy's smoking again.

"Why do I always got to think for both of us?"

"You're good at it," he says. "Good at using your head, ha ha."

I want to punch him, but instead I swallow hard. I don't want to be alone tonight. "Bathhouse?"

"Naw," says Darcy. "I'm not in the mood for those fuckers. No clubs, no bullshit."

"Underpass?" But we both owe money to some dealers over there, so I know that won't fly. It's too late for the drop-in where we crash sometimes. Darcy's sister put out an R.O. on him so we can't go there, and Henry, well, Henry is definitely out of the question.

"What about your vegan hippies? Can we go there?"

"Hmm." Darcy twiddles his fingers on his chin. "Probably not. Not supposed to hang there if you're fucked up. House rules."

I snort. "What are they, straight edge? No wonder you're never there."

"Too far, anyways." Darcy snaps his fingers and says, "What about the Professor?"

"Aw, that dude is away somewhere. Out of the country or something. Can't stay with him."

But we could stay at his place, right?

"No, goof, it's *this* street." I stop on the corner, but Darcy keeps going. "Fine, be that way," I shout after him.

He keeps walking down the main drag of the gaybourhood. He's stubborn, but he's usually wrong when it comes to directions. He'll come back when he figures it out. I lean on a parking meter and pull up my hood. It's getting colder.

It's dinner time, that lonely twilight hour. Gay men run in and out of the expensive shops. There's a cheerful sign in the butcher's window right in front: "Our meat's not cheap but neither are you." Inside, a well-dressed man leans over the counter and points: organic beef, lamb shanks, lean spiced sausage.

My stomach growls. Looking at that meat reminds me of the time Darcy got the great idea to go cattle rustling. We had this rich old trick in Cabbagetown who had a nice big patio for summer parties. We discovered his deluxe new barbecue while squatting his garage last spring. Darcy's idea was to steal raw meat from the grocery store. So we smuggled it out in our pants, right, and carried it bare-handed all the way down to the old man's house to try and talk him into buying it, cash on the spot. *Ha ha*. Made some money that day, didn't we?

Me and Darcy have panhandled this whole strip long enough to know the drill: Starbucks' lattes in the morning, brunch at noon, afternoon shopping, dinner with a friend. Then a long night of drinking, dancing, and debauchery. Around here, most men like their meat as fresh and pink as the boys they invite over later, after the scraps are tossed.

Darcy runs back down the street toward me as the sky opens up. "Shit, you were right," he yells. I'd laugh, but we're busy running. Down comes the rain: big drops, surprisingly cold and stinging. Almost hail.

"There," he shouts. He points to a tiny fenced-in front yard with a large boulder as a centrepiece. He leaps over the wrought iron and lunges around several flower pots.

"There was no rock!" Darcy's not listening. This thing is so large it must have been driven from goddamn Sudbury, driven down Highway 69 in some kind of reinforced flatbed four-by-four, a truck from my ghostly past.

He says, "It was this place with the rock, so shut up," and I cuff him. I'm still kind of mad about the courier. Darcy looks around for the spare key. He peers under the doormat and in the mailbox and digs up some of the orange flowers from the garden. "Fuck," he yells.

The rain is pouring down his face, drilling into the ground, slopping mud all over his sneakers and the draggy hems of his pants. He's about to smash the wee glass pane on the front door when we notice a man inside, staring at us. He's wearing an apron and oven mitts and he's holding a frying pan in one hand. In the other is an oven-mitted cell phone. He looks a bit scared but mostly surprised. He waves the phone down towards the mess of flowers at Darcy's feet. Now he's pissed.

"I told you it's the wrong house." I book it.

"I coulda sworn that was it," he says, when he catches up to me. He's laughing, imitating the dude. His hair is plastered to his forehead. That awful shirt is completely soaked.

"Shut up." I cut across another fenced yard and duck behind the shrubs that block the front door. I move the mat. The key is right there, small and hopeful. It isn't breaking and entering if you got a key, right?

Inside it's quiet and dark. It smells musty. Darcy locks the door and puts the chain across. He squeaks his wet shoes down the hall and into the living room.

"Take your shoes off," I yell. "Seriously."

"What are you, my mom?"

I take mine off, pull the wet hoodie over my head, and peek around the corner into the living room. There are bookshelves all around. Stacks of books lay on the floor in front of them. Books spill off the coffee table. Books support a dying plant. Books underneath the phone. There's a small TV covered in more books. There are a couple of old chairs. Darcy collapses on the professor's big leather couch, muddy shoes smearing the little pillow at one end.

"Fuckwad. Look at the mess."

Darcy sucks his teeth. He slowly reaches for his shoes, one then the next, and tosses them at my head. I catch and drop them on the plastic tray by the door. The small recycling bin beside the boot tray is full of old newspapers. And on the very top is the temporary cancellation notice—for one whole month.

"Uh, this dude is away for a while," I say.

"Awesome."

"Well, I'm washing my clothes, right?" I know where the machines are from the last time I came over. The professor gently touched my clothes and asked if I wanted them cleaned. He didn't make a big fuss about it, just showed me where everything was and how to turn on the washer. *He wouldn't mind*, I think. I go straight down the hall, through the small kitchen, open the closet door, and there it still is.

"Do mine, too," says Darcy. He follows me to the kitchen. He rips off the preppy shirt, his pants fall around his feet. He pulls his dirty socks off, then his Tasmanian Devil boxers, not a blink of an eye. He's naked and absentmindedly tugs his ball sac, scratches his bony chest. His skin is so white, the veins show through. Blue veiner: that's what chicken hawks call him at the bathhouse. When Darcy first got to town, he sure made some money. The men couldn't keep off him. Now, he's no runway model, but at least his arm sores aren't oozing.

"I'm hungry, yo." Darcy opens one cupboard, pokes around, slams the door, opens another. "Fuck, this guy has no food." He tosses a few things onto the counter, packages of ramen. They fall to the kitchen floor. "I want Kraft dinner."

I dump soap into the washer, turn the dials, and start the water flowing. Darcy's stuff is all in there. My socks: one, two. My hoodie: empty the pockets. My shirt goes in. I duck and check my chest from habit. The scars are healed up pretty good now, faint lines near my jujube nipples. I never had tits to speak of, always more like pecs anyways, so the surgery wasn't too drastic. Like, I can take my shirt off in public if I want, and no one is any the wiser. Except other trans guys, right? I don't know how we can tell. Smell it, probably. Sniff each other right out of a crowd, we can. My muddy jeans get slogged into the machine, and I debate the underwear. They're wet, not fresh either. But I hate even Darcy seeing me.

"Take it off, sugar loaf." He swings his bony hips at me.

"Shut up." But he's not even looking.

"Can you believe this dude doesn't even have proper cereal? Like, what is this shit?" He shakes a box of bran into a pile on the floor. "I want Cocoa Puffs!"

Fuck it. I pull off the tighty whities and toss them in. I slam the washer lid down. I cup my hands in front to hold my dick in place and head for the bathroom. "Just don't make a friggin' mess," I say before shutting the door. I put in the stopper and fill the tub with hot water. There's a bottle of something smelly so I squeeze a bit under the tap: a real bath with bubbles. I step in, jump out, hop around holding my burned foot. *Shit shit shit shit.* I take a dump while the water cools. It's been a while since I got to use such a nice clean toilet. With soft paper, too. I flush and even spray the air a bit with the faggy freshener. Now the water is perfect. I hunker down so it covers me, comes right up to my bottom lip when I lie back. I decide my dick should have a bit of a rinse, too. I soap it up and wring it. Dirty water runs out. I rinse it a few more times, and it starts to look pinker. It looks less like a part of me and more like something I once paid money for. I prop it on the edge of the tub and lie back again. I look at it up there. It looks at me. Then I submerge myself totally.

Lying underwater I can hear Darcy cranking the knobs on the TV. "This shit don't work," he yells. He comes into the bathroom. "I'm bored."

"Knock much?"

Darcy yawns in the mirror. His eyes crinkle up and his mouth stretches wide. The red hair sprays around his face like a demented halo. He leans forward and starts picking at his teeth. He finds a toothbrush in the drawer and loads it up with minty paste. He scrubs carefully, like he's remembering the instructions from a long ago manual. I gather up what's left of the bubbles and station them above my crotch. Darcy spits and rinses. He smiles at me in the mirror. "I can see your boobies," he says.

"Shut up."

He looks hurt. "I didn't mean it like that. I meant boy boobies. Boys have boobs, too, you know." He puts his big toe in the tub water and wiggles it around. He splashes me and I grab his cold foot.

"You stink."

"So clean me," he says, and plops right on top, knees and elbows cracking against the porcelain tub. We wrestle a bit, send waves over the edge, onto the tile floor. Our bones clack together; it's a tight squeeze even for two skinny boys. Finally Darcy settles himself at one end, his head resting on one side of the faucet, his legs stretched out so his feet pop up beside my shoulders. My legs rest over his narrow torso, my feet near his face. He blows bubbles with his mouth. He smiles at me strangely, then up pop a series of large bubbles from the middle of the tub.

"Gross!"

He says, "Ha ha. There's your bubble bath."

"Your feet stink," I say. He waggles them on either side of me.

"Yours are dirty, too."

"So wash them." I chuck the wet cloth in his face.

"Don't be like that," he says. "You get so mad all the time." He looks at me for a minute. Then he sends another loud bubble to the surface by my leg.

"What the—?"

Darcy is in hysterics.

He grabs my foot and slides the soap bar in between my toes. When he gets near the little one, my foot twitches, and he holds it tight in his hands. He rubs along the bottom, all the way to my rough heel. He presses around the heel, traces the sides of my foot, massages deep in the arch and in the sore, neglected ball of it. He pulls the toes again, slowly, twisting them a tiny bit just before letting go.

My voice wobbles when I ask him where he learned to do that.

"My mom used to make me rub her feet all the time when I was little," he says. "They got sore from hookin' in high heels." He sings this last part and rolls his shoulder, shakes his wet hair like a dog. "My sister bossed me around and made me paint her nails. No wonder I'm queer."

We laugh. Darcy adds more hot water. He has to stand up so he doesn't get burned. He sits in front of me, my legs cramped around his, like we're riding a toboggan downhill. I soap up the cloth again and slop it loudly against his narrow back.

"What would happen if the King caught us?"

Darcy flinches. "Seriously?"

"Uh huh." I wash his pale back, long strokes, up and down.

"Well, the first time I heard about him was from this kid. This cute little hustler, Jake. He had some story about the King snatching up kids and selling them off. Like permanently. For snuff or other fucked-up movies, for dungeon boys, that sort of thing. Everyone thought Jake was on the pipe too much, though. He was always borrowing money and scamming, right?"

This Jake sounds a lot like someone else I know. I trace my finger from one freckle to the next on Darcy's back, past his sharp shoulder blades and the knobby bumps of his spine.

"So Jake was going on about it, right, saying the King was on the hunt. He was scared shitless, trying to hide, even trying to get out of town, trying to bum more money off everyone, but no one would give him any. Cuz he already owed."

Darcy sighs and shivers when I dribble more water down his back.

"Then what happened?"

"Then he disappeared, all of a sudden. Nobody's seen him since."

"Maybe he did leave town," I say. "Maybe he went home."

"Naw. He wouldn't. Not if half the shit he said about his parents was true."

"Maybe the social workers got him. Maybe he went to fosters," I say.

"Nope." Darcy wriggles his shoulders. "Rub me."

I slop the wet cloth on his skinny back again. We sit in silence for a while.

"Well, he could've gone anywhere," I say.

"Who?"

"That kid," I say. "Jake."

"Oh, him. Well, he could've, but he didn't." Darcy sounds pretty sure of himself.

"How the hell do you know?" I don't know why this makes me so mad. It scares me, more than anything.

"Because I know. I saw pictures." Darcy's voice is tight, scratchier than usual.

"What kind of pictures?" I say.

"The dead kind."

I drop the cloth in the water. "Where'd you see those? At some creep's place?"

"No." Darcy's voice sounds strangled. His shoulders hunch forward.

"Are you crying?" I try to twist him around but we're rammed in that tub, and there's no room.

"No," he says loudly. Darcy's shoulders start to shake. He gasps. A high-pitched sound squeezes out of him. I don't know what to do. I've never seen him like this.

"What's wrong?" I say, but that's dumb. *Everything's* wrong and we both know it.

Darcy sobs while he talks. He sounds just like a little kid. "I-I just feel bad. I never believed that boy, and now he's fucking dead."

Finally we twist around a bit so I can hold his wet face against me. His boney white self jabs at me, all angles. He knocks against the tub and splashes water around. The ugly sounds that cough out of him are more like a dog barking than a boy crying.

I ask him more questions, but Darcy just howls. He won't say anything else. Like where he saw the pictures, or who had them. Or what exactly happened to Jake. I get the feeling he knows a whole lot more, though. He's scared. *Wigged right out.* As though it could happen to him.

And it could, I think. To any of us.

His terrible fear infects me, quick as the hep, quick as the bug, quick as any bad thing at all. I think about Lil' Brat, smart as a fox and twice as mean, gone with the King today. *What will happen to him?*

Darcy calms down after a while and we add more hot to the tub. His dirt and stink are finally washing off. He fiddles with the cloth for a bit but eventually settles against my chest again. His wet hair pokes in my eyes and mouth but I don't mind. I lean back and let the water do its thing. I don't know where to put my arms so I just kind of hug them around his front. It feels nice. My dick falls in the water and he picks it up, squeezes it softly, and holds onto it.

"You don't mind, do you, Sly?"

"What, you playing with my dick again?" We chuckle. I can feel his laugh rumble against me and it's better than before, better than his heaving, awful cries.

"Let's stay here for a long time, Sly."

"Okay. 'Til the Professor comes back." But I wonder how soon it'll be before he gets bored or starts jonesing, before he paces up and down the hall, restless, edgy, and needing some kind of fix.

"No, I mean the tub. Let's stay in this tub forever."

I say, "Okay."

Because in this business, you just never fucking know.

Happy House

Home is the Factory squat. From the first time I climbed through that broken window with some kids from the shelter, I knew it was my place. I could take my boots off here. Maybe even sleep a whole night without getting my shit fucked with. Just like the first night I met Oreo. When I saw her—a gorgeous punk warrior smiling brightly—a light turned on in that empty inside space, and I knew she was meant for me.

The Factory is not an address you can write on social worker forms. Can't get your welfare delivered here. It's totally under the radar, a boarded-up chair factory in the Junction. It's hidden from the rest of the city by a wall of trees and tangled bush, like a prickly moat in some fairy tale. The slaughterhouse next door is a small, sinister-looking thing. It reeks. An abandoned lot separates us from them, but that smell is everywhere. Not like meat, or even raw meat, but the gag-worthy smell of pig shit and rotting entrails and old blood. No one else would even try to live up here, not with that stink.

So, home is a smelly, red-bricked fortress with giant padlocked warehouse doors on one side. We use the regular-sized door at the back; locks stripped off, doorknob gone. We got electricity—some kid wired it up a year or so ago—but there's lots of natural light. We ripped boards off some of the windows. Up high in the loft section there are even more windows, not all broke. It's a mess, but we're slowly clearing it out. Some kids call it the Pig House on account of next door, but we're against that. One, we're vegans and don't insult animals. Two, we totally hate cops. Three, the *slaughterhouse* is the Pig House and *our place* is the Factory, end of story. Someone started calling it Fairy Mountain since our squat is now fully gay, but people started thinking F.M. was a completely different place, like a whole new squat someplace else in Toronto. Totally confusing! So really, we are just the Factory squatters, and that's that.

The Factory has rules like anyplace, but it's better than shelters and foster care and the Boys' and Girls' Home before that. Obviously, it's way better than living on the street, getting beat on and hassled and eating rape for breakfast, like you do. Going hungry and losing your mind, friends turning on you. Always on the make. At the Factory we do chores to fix the place up. We dumpster dive food and cook together, have house meetings, that sort of thing. Sometimes we have punk shows in the main space, or DIY workshops about silk-screening, basic plumbing, worm composting, whatever. Lots of kids pass through in the summer: rail riders, touring bands, punk nomads. If they stay, they got to cook or fix shit or teach stuff. They got to make the Factory a better place for being there. That's rule number one.

Also up there, not exactly number two or anything, but up near the top, is this other rule about not oppressing other people with your bullshit. I thought that would mean not being a racist asshole or a homophobe and stuff like that. Apparently it also means not rubbing your "monogamous romance" in other people's faces because this can be boring and offensive. You can have all the sex you want with as many people as possible, but so help you if you fall for one girl and want to be with *just* her. Like, as a couple, which is seriously my situation with Oreo. Personally, I don't think it's fair, but that's what it is to live in a freegan collective— plenty of compromise!

So here we are again, me and Oreo, standing in the gravel driveway *outside* the Factory for another Relationship Talk. At least it's not raining.

"Oh, shit." Oreo, adorable as she is, looks totally guilty when I wave the paper.

"You wrote this, don't pretend you didn't," I say. "That's your handwriting." Not to mention her signature skull and crossbones decorating the page.

She opens her mouth but a truck downshifts, brakes, and pulls onto our little road. I can't hear her, just see her mouth moving. We dive behind the corner. The truck churns up small stones and spits them out as it passes. I hear squealing, and when I peek, I see all those round snouts through the dirty cages. They're heading next door.

Poor little piggies.

We wait for the dust to settle and the truck to park itself and the roaring engine to quiet before we continue.

"It's supposed to be a surprise." Muscles ripple along Oreo's arm when she points at the large heading. "See? Ferret's *surprise* birthday party. It's a to-do list, babe."

"Obviously," I say. "But you shouldn't have left it lying around where I'd see it."

"Yeah," she says. She looks pretty bummed. "That sucks."

She has written everything out carefully with extra swirls and lightning bolts around each number on the list:

1. dumpster dive vegan cake
2. draw a funny birthday card
3. write love poem for Ferret
4. make brilliant playlist for party
5. check with squat about party!!

"Oreo, I don't want a birthday party." My stomach knots just thinking about it.

"How do you know? You've never had one." Oreo kisses me. She tugs my blue dreadlocks, twirls one end between her fingers.

"I shouldn't have told you that. Just cuz I haven't *had* something doesn't mean I *want* it."

Oreo chuckles. "You sure about that, babe?" She flashes a perfect, flirty smile.

"Uh, yeah." I think about every creep who says I'm only a dyke because I haven't had "the right one" yet.

Her warm hands creep playfully inside the waistband of my combat pants. Her fingers rub the tickly spot above my crack. "Come on, Ferret." She gives me a slobbery zerbert on the cheek. "It'll be fun." She smiles. Oreo has really nice teeth—evenly spaced, white. The tip of her tongue pokes out at me. Farther back I see the silver flash of her piercing. She says, "You'll get to be the centre of attention."

"I hate that." My head droops onto her shoulder.

"Okay, you'll get to sit on the sidelines and see your friends having a great time."

"Hmm." I squish my face into the crook of her neck and tug her long braid. She smells like honey cake, the lotion we shoplifted at the pharmacy. When she talks, I feel her voice rumbling from inside her chest. I trace the neckline of her ripped Slayer shirt, touch her warm skin with my finger. She is the most beautiful colour ever: coffee with cream. She is taller and darker, bigger and braver than me.

"If you don't like it, you don't have to have another one." Oreo looks hopeful, something I don't feel too often. "I already made my list. Please?"

"I just want to be with you."

"Me and you are together all the time. You should have fun with friends." Her smile and her shining eyes and the way her beautiful face lights up when she has her hands shoved down my pants make me buckle.

"I don't even know when my real birthday is." If you get dumped at the Boys' and Girls' Home without a proper birth certificate, without a note or some weeping, incapable mother to tell them about you, they just assign a date.

"Saturday night sounds good."

"Maybe." I hate to disappoint her.

"I'll get you Sour Cherry Blasters." She wiggles an eyebrow.

I sigh. "Oh, all right."

"Ferret's having a party!" Oreo bounces up and down. "It's gonna be sick. You wait."

My knees wobble when she kisses me. Heat spreads in my belly. Oreo smiles and pulls me towards the Factory door. Like I said, you can have all the sex you want in there, just don't flaunt a Meaningful Relationship.

We step from the hot, bright outside world with its sun and its buzzing, flying creatures into the dark, dank Factory.

Cement floors and boarded windows make it cool inside, even though it's the blazing end of August. The Factory smells musty. Old. Exposed brick with oversized storage units line the walls. Giant iron chains hang off pulleys in the corner by the padlocked loading dock. Oreo and I zip past the open kitchen area with the long dinner table to the back corner where our mattress is hidden behind shelves and a tall wall unit. Oreo's shirt is already off. She yanks my studded belt. I pull our makeshift curtain across the rope guide and hook it in place. Our corner smells like incense sticks and vanilla candle wax and patchouli oil and sawdust and, of course, slaughterhouse. Oreo pulls me down on top of her. We roll and giggle and kiss. Oreo whispers into my mouth, "Happy beerthday, dear Ferret, happy beerthday to you."

Later that afternoon, we're crashing through the tangled bush that surrounds the squat. We're taking the back way to Special Friend Discount, the sketchy convenience store, to get my Sour Cherry Blasters. At night, we cut through the open field and just walk down the gravel lane that the pig trucks use, which is faster. But during daylight we keep it on the down-low.

Special Friend has the basics: dust-covered groceries, porn, tampons, and junk food. Most Special Friend customers buy cartons of illegal cigarettes straight from the reserve, cash only, and only if no one else is in the store. And only if the cashier recognizes you. And not if they think you might be a narco, out to bust their ass.

"Out of everything we've ever dumpstered, how come

there's never been any Sour Cherry Blasters? Don't you think that's weird?"

Oreo thinks about it for a minute as we continue down the steep hill, crushing overgrown weeds with each step.

"We always have more food at the Factory than we need, right?"

"Yeah," she says. The path widens and she grabs my hand so we can walk side by side.

"All the ripe fruits and veggies we can eat, tons of it organic. Day-old bread, doughnuts, noodles, you name it. But no Sour Cherry Blasters, not ever."

Oreo says, "Maybe stores never throw them out. Maybe people like us are so busy eating them, they never get wasted. If you stop buying them, you could maybe score them for free."

"Maybe. I can't wait, though. I want some now."

We cross the railway tracks and pop out of some greenery onto the sidewalk of a small street that leads to the Junction, past all these old homes. Most are dilapidated, renovated into cheap rooming houses or bizarre churches with long names. Some are yuppie investments, with new roofs and pretty front gardens. One or two are boarded-up wrecks. Special Friend is only a couple blocks farther.

"Surreal," says Oreo, looking back at the now-hidden path that leads to the squat.

"We're invisible in there." Oreo rubs her neck where my mouth marked her. "It's like we don't even exist."

"In a good way, though." I laugh and swing her hand in mine. It's still sunny, hot. I'm with my girl. I have a safe place to live and good food, even some friends. I'm happy, for once in my life, invisible or not. That feeling—the sudden realization that things could maybe get better for me—tingles in my spine.

Oreo giggles. "Ferret, you got burrs all over." She pulls one off my sleeve. "There's more." She crouches down and works at the ones on my combat pants.

"You, too." We pick them off each other for a minute or two. I can't reach the ones on the back of my shirt. The street is deserted except for us. The houses on either side have blinds or curtains in the windows. Nobody's spying, so I take my shirt right off and keep picking at the burrs. Oreo inspects my pant seams, all the way up to the crotch.

"Whoa," I say, smiling at her.

Oreo laughs and lifts me up. I wrap my legs around her. We kiss for a long time. My shirt flutters to the ground. I forget what we're doing, where we're supposed to be going.

There's the sound of an engine. There are brakes.

"Well, well. Looky here." The low voice cuts through our lips, severs our bodies. We'd recognize it anywhere. I scramble down, and Oreo steps in front of me.

It's the King. He likes to be called the King because he sounds like Elvis. He does his black hair the same way, too, greased up with sideburns. He is also the King because he rules this city, at least as far as junkies and hookers and street kids go. The cop car is parked beside the curb facing the wrong way. The King leans out his open window. The door opens, and he stands up, and up. When he walks toward us he grows even taller; his blue uniform gets bigger with each step.

My leg shakes. My mouth goes dry. My shirt is only a

pace or two away on the other side of Oreo, but my feet are heavy cement blocks that won't budge.

"Some reason you're not wearing a shirt?" He stands close to us, too close, and he rests one large hand on his hip, right near the black holster that holds his shiny gun.

Oreo says, "It's not against the law. Not in Ontario." Her chin juts out. Anger pinks her cheeks.

Oh, shit.

"You think people want to look at your flat tits?" He looks disgusted, like I'm a bug he'll squash. "Think everyone wants to watch your disgusting lezzie show?"

"Put your shirt on, Ferret." There's a tic in Oreo's cheek. *She might blow.*

I bend down for the shirt, but the King steps on it with his huge polished shoe. "You'll put that on when I say so." He's not even looking at me, just staring right back at Oreo.

I keep my hold on the fabric, in case he lifts his foot. I'm crouched low, trying to cover myself. I have a close-up of his shiny cop shoes and his hemmed pants.

"Get up." His voice is mean. It feels like a stomach kick; it hurts all the way through. He snaps his meaty fingers in my face. He's standing so close to Oreo that he's pressed against her.

"Don't talk to her like that," says Oreo.

The King puts one large hand around Oreo's neck and grabs my bare shoulder with the other. His squeeze sends spasms through my dangling arm. His fingers could break me. "I'll talk to her any goddamn way I please, dyke. I will say and do whatever I like. I'm the law."

Oreo struggles to get away, but he presses harder. Her face

darkens. She makes awful sounds, choking, gasping for air.

"You unfuckable little sluts make me sick, you know that?" He covers us both with his coffee breath. His nose is red and veiny at the end. Spit flies from the corner of his mouth when he talks. "Now. Put your filthy shirt back on."

I would. I want to have as many layers as possible between my insides and him, but he's still holding me, threatening to snap my very bones.

He shoves me. I stumble. I land half on the sidewalk, half on the grass. He's got Oreo by the throat with both hands now. He lowers his face and he's saying something, I don't know what. He's squeezing the life out of her, right in front of me, and there's nothing I can do. I grab my top and try to put it on. My fingers tremble. My left arm, the one he hurt, hangs numb. I might be crying. Every inch of me screams to run, run, but I can't leave Oreo with this monster.

"Please." My voice falters. "We'll go, okay?"

He squeezes harder. Oreo's eyes bulge. One of her boots kicks out like a puppet dancing. I panic. My breath shortens into small gasps. I feel dizzy watching, but can't look away.

"You'll go when I say so."

Oreo's face is a terrible colour. Veins stand out on her temples. Finally the King releases his hold. That's when I exhale.

Oreo collapses. She retches. Her hands flutter to her throat. She stays curled on the ground. This is terrible, to see her humiliated like this.

"Public indecency, mischief, loitering ... I could nail you with any of those. But you're not worth the paperwork. So get the fuck outta here before I change my mind!"

I'm beside her, hands petting, trying to calm her down. I tug on her arm. I try to lift her. Her eyes snap open. Now she's up. We run down the street, past the shuttered old houses with the sagging porches, toward Special Friend. The King follows us to the corner in his car. Then the car turns and slowly chugs away in the other direction. Oreo coughs. She spits on the sidewalk. There are marks coming up around her neck that cover my love bite completely.

What happens next is terrible, too heartbreaking to watch. Oreo kicks the newspaper machine on the corner over and over, denting the side of it. She howls. That probably really hurt. Oreo paces the sidewalk punching the air, swearing, screaming, pulling her long black hair out of its braid.

I sit on the cement stairs of the convenience store and wait for it to pass. She's in a rage, that's for sure. She can't help it. You just got to know that about her and when it comes, you step away. Let her do her thing. You definitely do not want to be up in her face. The first time I even saw Oreo she was in the pit at an all-ages hardcore show downtown. She noticed how some guy wouldn't leave me alone. She gave him what for and, of course, he snotted back to her. So she slugged him. To be punched by a girl, even a butch one, was embarrassing for a punk. But when he hit Oreo back, he invited the beat down of his puny existence. Oreo knew how to fight, and that day she did it for me.

Today, though, there's no one else to hit. No physical release to extinguish this hate inferno the King sparked up.

The store owner comes outside and waves a cell phone around. Oreo stops yelling.

"No trouble," he says. He turns and says something in

Korean to his wife, who is huddled inside, peering out from behind the long-distance phone-card posters on the front door.

"Please," I say to him. "No phone."

"No trouble, no phone," he says, looking warily at Oreo. She's standing in the street, her back to us. Her torso heaves with each breath. Her hands hang at her sides in loose fists, defeated.

"Please." I feel my eyes well up and have to look away from him.

Eventually he goes back inside with his wife and they both stare out the front door until I walk towards Oreo.

"Hey."

She sniffs loudly.

"I don't feel like candy anymore," I say.

She nods.

"Let's go home." I touch her back lightly. She flinches. I wait. She wipes her face with her sleeve. She spits into the street. Then she takes my hand and we walk back the way we came. We don't say a word when we pass the spot where it all went down, we just keep walking.

Oreo hits the path first. She moves fast in long robotic strides. One of her steps flattens a patch of long grass. In its wake I notice a small piece of paper. I stop to pick it up. It's a typed message from a fortune cookie. It says, "Happy celebration happy, Wong's House of Love."

"Yeah, right," I mutter. But still, I fold it and put it in my pocket for safekeeping.

Toddlers and Tiaras

(For Doris)

Me and Darcy sit on the rusty fire escape outside the old lady's apartment window. We're waiting for our show to start. It's sweaty hot; the night air is heavy, with no breeze at all, not even five floors up. I shift. My bony ass hurts and angry red stripes mark the backs of my bare legs. Darcy pulls his T-shirt up over his face but keeps the collar around his forehead, tucked behind his ears. Then he twists the cotton material into a thing that he ties up like a turban on his head, covering his greasy red hair.

"Freak."

"It's my tiara, Sly," he says. He tries to grab a cigarette from my pack, but I slap him. He sighs. We both know the smoke would snake right in there, through the open window, and the old lady would smell it, and she'd know we were perched out here again. Last week she threw a pot of dirty dishwater at us, and that was not great.

"Wish we had some chips." He farts.

"Shut up, Darcy. She'll hear us."

"As if. She's fucking deaf." He does it again, louder and longer.

"Yeah? I bet her nose works just fine."

He laughs. "Listen, if your Professor friend had an ef-fing TV we wouldn't have to be here. I'll probably get a disease sitting on this contraption."

I don't say anything, but we both know Darcy already has the hep, and he didn't get it climbing fire escapes. Plus, we're *lucky* we can stay at the Professor's. We're *lucky* we're not out on the street getting our asses beat by people we owe or by the cops, who hate us. We're lucky the frigging King didn't scoop us up in his latest raid and that he hasn't tracked us down since.

"It better not be a highlights show," says Darcy.

"Shh. It's starting," I say, as canned laughter bursts out. We sneak right up to the window, lean our elbows on the sill. We're a foot away from the back of her couch with the crocheted blanket on it, maybe two from the back of her head. Her white hair is combed neatly, and she's got a long braid wrapped around, tucked into a bun, and pinned in place. If we lean to one side, we can see her big old TV directly in front. It's like we're at the drive-in, sitting in the back seat.

The theme song swells, the trailer rolls, and we hunch closer. We shimmy our shoulders in time to the music. Darcy claps his hands lightly to the beat. Inside, the old lady hums off key. After the song, the show host announces this is the second-last show of the season—they're kicking three more girls off tonight. Then there's a commercial break, time for the old lady to make her sandwich. She grunts when she leans forward and slowly stands. She shuffles into the kitchen. We hear plates banging around and the fridge door slam.

Now we lean right through the window, everything from the waist up. We reach over the back of the couch to pet the stuffed dogs all piled up on it. One of them, a worn-out Dalmatian, stares its googly eyes at me. I make it growl softly, then bite Darcy's scabby arm.

"Quit it," he whispers.

"Arrrugh," I bark back.

The glow of the television lights up the shelves around the stand. There are dozens of ceramic dogs flickering in the blue light, all sitting on old lady doilies. Some of them beg paws-up, some have tongues flapping out the side of their china mouths, some leap with painted frisbees in their teeth. She has a Dogs of the Year calendar up on the wall—from 1987.

"Think she has any weed stashed?" he asks hopefully.

"Yeah, right." Last week, when we first came here, it was to score pills from the bathroom cabinet. But as it turned out, the old lady was watching Darcy's favourite show. So instead of robbing her, we just chilled and watched from outside until she caught us, like.

The fridge door bangs again. We crouch down. The lady has it timed pretty good. She shuffles back into the living room just as the commercials end. The couch springs creak when she plops down, and we peek our heads up. She's got her sandwich on a small plate. It's cut in half diagonally. She picks one triangle up and stuffs it in her mouth.

"Onions?" whispers Darcy. He wrinkles his nose.

I elbow him.

The old lady sets her plate with half a sandwich down on the side table. She flicks crumbs off her lap. She claps as they open the curtain and the little girls stand ready, toes pointed, hands clasped, those concrete smiles holding up their faces. Beady-eyed mothers hover on the sidelines. The host waves from centre stage and trills out names: Ashleigh, Morghan, Rhianna, Tressa. Lyndsey, Tarabelle, Crystal Dawn.

The old lady heaves herself up and raises a fist toward the television.

"Aw, why she got to stand right there?" Darcy sucks his teeth.

We lean to the right, to the left, to opposite sides at the same time, trying to see past her. She's short and wide. She's got her hands on her hips and she's yelling at the judges. Not in English, in some other language.

"She sure sounds mad," says Darcy.

"Seriously."

Darcy crosses his arms over his bare chest. "I mean, why have a couch if you're not going to sit on it?"

"Beats me."

She waves her hand one last time in disgust, then slowly bends to sit back down. She lands heavily and some of the stuffed dogs avalanche into a pile around her. "Bah," she says. She picks up the Dalmatian and sniffs it.

On television, the girls move stiffly around the tiny stage and wave. We get close-ups of each one, cut to prerecorded snippets when the girls forget they are on camera. Rhianna rolls her shoulder: Rhianna, collapsed in her hotel room as the adults argue about which dress she should wear. Morghan and Tressa, the prudey sisters, twirling: Morghan and Tressa eating too much cake and getting yelled at by their mother. Tarabelle shuffle-steps: Tarabelle falls asleep while her arch-nemesis practices walking in the hallway, her mother shaking her head: "No, do it again. No. Do you want to keep your pretty dress? So do it right."

Then there's Crystal Dawn. Darcy and the old woman start clapping. Crystal Dawn is definitely their favourite. She's the creepiest, only three and a half, but she has the plastic made-up face of a forty-year-old. Her smile is frosty, and her eyes shine like a store-bought doll, like all the little girls who compete in these pageants. She waves triumphantly. Crystal Dawn is so outrageous, she gets an entire shame video all to herself. They edit seconds from each of her temper tantrums to recreate the whole gorgeous mess. It's like flip books you make in school when you're bored. It starts with the first bottom lip twitch. Then the shaking, silent, stretching open mouth as her face gets red and wrinkly. She sucks in air—we all hold our breaths. Finally, it's the money shot: the unapologetic howl! Her drooling, snotting, rage assault! We're addicted to it, all three of us. The whole continent, really.

"Wow," I say. "That never gets dull."

Darcy nods. "I wish *I* could cry like that."

I don't say it, but he pretty much *did* cry like that, just last week when we first landed at the Professor's.

"Oh, not again," groans Darcy.

As if the tantrum video is not enough, the show producers cut back to Crystal Dawn's notorious piss scene. Inside, the old lady sighs loudly. She reaches for the other half of her sandwich. She doesn't want to watch this either.

"There she goes," I say happily.

Flashback: Crystal Dawn crouches backstage, sticks out her bum, and pees through her lace-trimmed Christian Lacroix panties. She looks like an angry animal, red-faced, fists clenched, yellow curls bobbing. Crystal Dawn's mother, a hefty lump of a woman, screams and shakes her. "Those cost 425 bucks, you brat! That's coming out of your prize money!"

The old lady hollers.

Darcy almost gives up on Crystal Dawn every time he sees this clip. "She has no respect for French design!"

"She's not even in kindergarten. How's she supposed to respect anything?"

Inside, the lady drops her plate; it clatters to the floor and she bellows. We duck. We stay crouched down 'til she's quiet, just the show blasting. The host says the panty pee scene has had more YouTube hits than the inaugural address. Crystal Dawn's baby voice booms: "I did a bad mistake, but tonight I'm gonna be perfect."

The old lady murmurs. We peek over the sill. Darcy gurgles with excitement. Crystal Dawn *is* in top form. Her helmeted up-do sparkles with rhinestones, golden ringlets pasted into place. Her eyes shine from the lubricating drops her mother puts in right before she hits the stage. She's got her tan sprayed on, and her flippers tucked in her mouth to cover those crooked teeth. She's wearing a pink and white cupcake, the short tutu all the littlest girls wear. When she walks across the stage, she swivels her hips. Her hands flit like birds with rigor mortis. Her shoulders roll aggressively. She winks at the judges. She's killing the competition, and she knows it!

"Oh, she's wearing the Jon Benét booties," squeals Darcy. "Bold move. She'll totally win now."

"Not if they call Children's Aid, she won't."

"Children's Hate? You want to sic those dried-up social workers on Crystal Dawn? What's wrong with you?"

He thinks I despise these girls since I hated being one myself.

"Crystal Dawn's mother is a great manager, Sly. Her stylist has impeccable taste!"

"Whatever."

"You know, I used to dream about being in pageants. Only *my* mom didn't care enough to put me in them."

"You want a mother like that? That can't stay out of her track pants long enough to make another baby to pimp out?"

"At least they can see their children's *potential*."

"Potential of a cum-crusted death in a scary basement?"

The lady stiffens. I duck down again instinctively.

Darcy whispers, "It's swimsuit time. Look."

They're all lined up in their fruity two pieces, but I stare at the space off-stage and at the crowd during the sweeping camera shots. I'm looking for the forgotten siblings: a truly ugly step-sister, some invisible brother, or unloved cousin. Maybe a henpecked husband, guarding the miniature designer dresses, yawning. Somebody real. Someone you can sink your teeth into.

During the next commercial break, the lady goes into her kitchen. We lie flat on our backs. Darcy tries to think who we can score off of.

"I thought you wanted to get clean."

"I did. But now I'm not so sure," he says. "Being sober is boring."

"Oh, so I'm boring?" I ask, pouting.

"I didn't say that. You're so touchy."

"Anyways," I say, "being bored is better than being dead."

"Ooh." Darcy pokes my arm.

I push his finger away. One week hiding out at the Professor's and Darcy has forgotten all about being scared to death, about being hunted by the King. He wants back in the game.

He says, "I know I freaked. I was wigging. But I'm fine now. I just want to get high."

I did a bad mistake but tonight I'm gonna be perfect.

I shrug Crystal Dawn's voice out of my head. "Well, we're shit outta luck, man."

"Maybe not. A lot can change in a few days," he says.

"We're still broke. We still owe a lot of money. Actually, *you* owe a lot of money, but somehow I always get stuck paying." Fuck if that don't piss me off.

"You make me sound like an asshole," he says cheerfully.

"The pigs are probably still looking for us. So we won't be making any money tonight."

"Fuck," says Darcy.

"Pretend we're on *Celebrity Rehab*. Famous people pay a lot to be someplace they can't get high. We got it for free."

"You're whack." Darcy snaps his fingers. "The courier! We could stop by his place, see what he's got." Darcy sparkles just thinking of that big blond boy.

"He took you to his place?" A lump hardens in my stomach.

"So?" Darcy's eyes shift. "How do you think I got his

sweater?" His lip curls into a sneer.

I remember the night he showed up wearing it, while I was working double time. The night of the storm, when we ended up crashing the Professor's pad.

"Well, without a GPS tracker you'll never find your way back there." I try to joke, but there's an edge to my voice.

His face tightens. He knows it's true, so he can't exactly argue. Darcy sighs. "I wish I was a girl model. I bet they get all the drugs they want. Plus I'd wear dresses everyday."

"Why?" I snort.

"My legs look good in them. And they come off lickety-split." He smiles prettily. "When's the last time you wore one?"

"First day of kindergarten. My mom made me. Teacher made me line up with the girls and I was like, *No, I'm a boy*. I kept going into the boys' line, and she kept pulling me out, so I kicked her. I put the frigging dress in the garbage. They called my mom cuz I was running around in my underwear, yelling."

"Troublemaker."

"Yeah, we used to fight all the time. She didn't get it." I chuck a small stone over the edge of the stairs, hear it hit the gravel parking lane below.

"She probably *got* it, she just didn't *like* it."

"I guess."

"So, you hate this show?"

"Kind of," I say. "It's so fake, all the stuff they do to them. But it's like they're making little girly monsters, which is cool."

"If you hate it so much, why watch it?"

"Well, you love it. So it reminds me what a Gaylord you are!" I laugh and Darcy steamrolls me, and that makes me laugh even harder.

"Hallo!" There's a sharp rap on the window ledge.

We sit up. The old lady must be standing behind the couch. She's right at the window. I put my hands up to block whatever she'll throw this time.

"Okay, we're leaving," says Darcy. He scrambles toward the steps, grabs the railing for balance.

"S'okay. S'okay," she says and motions us to come closer. I don't move.

"Hold dat." She passes two flowered plates through the open window. Each one has a little sandwich on it, cut diagonally. Darcy takes them, his mouth hanging open. "You gif me plates beck after."

"Thanks," I say finally. We sit back down on the stairs with our snack. Darcy sniffs his like a hungry dog. He looks at me. I shrug. She nods and waves: *go ahead.* The bread is strange—dark, heavy. When I put a bit in my mouth, it is soft and good. Darcy digs in, takes a big bite, and hums while he chews. I take another small mouthful. There are slabs of cold butter on it. Then there's some kind of filling, cream cheese with chopped green onions. Nothing I ever ate before. The creamy part is salty and also a bit sweet. It tastes good. The lady smiles at us and then she sits back down on the couch.

For the final few minutes of the show, we actually lean farther in the window. We don't have to be quiet or anything. "Kreestal Don, number von," says the lady. She sticks her wrinkly thumb up. Darcy sticks his thumb up, too. I'm out-voted.

"Crystal Dawn definitely has personality," I say.

"Charisma," says Darcy.

"She can't take the pressure," I say. "Not of being Little Miss West Virginia."

"Vat you say." The lady frowns at me. "Shoosh."

Darcy says, "Yeah, Sly. *Shoosh*."

The host is about to announce the results. "Which three will it be tonight?" There is a drum roll. The mothers rub their good luck charms. Tarabelle, who forgot her choreography half-way through the song, she's gone. No surprise there. She wails as one of the handlers leads her off stage. The camera bounces back and forth over the tense faces of the remaining contestants. The cake eaters, Morghan and Tressa, look terrified. Rhianna is pale. *Did she wear the right dress after all?* Apparently. It's Morghan and Tressa who get kicked off for poor performances and bad attitude, according to the judges. They leave the stage shame-faced, one biting her lower lip, the other wiping at tears.

Crystal Dawn is safe! Darcy and the old lady cheer. The host reminds us there are only four girls left—the heat is on! Next week promises to be even more scandalous. One of the parents is caught sabotaging another girl's props in the green room.

Darcy hands back our plates. "That was really good," he says.

The lady looks at us. Her old blue eyes see past our dirt and bruises, my messy hair, and the sores on Darcy's arms. "Next veek, you bring cheeps. I like peekle flavour, yes?"

We nod. *Yes.*

Pig House Party

Everyone who squats the Factory has to agree on something like having a party, so I figure it'll never happen. Which is perfect because it won't be *my* fault. It'll be the fault of our dumb-ass collective who can't agree on anything, not even what to have for breakfast. So I write "party" on the house meeting agenda, right after "dishes."

"Washing dishes is bougie," says Cricket. We're all sitting at the kitchen table except for Cricket, who sits cross-legged *on* the table, painting his nails bright blue to match his mohawk. "The bougie middle class, afraid of germs, so scared to think about what happens to stuff once it's no longer perfect. That's why they obsess on dishwashing and laundry and floor cleaners. They don't want to face the reality that life is one big organic mess and we're all going to die." He blows on his nails.

Digit scratches his facial hair. He is trying to grow a goatee like Anton LaVey so he will look more evil for his future black metal band, but right now it's just itchy chin scruff. He sighs and finally pipes up in his heavy Acadian accent. "What's the big deal? Hif you need someting, take it. Hif it's dirty, wash it! We got to be more independent, *tabarnak*." He adjusts his bullet belt, which hangs around the hips of his skinny jeans.

"Exactly," says Oreo. She chews the end of her long

black braid. She's been quiet all meeting, hardly even paying attention. Her voice is hoarse, still messed up from yesterday's run-in with the King. Bruises are coming up on her pretty brown skin. "Even Zapatistas wash their plates." She points to the photo taped above the sink; guerrillas cleaning their dishes in a river, their semi-automatic weapons lying on the grassy bank.

"Yuppie propaganda," says Cricket. He tightens the lid on the nail polish and flutters his hands.

Oreo says, "That's authentic revolutionary footage."

Cricket says, "Whatever. It's not like we have an entire military campaign hunting us like the Zapatistas did. We can afford to leave a few plates around. What about our grey water politics?"

We look at the propped-open window where we scoop water from the rain barrel outside. We use rainwater to wash dishes and ourselves. The leftover dish and bath water is for plants and to flush the toilet when it's full.

"The entire planet is in a water crisis, and Oreo wants us to wash dishes? Unreal."

Oreo's eyes narrow. "I just want everyone to pull *his* own weight."

"Point taken," I say quickly. I signal Cricket to cut it out. Oreo is in no mood. That cop fucked us up, and not just physically. The King broke something inside Oreo, something I don't know how to fix.

"Oh, don't get all essentialist on me, Oreo. Gender is a social construct; this squat is living proof. Washing dishes has nothing to do with whatever I might have between my legs!" Cricket rolls his eyes.

"Not today," says Oreo. Her voice breaks.

"Fine," he says loudly. Cricket yanks up his patched hood and pulls the drawstrings tight, so his face disappears completely. There are funny lumps where his mohawk bends under the weight of the fabric.

"Man, you always got to talk about penis," says Digit. "Why you don't just wash your plate? Hit's easy."

Oreo has a spark of life back in her now. "Yeah, don't start what you can't finish, Cricket. I'm sick of cleaning up after white boys."

Digit sighs again, loudly. "Alright, everyone *try* to wash their own dish, and also *try* not to be total jerks." He drums his knuckles on the table in front of him. "*Ça marche?*"

Silence.

"Seriously, guys. I want dat in the minutes," says Digit. "For the people who *isn't* here, who probably *should* be more *serieux* about the collective. In New Brunswick, we don't have dis kind of ting. You get in the group or you get out, you know?"

He means red-headed Darcy. Darcy used to panhandle at the underpass with me, over a year ago. He's been around town and then some, always got his hand in some shit or other. He came to a punk show a while back and decided he was moving in, at least part time.

"Are we gonna talk about him or what?" says Oreo.

"It's not on the agenda," says Cricket in a muffled voice. "And we don't talk about people when they aren't here, remember?"

Oreo says, "That kid is sketch. We said no junkies in the squat. We *have* to talk about it."

Digit says, "He have some bad friends. He owe a lot of money, I hear that for sure."

I say, "He needs someplace safe. He seems sick. Where else can he go?"

Cricket says, "Well, where is he right now for our meeting? We're not an effing drop-in, we're a intentional freegan community!"

I say, "So we want to change the world but not help the people who live in it?"

Cricket sighs loudly.

Digit scratches his face again. "Who's writing da minutes?"

Cricket loosens his hoodie and peers out. "Oh crap, I'm supposed to." He rummages for a pen that works and for paper in the recycling box. There is a terrific lull while he scribbles down the stuff we've been talking about for the past hour: *Don't forget to compost. Worm bucket is outside, other organics in the back field. Whose turn is it to water the plants? Our tomatoes are almost ripe! Let's dumpster less food so we waste less, or let's invite people over so they can help us eat it all.* And: *Oreo wants us to wash our dishes so she can stop being an uptight bougie twat.*

"Okay, I'm ready," he says. "Damn, I wrecked a nail."

Digit says, "Who's chairing the meeting?"

"Oh. I am." I clear my throat. "So, uh, next item. Oreo was thinking we should have a party for my birthday next Saturday. What do you think? Probably a big hassle. Imagine how many dirty dishes there'll be."

"Very funny," says Oreo.

Cricket stops flitting his blue fingernails around, and

says it's a *great* idea. "Maybe we can even make some cash, selling beers and whatnot."

I cringe.

Oreo frowns. "No money. This is for Ferret."

Cricket says, "So, how you gonna pay back that fifty bucks you owe?"

Oreo says nothing, and I say nothing. Fifty bucks is a lot. I get my welfare in a few days, but Oreo wants to use some of it to get stuff for the party. Stuff we can't barter or beg or dumpster for ourselves.

Digit yawns, says we should get some bands to play, like *his* new band, only they haven't really started jamming yet, but they'd be able to *maybe* play some songs by then. "Maybe one or two. Black fucking metal." He makes devil horns with his fingers.

Oreo says, "No way, man. I'm DJing for Ferret so she can dance. We need something with a beat."

Then Digit says, "Maybe we should have other DJs, too, for *musicale diversité*," and Oreo says, "Like *who*? Who is more diverse than an Ojibwe lesbian dance party like me?"

Digit says, "Not a more diverse person, I mean some good music."

Oreo sticks her tongue out and crosses her eyes.

I laugh.

Digit says that at his first band practice, which turned into a tremendous beer and barf festival, he met Nefarious Rancor who's visiting *from New York*. "I can probably hook that up," he says. "He does brutal solo shit. The band is usually booked for, like, months, but he's in town right now. Only he *might* want some money to play."

And Cricket says, "Oh yeah? Well, I heard that dude's in rehab, and his rich Thornhill parents are paying for it, and that's the *only* reason he's here. Anyway, how are we gonna pay some metal Gaylord if we don't even charge cover?"

"He's not gay, he's bisexual," says Digit quickly. "I hear dat, anyways."

"We're not charging cover," says Oreo. "It's a birthday party. And I wouldn't complain about rich parents if I were you, Cricket."

Cricket ignores her completely. "What about hot Geraldo's band, Migrant? That would be wicked. People will totally come for that."

"I love Migrant!" I say.

"Why don't you ask your mom for some cash?" Oreo asks Cricket, sneering.

"Okay, let's not talk about parents," I say quickly.

I don't have any, so it doesn't matter to me. But this is the kind of thing that can get ugly fast. Digit grew up between the curb and the closet, no joke. Oreo's mom and aunt were killed by a drunk driver on New Year's Eve two years ago in Sudbury. But Cricket's family wires him money whenever he needs it, thinking he lives in residence at the university. The fact that he chooses to live the freegan life strictly for political reasons while still attending classes is great and all, but sometimes it rubs Oreo the wrong way.

"All right, I'm sorry." Cricket is quiet for almost an entire minute.

"Happy break," I say. We do that sometimes if stuff gets tense. Just move around in that big old building, skateboard up and down the long length of it, maybe have a snack.

Cricket stays put, dejected. He hates being reminded of his race, gender, and class privilege. It makes him feel less radical. Digit shrugs and says he'll make everybody peanut butter sandwiches on the bagels we scored today. *Typical Digit, always thinking of the group.* Oreo lies on the floor and stretches like a cat.

I go for a walk in the field between the Factory and the slaughterhouse. Really it's just an empty lot, a no-man's land where folks have been dumping shit for years. I like to look at our brick building, especially on a night like tonight with all those pretty stars out and with an almost-full moon pouring down, lighting up our house from space.

"Hey, Ferret."

The voice comes from over by the slaughterhouse. It's Eddie, sitting on the ledge having a smoke break. When he waves, the motion-sensitive outdoor security light blinks on. He's in the spotlight now, wearing coveralls and the long, bloody rubber apron and tall rubber boots. I don't want to be rude so I go over, even though I hate the whole pig blood situation.

"What up?" Eddie smiles and his buck teeth gleam. There's gore smeared on his chin. Eddie is tall and thin with skin darker than Oreo's. Blurry ink—homemade tattoos—decorate the sides of his shaved head, neck, and hands. Probably covers everything in between, too. Eddie lets anyone practice on him as long as it's free.

"Looks like we're having a party Saturday. You should come."

"Hmm. We don't go out too much."

"But it's my birthday. You got to come. Bring your boy-friend."

"Oh, Ray-Ray? Yeah. He's pretty shy, but ..." Eddie wipes his nose with his forearm. Blood smears across his cheek.

I nod. *Me, too.*

If you can get past his stutter, Ray-Ray is totally cool. His delicate hands, big eyes, that long, white-blond hair—he's like some fragile princess from a far-off time. Eddie is his dragon-slayer prince.

"I don't really party anymore," he says, like an apology. "Gave up the crank, all that shit. I'm doing good, too."

"Way to go. Just come say hi. It'd be nice."

Eddie takes one last drag off his smoke and flicks the butt to the ground where all the others are. "Break's over." He smiles again. Then he goes through the side door, back into the killing machine, and I cross the field toward our place.

Eddie's probation officer got him the job, and it's true, he's been on the straight-and-narrow ever since, working hard, looking after his boy. He told me the saddest thing about working the slaughterhouse was that he had to give up bacon, which he used to love. His mother bitched when he visited the trailer park, "Why didn't you bring some meat fresh off the conveyor?" Something about watching hundreds of animals get lined up, hosed off, then electro-cuted or bashed on the head every day, something about that changes you, I guess. Eddie's job is to reach up and, in that flickering moment when the pigs are harnessed into submission and hopefully stunned, to gut them, one after the other. I've seen him work, and it's not pretty. His gloved arms go right inside the steaming hot mess of their insides while they are technically still alive. The smell never leaves him, the stench of their blood and their shit as it pours out onto his boots and onto the concrete floor, the screaming and grunting. That killed his love of bacon.

I re-read the fortune from my pocket, the one I found on the path yesterday: *happy celebration happy*. Then I light a match and set it on fire. I whisper the phrase for luck while it burns in my fingers. I drop the last piece in the grass and watch 'til it's nothing but ash. *There.* I walk past mattresses with rusting coils popped out, old fridges, trashed cars with weeds growing up though the busted-out parts in their dented frames. Something scurries past—probably a rat, the way it skitters and bounces. I feel better. Being in nature always clears my head.

Back at the Factory, Cricket draws happily. Oreo blasts her favourite Dirt EP. She and Cricket shout the final chorus: "Object Refuse Reject Abuse!"

In the ensuing silence Digit pouts because his band got nixed from the lineup. "What does Migrant got dat we don't?" he says.

Cricket says, "First of all, you don't have a name. You don't even have a guitar, man. You're not a band 'til you have something to play and an effing name. Then by all means, call me." Cricket shrieks and waves his cellphone in the air. "Geraldo texted back—Migrant is totally in!"

Digit grunts. He fiddles with some metal piping he found in the dump.

Oreo says, "DJ Silo's said yes, too. We'll alternate spinning. She's awesome."

Cricket says, "No club kids. No fucking poseurs, no way. I'm putting that on the flyer—they'll bring the bougie pigs."

I say, "Flyer?"

Everyone looks up, startled, like they've forgotten me.

"Why do we need a flyer if it's just a few folks getting together for my birthday? I don't even have that many friends."

"Sure you do, Ferret. There's everyone at the drop-in and the underpass, there's the Frenchies in Parkdale, and our girl posse." Oreo is ticking off one finger for each group. She waves four fingers at me.

"Those people don't even know me. They're your friends."

Cricket says, "Girls, can you keep your monogamous relationship issues private?"

I say, "It's not about our relationship, it's about how many people do you want in our place? Like, is this party for me or is it for the squat or what?"

"Hit's for all of us," says Digit. "But let's not go crazy." He picks up a piece of wood that was lying around, and balances it on top of the metal he's wired together. "Hey, if I sand dis and attach hit like dis, we can use hit for the birtday cake. Look." The wood rotates smoothly on its new-found perch; it's a punk-rock, custom-built Lazy Susan.

"Wow," I say. "Digit, you're the best."

"Just what we need. More bougie kitchen crap!" says Cricket. "Well, I'm definitely inviting my new boyfriend. Oh my god, he is so hot. Maybe he'll bring his courier friends."

"Your imaginary boyfriend," says Digit. He rolls his eyes.

"Oh, he exists," says Cricket. "And he's going to be existing in my pants on Saturday night, so get *über* it."

"Word," says Oreo. They high five, which is nice, since they've been bickering all night.

"Okay," I say. "Invite whoever you want; it's for all of us. Let's not get busted, though."

Everyone is like, *Fuck that, we're not having no cops here.*

An image of the King pops into my head. I feel that sore spot on my shoulder where he bruised me. Oreo and I look at each other. No way do we want to run into that pig again. Suddenly, Oreo laughs, something I haven't heard in a while. She cues up N.W.A.'s "Fuck tha Police."

"Spin it, girlfriend!" Cricket leaps off the table. He spanks his own bum as he dances around the room. Oreo joins in, laughing. *That's better.*

"Eh. Can we ave hardcore and metal, or is dat too much to hask?" Digit hates dance music. "Otherwise I won't bodder inviting anyone." He's sanding the board now, and it looks pretty good.

"Maybe," shouts Cricket.

"Maybe not," shouts Oreo.

I say, "What should I do?"

Oreo pulls me close and sways in time to the music. "You just figure out what you're gonna wear, Ferret. It's your party."

"Hmm. This *is* what I wear." I look down: dirty patched combat pants, heavy metal belt, scuffed boots, some ripped stinking shirt over a vintage bra I've never washed, a few pounds of leather and metal jewellery. Oreo hugs me tighter.

Cricket shouts, "Some girls wear skirts. They're hot.

You should try it."

Oreo nods and smiles.

I don't say anything, but I wonder.

By Saturday night, we are wired. We take turns washing our crusty dishes. When no one is looking, I throw a couple into the dump—they're just too disgusting. Oreo stacks her second-hand speakers around the room, tapes down the wiring, sets her turntables out, lines up her vinyl underneath. We haul out the generator for this, since we'd probably blow the low power still humming in this building. Oreo tests the system, and it sounds amazing. We have some serious bass happening in the Factory. Digit clamps an old lamp to the table for light. He sets his homemade Lazy Susan on the kitchen table and the big cake on top. Oreo scored it from the health food dumpster. It's gorgeous vegan, gluten-free fudge, and it smells incredible. Some loser would have paid forty bucks for it, but technically it's past the expiry date. The top isn't even crushed. I lick some icing off the box. *Mmm*. Cricket clears a dance floor. Digit and me put our stuff away in cupboards and staple fabric over the fronts so people won't go through our shit.

At the last minute, I change into a short skirt from the free bin at the drop-in. I pull fishnets over my bruised legs and put on more makeup than usual. I feel like some drag queen, lurching around in borrowed shoes with a two-inch heel. But there's something else. I feel—not exactly pretty, but *special*. Like something good could happen to me, now that I'm paying attention. *Happy celebration happy*.

"Hooka, what?" Cricket slaps my behind when I stagger past.

"Seriously, Cricket. Do I look alright?"

"Yep, you clean up pretty good, Ferret," and that makes me smile.

Oreo's eyes light up when she sees me. She whistles at my short skirt. There's that electric thing again, that zap of possibility. "You look good enough to eat." In these shoes, we're the same height, eye to eye, boob to boob. I kiss her at this new angle and that calms me. It reminds me of the only things that matter: this place, our friends, and us.

"I still wish we were alone."

"Oh we *will* be, don't you worry." She kisses me again and trails her fingers down my back. She rubs my neck, my shoulders, even the one that is still sore from the King. She tugs on my skirt and smiles, and I'm glad I did it. I'm glad I tried something new.

Soon people drop by. Kids who used to live here, who did workshops, shows, that sort of thing. There are kids from downtown, from the hardcore scene, and the drop-in. Some bring their dogs, and most of them get along. Geraldo arrives in an old van with his gear, and Digit helps set up the drum kit and plug in the PA and mic. Crust punks pile to the front of the long room as Geraldo tunes his guitar. Then the small girl playing bass fills the Factory with a subterranean rumble. The dreadlocked drummer clicks his sticks together and suddenly the band explodes in a frenzy of sound. Kids drop their bags and push into each another, they writhe and slam, and the more everyone moves, the warmer it gets. The music stops as suddenly as it begins.

People whistle and cheer. "This song is for the keeds in my country," Geraldo says breathlessly into the mic. "It's called, 'Food Not Clowns: We Can't Eat Your Bombs.'" Drumsticks click again, bass and guitar barf an onslaught of high-speed chords into the air, kids sweat and shout and bash into each other in a joyous frenzy. I can hardly breathe until the song's over two minutes later.

"Migrant kicks *ass*!" I shout to Oreo. She smiles and squeezes me, shields me from a spazzed-out boy in the make-shift pit. When the set ends a few songs later, kids pour outside to get air, to cool off, and Geraldo starts packing up the cords and pedals while wiping sweat from his face and neck. Oreo helps them clear out their gear—so does Digit, who is apparently not holding a grudge about the whole band thing. In fact, he looks downright friendly, chatting up Geraldo, who apologizes for cutting out early. Migrant has another gig across town tonight and they have to jet. Oreo switches a patchcord and gets a CD playing, and kids gradually drift back inside.

Everyone is excited to be at the Factory for one big bash before summer ends. Oreo turns up the music and people dance. *This is fun*, I think. Kids tell me happy birthday; they go out of their way to be friendly, and I think, *Oreo was right. They do like me!*

More people come, people I don't recognize. They barrel through the back door. They bring fancy beer and expensive booze. Some of them make fun of our place, wrinkle their noses. They pile their purses and bags near the door. It's hard to get in and out with all their stuff in the way. They scare off the crust punks with their perfume and soap and the smells of their hairspray and who knows what else. Clean, shiny people sit on the couches we pulled from the dump, on our makeshift chairs, and up the ladder rungs that lead to the loft. Rich kids dance in the main room of the Factory. They laugh and gossip and gulp fruity drinks. Girls wear sparkly clothes with large earrings, tight pants, and strappy, bright sandals. Some of them want different music, and they start to bug Oreo, asking for shit we'd never play here—Britney and Fergie and Beyoncé. I see that tic in Oreo's cheek, which is not good. Oreo plays it cool, though. No fighting; she just tells them to go fuck her mother if they don't like her tunes.

"Did you hear what she said to me?" A whiny blonde gets pulled by the arm. Her friends glare at Oreo.

A couple punks sneak over to the rich kids' pile, start sifting through the designer bags. I could say something, but fuck it. It's not like those clean kids belong here.

"Are they from your university?" I whisper to Cricket. He's pouring vodka from one of their large bottles.

"Fuck, yeah. Bougie poseurs. I'm making you a birthday drink. It's on them."

"But how did they find our place?"

"Probably DJ Silo, that top-forty sellout. She's in my queer studies class."

"You think *they're* queer?" I can't believe it. They're so shiny.

"Oh, honey, they're not queer; they're the gay-lesbian enemy—mainstreaming homos. We're nothing like them, don't worry."

"Huh." I look at all these girls again. Some of them are

pretty touchy-feely, kissing and standing close. Some of them are definitely checking Oreo out; they blush and giggle and try to talk to her. My stomach tightens with worry. I grab a beer from the fridge and gulp it. I don't want to ruin anyone's fun, but seriously.

"Digit!" I have to yell, and he still can't hear me over the music and all those voices. I chuck my beer cap and hit him square in the back of the head. He grins when he sees that it's me.

"Ay, *bonne fête, ma fille!*" He pushes his way over to me, beside the cake.

"Digit, are these your friends?" I trace the cake edge with my finger and lick the icing.

"*Absolument non.* Great party, eh?" He swigs some beer. "This is nothing. More than 200 people reply on Facebook."

I'm speechless.

"Don't worry, it's not like I attach a map or someting. It's cool."

But I wonder. Crickets' flyers are all over the place. The slaughterhouse is marked with a drawing of a pig, and there's a giant X for the Factory. It says: Pig House Party, B.Y.O.E. Fuck you, Club Kid Poseurs.

"*Salut, toi!*" Digit gives devil horns to someone in the crowd.

I take my heels off and climb onto the ledge by the kitchen sink. I wobble. Now I'm taller than everyone, and I can see almost the whole main room. I try to count—in twos, in small groups—but nobody stands still long enough. I get sixty, then almost eighty; that can't be right. I forgot the upstairs. Maybe seventy. I round up, I round down, I give up. The Factory is full.

"Whatcha doin,' girl?" Cricket's obviously had another drink.

"Trying to count. Digit says 200 people replied on Facebook …"

"Digit posted on Facebook? He's such an ass." Cricket helps me down and holds my arm while I put the dreaded shoes back on.

"We should eat that cake, honey."

"Everyone?"

"Uh-uh. Just you and me. Fuck Facebook. Fuck the bourgeoisie!" With that, Cricket stabs the cake's dark centre with our butcher knife. "I killed the cake," he shouts, and a few people turn to watch. He keeps stabbing. We laugh and grab handfuls, rich and moist. I smear some on his mouth. Cricket plasters my face.

"Mmmmmph." I'm chewing and swallowing and savouring this thing like love that fills my mouth. "Wow."

"Ferret, itsh all over yer fash," he says, and slobbers up another dollop of frosting.

Digit is suddenly there, mouth open. "*Qu'est-ce que vous faites?*"

Cricket scoops and smears it on Digit.

Digit grabs the knife from Cricket and accuses him, "English cake killer!"

Cricket shoves another handful into Digit's open mouth. "Born again! Cake resurrection!"

Digit howls. He doesn't laugh often, but once he gets going he can't stop. His face turns red, veins pop on his temples like angry worms. He coughs and snorts and drools. Saliva strands hang from his open, cake-filled mouth. Tears stream from his squinty eyes. He collapses on the table, shaking. It's contagious. I can't stop either, not even when Oreo is beside us, not even when she grabs my hair and licks that cake right off and smooshes her clean face into my dirty chocolate mouth. *Our best house meeting ever.*

The back door opens. A new crowd pushes in through the people who are trying to push out. People want to smoke outside or take a piss and can't find our toilet. Some complain about the no-flushing rule. Tall Eddie comes in, dragging Ray-Ray. I wave. Eddie raises his bottle.

Cricket shakes off his carb coma when he sees the big blond head of the new guy he likes, that bike courier. He pushes through some bum-shaking dancers, dragging me along behind. He smiles and the blond brick wall of a man smiles back. Cricket introduces me; Two Ton tips his cap.

"Ah, your birthday cake," he says, and wipes a bit of chocolate from my cheek.

We drink to that. Cricket offers pills. I can tell he likes the guy cuz he doesn't even get mad when Two Ton takes more than one. In fact, Cricket *smiles*. What an E-tard.

"I hope you don't mind, Ferret. I invite a little friend to come for your party. Darcy, a skinny red-haired boy."

I smile. "That's the kid who moved in. I haven't seen him all week. I hope he's okay." The pill sticks in my throat so I wash it down with beer. Maybe it's the free booze talking, but right now I decide I don't mind all these people any more.

Cricket says, "I heard he got picked up by the cops."

"Really?" Two Ton looks confused. "I see him today. He says he gonna bring his other friend tonight. I forget his name. Cute boy," he says and winks at me.

"I like cute girls."

Two Ton shrugs. "Oh well. More of them for me and Creek-it." And then he cracks that big smile of his, mesmerizing Cricket even more.

Strangers keep coming. I stop counting. There's probably double the number of people there were earlier. The Factory is overrun. Scuffles break out—someone can't find their wallet, their cell phone. Some other gadget goes missing, a purse is lost. Accusations are loud, fingers point. Oreo just bumps up the volume. Cricket pours drinks for the victims, for the accused—from other people's bottles. People shed layers of clothing they don't need; it's hard to keep the beers cold. The walls sweat.

Suddenly I feel the swell inside; the tingly numbness spreads, and my skin feels warm. Cricket's pills are kicking in. Everything is magic now. Little Darcy shows up, beaten and sketched out, nervous as a mouse; I pull him onto the dance floor and twirl.

"You okay?" The words fill my mouth and take longer to say than they should.

He tries to shake my hand loose, but I pull him closer. "I heard you got nabbed by the cops."

He licks his swollen lip. His eyes shift back and forth; he blurts something then stops.

The music is wicked intense—Oreo is smokin' the heavy beats. I dance Darcy over to the turntables, and he disappears while I kiss Oreo. She looks so hot with her headphones on, her smile lighting up the place. All those other girls, those fancy rich girls, they can fuck off. Oreo kisses me back, and I can't wait to be alone with her. The floorboards bounce back up against my shoes. I move to the middle of the throng, strangers dancing close. We crush together, apart, together, for hours, it seems, world without end. Oreo spins fast breaks, stutters the vinyl, teases metal classics into her electronic weirdness, then lets the drum and bass kick heavy and dark. I am smiling. *I'm really having fun.* Even if all these people don't know me, even if they don't know who we are, everybody's having an awesome time together in *our* house. It's a brilliant party.

I don't even notice them at first, the sirens blend so beautifully. The spinning red lights reflect off skin: faces, closed eyes, bare bellies. Then the snare drum pops over our heads, so much like gunfire. I'm dancing slowly, swaying, my eyes are open, taking it all in. My arms outstretched, I'm in the middle of all those hot bodies, sucking up the sounds, the pictures. It is some sick dance video: Cricket's arms up flailing, a raised stick, his face contorting.

Tall Eddie sees over the whole crowd, he yells something to me—I don't hear him, but we talk with our eyes; he's freaking out. I don't understand. He pushes Ray-Ray through the people, tosses him toward the open kitchen window. Ray-Ray is up on the ledge. He looks back at Eddie, then he jumps, his long white hair streaking after him. *Eddie.* Someone hits Eddie on the shoulder with a long stick. Eddie turns, ready to throw a punch, but instead his body pulsates with electricity, he sails backwards, limbs flailing, his eyes roll to white. I'm staring, surprised at his funny dance. *Who came dressed up like that?* I think. *Who came in a uniform?*

Two Ton throws his beer in the uniform's face and dives out the same window as Ray-Ray, the one near our rain barrel. He's gone. People stare. Uniforms—there's more than one—move through the crowd, and bodies part like water. There's pushing and shoving and the sticks come out: bodies jerk and twitch. Feet shoot out from underneath, they kick and slide to the killer music. Kids push me, step on me. I'm swarmed, can't move. Suddenly, people fall down in front of me.

I see Digit's back; he's still eating the rest of that cake in the corner, he's licking icing off that butcher knife, and men are yelling at him. He turns, slowly, knife raised, and there's a loud pop, a sound that cracks over top of the music, and Digit's head snaps backwards; there's a dark spot spreading across his chest. The knife goes flying and his body lands by the sink. He convulses, red spurts streak the walls and broken window behind him. Kids scream. A girl beside me vomits. There's that pig we hate. The King is standing over there, gun still raised, the smell of it burning my nostrils. The King turns and stares at me. *He sees me see.*

I need Oreo. She's shaking those dreads, cueing up something new. I yell, but her headphones block me. She's zoned. The King is behind her. She has no idea. I run. My heels catch in a pile of clothes. I wave my arms as I fall— I'm frantic. Then Oreo sees me, sees my terror, and so does the King. I'm trapped by the couch, trying to kick off those shoes. They both watch me flail, one behind the other. The King smiles as his stick lands on Oreo's temple. Pain flashes across her face, I feel it. Oreo's mouth goes slack; she crumples out of sight. I roar. The pretty inside light that only Oreo brings me flares up and out; it burns to black and is gone.

The King gives a hand signal. Someone cuts the generator: music stops, lights go out. Ghosts of kids are screaming, grabbing their stuff, and running in the blue black. They move fast, but not fast enough. The back door is blocked. Headlights beam through the windows, red lights spin. A line of cops grab and handcuff kids when they push their way out. Kids are freaking. Their silhouettes pile out the windows then scramble right back in; they're getting beaten out there, they're getting tased.

Meanwhile, kids trample me. I crawl toward the last place I saw Oreo, calling her name, trying to protect myself. High-heeled shoes snap my wrist, Docs smash my face. I curl up underneath the turntables—no Oreo. Shoes stampede on all sides; they stomp past me in a blur. But one polished pair stops right in front. Big black cop shoes, with hemmed blue pants. I know exactly whose they are, too.

Shakler Bakler

Nothing.

That's all there is at first.

I'm dead, I think. Finally.

Then the pain kicks in: the rolling ache in my head builds to stabbing points in each eye socket. My stomach twists and bloats with gas. The crazy-making itch starts up again, like worms chewing through sub-layers of skin, skin that holds my bones and bruises all together. I massage my jaw; it's sore from clenching my teeth. I clear my throat and hork out chemical-flavoured post nasal drip.

Okay. I sigh. So I'm alive.

Wherever I am in the world, I'm also lying on the floor between a wall and an old couch. Actually, I'm halfway inside the back of the couch. *Hiding from the cops.* The fabric is torn away. I can see the wood frame, springs above me, little bugs crawling around, the stuffing pulled out of cushions and neatly piled up in tiny rolled balls of fluff. A pyramid of fluff balls, all the same size, all carefully stacked and counted. That was me, last night, tweaked, fiddling with that stuffing for hours, right after taking my transistor radio apart and lining up the pieces along the baseboard, biggest to smallest, darkest to lightest. Wires and plastic parts, dials and buttons, the coded flat metal pieces all glare at me. *What the hell was I thinking?*

I pat the chest pocket of my cotton shirt. I can feel the baggies in there, should be two of them left, with clear chunks of beautiful Vancouver meth—an eighth of an ounce, at least. I wiggle my toes. Packets of other stuff I picked up during the raid are hidden in my shoes. *My stash.*

I pull myself out from behind the couch slowly. My stick legs drag behind, heavy and numb, like they're somebody else's. Sunlight blasts through open windows. It's squinty bright and way too quiet. *Morning.* I'm in the Factory, alright, even if it's unrecognizable. I know the smells: sawdust and sheet metal, spilled beer, dirty laundry, rotting bags of dumpstered food. Over top it all is the hot stench of pig shit from the slaughterhouse next door.

I remember Ferret twirling me around last night at the party, trying to get me on the dance floor. She always stood up for me. Cricket and Oreo, even Digit—a hell of a nice boy—knew better than to trust a basehead like me. *How could I dance?* Me, tweaked, knowing the cops were right outside, knowing I brought them to the doorstep. Desperate to find Sly before the raid. My stomach cramps just thinking about it. I freeze, hold my gut. My ass puckers, but I don't shit myself. The cramp loosens, the pain rolls away again. I scratch my scabby arms. I pick at my lips.

"Ferret? Anybody?" My voice is a screechy mess.

No one answers. Pigeons purr in the loft. Water drips steadily. Outside, a truck downshifts. Its brakes squeal, just like the pigs it carries. I hear it chug up the long gravel drive.

My legs tingle pins and needles. I limp along the dirty floor, past Oreo's smashed turntable, all that broken vinyl.

There's glass from the side windows everywhere. Boards hang by rusty nails where the other pigs, the cops, bashed them with sticks. There's yellow tape across the doors, the windows. I lean against a fallen speaker, pick up a half empty beer. It's warm, but there's no cigarette floating inside. I rinse my mouth and spit on the floor. The chemical taste doesn't go away, but at least I'm not as dry. My hands shake when I set the bottle back down. *I need water*.

The Factory is a big old mess. Shelves collapsed in a heap when one cop took an axe to them. That was terrible; the loud whacks, the looks on all those kids' faces. Clothes, art, photographs—everything they had, pulled from the broken shelves, thrown into piles on the floor. The big room reeks like piss, and I remember seeing one cop whip it out and spray the piles. An axe blade trail leads along the food cupboards, across the makeshift kitchen counter, up the bloodsplattered wall. *Blood*. I shudder. *The shooting*. I pick my lips some more. I stare at the floor, at the stains, for an hour or maybe only a minute—it's hard to tell.

Water.

I lick my bumpy dry lips. Water trickles out of a chopped-up pipe; it drips down and runs along the slanted floor, all the way over to the far side of the long room. A tiny man-made lake ripples with each new drop. I tilt my head back underneath the pipe and fill my mouth. It tastes weird, cool but tinny, a bit like earth. It reminds me that I have to pee.

Sly, I think miserably. *What happened to Sly?* I never saw him last night, not on the dance floor—as if he'd dance. Not in the bathroom lineup, not outside in the dark field, or upstairs in the make-out loft. Maybe he stayed at the

Professor's. Maybe he was still mad at me for taking off, for scoring and leaving. *Maybe.* After the cops burst in, the place was an effing zoo. Kids screaming, pushing, cops yelling, giving out the beats, handcuffs snapping shut. The best part was everyone dropping their stash.

Time for a wake-up call. I jiggle from one foot to the other. My bladder presses. A snort will get the brain cells working.

I touch my chest pocket; want to save the meth, but maybe a toot of that rich-kid coke ...

Outside, a car door slams shut. Then another. That snaps me awake. There's a digital *bleep* and radio static. Deep-down man voices. Gravel crunches under their heavy boots. I don't have time to climb to the loft, and there's nothing left to hide behind, so I scramble back to the couch and stuff my aching body behind it, though I can't crawl right inside it, back into the filth.

"Whew," one guy says as the door creaks open. "Stinks." He laughs nervously. His radio chirps. "So, what're we looking for exactly? The girl's probably long gone by now."

"Leftovers." This voice is lower than the other, hollow and mean like an ulcer. *Constable Earl King.* I listen to his deliberate steps as he walks through the Factory. They stop.

Air catches in my chest. I try to slow up my breathing, but I can't. I'm panting. My hands and feet run cold. There's no stopping it, hot piss soaks my jean shorts, pools under my bare leg. It runs along the downward slant of the old floor. It runs underneath the whole length of the couch. I can taste the sick at the back of my throat, but I swallow it down.

One pair of feet walks around the place. One stands still.

"What a mess," the other guy says. "God, don't these kids bathe?" He stomps his foot and sighs loudly. "Piss. Stinks like piss."

The King grunts. The King is climbing the loft ladder. I can tell by the sounds of his heavy steps on each creaking rung, by the ladder bouncing against the wall when he moves, by the way his deep voice echoes longer in the big room. He says, "Rats, roaches, pigeons, and street kids. City's full of vermin."

"Yep. We got our hands full." The second man sounds farther away. Maybe still near the entrance, or in the kitchen. He drops something, it clatters to the ground. It rolls and rolls all the way over to the couch. "Shit," he says. He walks slowly. His steps get louder; I feel each one through the floor boards. He stops. Leather creaks, and his knee pops when he bends down.

I feel his hand on my sneaker. He tugs hard, then drops it with a gasp. I hear him drag the couch away from the wall. "What the—"

There's no use pretending. I open my eyes. I waggle my fingers at him.

He's blond with pink cheeks and looks tall, especially because I'm sprawled down on the floor. The red stripe runs all the way up the outer seam of his dark pants. It's the nicer one, Officer P. Anderson, the King's partner. He inspects his fingers, the ones that touched my shoe, for cooties.

"Well, well," he says. "Not our girl. It's the informant."

I clear my throat. No words come out. I try to compose myself. I sit up, my back straight against the cement wall, like a debutante.

The King's voice booms from the upper loft. "So we got our redhead back."

My skin prickles.

The King climbs down the creaky ladder while he talks. "Darcy Jones. Good tip last night. We got a lot more than we expected."

I remember them beating their way through the party, having a field day.

"An unlawful gathering in a dangerous location—trespassing, drug trafficking, underage drinking, weapons ..." He lists them off on his big fingers.

Officer Anderson says, "*I* think this was a meth lab. Don't you, Earl?"

No way, I think. I'd have never left this place if they were cooking crystal.

I say, "The only thing they baked here was lentils. Tofu."

Anderson laughs meanly. "Darcy doesn't understand."

"Nobody likes a meth lab in their neighbourhood, Darcy," says the King. He speaks slowly, loudly, like I'm a retard. "People don't care *what* we do to them, as long as we get rid of them. So, for our purposes, this dump was a meth lab. Got it?"

My brain is hardly working. I'm still stuck thinking that they actually *had* a meth lab and were holding out on me. *Effing vegans.*

The King says, "We sent some scumbags back to jail last night. Hopefully their bitch lawyers won't spring them too soon."

"Oh, and the hospital," says Officer Anderson. "Right? Sent that kid to the ICU."

"Won't be walking out any time soon," says the King. "You came through for us, Darcy." His deep voice sounds almost proud of me.

I smile, but I'm not sure if I should.

"*I* didn't think you would, to be honest," says Anderson. His hands are fists on his hips. I'm staring at his belt buckle, a silver rectangle like a little doorframe leading nowhere nice.

"Didn't find your girl-boy, though," says the King. "Too bad. I wanted to get a closer look at that freak."

Sly. A guilt pang twists my guts. I told him about Sly being trans. How he is a boy born into the wrong girl body. "He wasn't here last night," I say, my voice cracking.

The King is right beside Anderson now. Two big men— one pale with pink cheeks, one dark with a big veiny nose— a wall of blue.

Anderson says, "Who would have thought so much could go down on Fairy Mountain?" He chuckles.

The King says, "Hmmph." Then he says, "Get up. What's in your pockets?"

I get up slowly. There's a wet stain on my jean shorts. I pull my front pockets inside out – nothing. I turn around and wiggle my hips slowly, to show him there's nothing back there either.

"Did you piss yourself?" The King looks disgusted. "Clean up. I still need you for a couple more jobs today, Darcy."

I clear my throat to talk. "But you said we'd be even if I told you about the party." My hidden foil packets are burning holes right through me. I got a crack attack coming on. I can make do with a joint to calm my nerves if I have to, but seriously? I need a bump, a line of coke, or a hit of something speedy, just to get back in the game.

He says, "Shut the fuck up." His hit sends me flat against the wall. *Whush.* All the things bumping around in my head fly clean out of there. "You're *never* gonna be even, got that? You do *what* I say, *when* I say it. You know what happens if you don't play? You're done. Permanently."

Photos of that boy he killed, him all cut up and beaten, that pretty hustler we don't see around anymore, bolt through my brain like lightning. I don't say anything. I don't cry. It's like that hit sends me back to myself, wakes me up and gets my brain working again, almost as good as a chemical.

I know all about hitting, I think. Oh, yes.

I pick up the first piece of clothing I find, a button-down shirt someone left on the arm of the couch, and shove my arms into the sleeves, pulling it over my T-shirt. I sidle behind the couch, away from them, and smooth the fabric over the pocket that holds my goods.

Anderson says, "We need you to find someone, Darcy. Someone who was at the party."

"Emily Stuart." The King pronounces it loud and sharp, so the last name sounds like a spit.

I say, "I don't know anyone named that." I cough. I'm looking for pants in all the stuff left behind by the party kids.

"Oh, yes you do. She was living here." Anderson steps toward me and waves papers in my face. "Having her welfare delivered to the drop-in centre."

"I already told you who lives here—Cricket, Oreo, Digit,

and Ferret." *And me.* "That's it. There's no Emily No One." I root through a pile of clothes. There's a silver scarf, a light jacket, a pair of giant white sunglasses.

Anderson checks something on his paper. "James David Smith, a.k.a. Cricket, the fag with the blue hair. Got him. Oreo Ahkwa-blah-blah-kwe—are they serious? More like Lesbo Broken Nose." He laughs meanly. "Digit is André Savoie, the kid on life support. Emily Stuart, missing in action."

"What do you mean life support?" I put the sunglasses on top of my head and drape the scarf over my shoulder. I can tell it looks good, even without a mirror.

The King grabs my arm and nearly rips it out of the socket. "Listen, you little fuck. She's a skinny dyke with dirty blue dreads. She was wearing fishnets and a skirt. Ring any bells?"

"Oh, that's Ferret. Why didn't you say so?"

The King drops my arm. I shake it out.

"That hurt," I say. Now I know. The King reminds me of someone—one of my long-ago dads. It's so familiar, all of it.

Officer Anderson scribbles in his notes. "Stuart, also known as Ferret."

"The best thing about these little cunts," says the King, "is they're like rats in a trap. They'll chew off their own legs to escape, never mind what they'll do to each other."

The King's eyes are flat, unblinking. I stare him down while I undo my wet shorts; they drop to the floor with a slap. My bare skin prickles into goose bumps. My thing shrivels up like a small turtle. I see his eyes drop down to look at me. I step out of the crumpled shorts and slowly walk past him toward another pile of stuff farther away.

"Hurry up, Princess," says Anderson. "It's not a fashion show. We got work to do."

I swish the silver scarf over my shoulder. The long end of it tickles my bare bum. I pick up a pair of red spandex shorts some girl probably wore under her skirt. I step into them, pull them up over my shoes, all the way to the waist. *Perfect.*

"Fine," I say. I put the sunglasses low on my nose and sashay over to the back door. "Coming, officers?"

The King opens the car door for me. I raise my hand, *Ta.* I slide across the wide back seat and cross my legs. I tap my sneaker on the divider that separates me from the front seat. I can feel the packages shimmy around in there. *I need a bump.* The King slams my door. He gets in the front, slams that door, too. I can see the grey in the back of his hair. I never noticed it before. *Salt and pepper, so distinguished.* The radio bleeps. Anderson gets in his side and, voilà, another slam. The King calls the dispatcher, says they're investigating the old chair factory crime scene. Tracking a witness. Following leads. He hangs up the radio. He opens his window, spits. Finally, he starts the engine.

Anderson says, "Fuck-load of paper work for one bullet, wouldn't you say?"

The King says, "Shut up."

"No, seriously. Was it worth it?"

"Maybe. If those douchebag lawyers don't screw it up."

One little bullet.

I remember the gun last night, the sound and smell of it, the way everyone freaked. Everyone else ploughing their way out of the Factory, and me with my eyes on the floor, on hands, pockets; me seeing flashes of silver, little clear baggies, and tiny pill boxes, the fancy ones those rich kids shake around. Crumb-snatcher me, picking it all up, hiding in the back of the couch for hours, quietly tweaking, organizing my fluff balls while chaos blew through the Factory, and later, while the cops did their thing and closed the place down.

Great party.

"We're taking you to all the hot spots, Darcy," says Officer Anderson. "The underpass, the drop-in, the parks. You'll be hitting the streets, asking around, then meeting up with us every hour or so."

Good, I think. I can totally get high and keep my buzz on. The only question is—back to crystal light, or should I save that for better times? Should I shake and bake the coke, cook up some crack, and sell it around? That'd be good for coin.

"We need you to find Emily. Uh—Ferret."

"Why?"

"Because we lost her," says Anderson.

"Shut up," says the King.

"Sorry. But we *had* her. Then we didn't."

The King turns around, his eyebrows hunch in toward the deep frown in the middle of his forehead. "She witnessed the shooting last night. We need her cooperation. Your job is to tell people, even if they don't ask, that André, uh, Digit needs her to come forward. Got it?"

"Hmm," I say. "That's easy."

"You tell people we got the shooter. Edward. But we need the witness."

I'm important. I pretend the King is my chauffeur. I sit very tall, chin up, my new sunglasses on. *I'm Lady Gaga. Beyoncé. I'm Michael Effing Jackson.*

The car rolls down the gravel laneway. We swerve to let another pig truck through. I fall against the door with the sudden movement.

"Shit," says the King.

The big truck stops and reverses, pulls up and stalls right beside the police car.

"Shit," says Anderson.

When the engine cuts, all you can hear is the animals squealing, snorting, and grunting. The smell of them and their manure fills the car. I cover my nose with the scarf.

"Phoo," says Anderson. He waves his hand in front of his face.

The truck revs up again. The engine shudders and chokes to life; it roars and partially drowns out the terrified pig sounds. The driver honks and gestures. He wants us to back up, to give him some more room. The King stays put. Dust churns up around us. Exhaust blasts out the back end of the big machine. The driver manages to squeeze his truck beside us after all.

I stare out the window—all those stacked crates, those round snouts, those big asses and flapping ears cruise past. One big pig, brown with lighter blobs on it, stares right back at me. We're only a couple feet apart, me and this pig, and only the cruiser glass and the crate wall between us.

Those small pink eyes find mine and won't look away. I take off my glasses. I blink. The pig blinks back. Then the cop car lurches ahead and I can't see it anymore, even when I twist to look out the back window. The King turns right at the end of the lane. My stomach cramps up again. I grit my teeth and squeeze my butt cheeks together 'til the pain rolls away. *Close call.*

The King lays on the accelerator. Dust blows in his window, wind fills my mouth. I put my glasses back on, wrap the silver scarf over my hair like a movie star.

This is nothing, I think. As long as I have shit to snort and shit to bake and shit to tell the cops, I'll be just fine.

The drop-in is usually packed on Sundays—free food, free laundry. It's warm and dry. It's loud. Kids trying to watch a movie, kids shooting pool, kids making a mess in the kitchen. Sundays you can work off your hangover, shower, catch up on the weekend gossip, crash out for a bit in the corner. Visit High Heaven. Chill with the gang. Most days, it'd be easy to get the word out about Ferret. Thing is, today there's no one, just the blonde social worker and the Knitter. I hear needles clickety-click from across the room.

"Hey," I say.

The Knitter nods.

"Where is everyone?"

He shrugs. His hands and those long needles keep moving. At his feet a ball of multi-coloured yarn unrolls a bit more with each jerk of his mammoth forearms. The finished knitting hangs down all the way to the floor. The Knitter is the largest security dude at the drop-in. Someone said he used to be a pro wrestler. I wouldn't be surprised. His neck is thicker than my thigh.

"Nice. You making a sweater-dress?"

He grunts.

"Wait, wait, let me guess. A poncho? I think they're in for fall."

His eyebrows bash into each other when he frowns. "Scarf," he says in his bottomless-pit voice.

"Wow," I say. "That's a pretty long scarf. Even for you."

He pauses and looks right at me. His eyes are close set in his huge face with his enormous bald head. "What do you mean?" he rumbles.

"Well, you're a big man and all. But it takes a certain *something* to pull off such an extreme scarf." I flick the end of my silver fabric for effect. "I can give you some tips, like for wrapping it and making turbans, that sort of thing. It's one of my specialties."

"I'm not gonna *wear* it," he says gruffly. "It's part of my recovery."

"Oh." I tap my shoe on the ground. "Recovery from what?"

"Smoking and drinking and stuff."

"Does it work?" I push my sunglasses up onto my head and peer closer at his big hands.

"Addictions, man. You never stop thinking about it, but if you keep your hands busy, you don't do it. See?"

"Hmm." Truth is, he's probably right. There's no *way* he could spark up a joint or open a bottle or shoot himself up with those gargantuan fingers fiddling away.

"When you give it up, you still got to recover from all

the damage you did. Mentally, physically, spiritually. I knit. It helps." He stops talking as abruptly as he started. He goes back to his work, clickety-clack, and I shrug my shoulders. *Who effing knew?*

"Hello, Darcy," says the chunky blonde in the kitchen area.

"Pame-lah," I sing her name. "Have you seen Fairy-Ferret?"

"Not today. You aren't the first to come looking for her, either. She in trouble?" She sets her knife down and gives me a hard stare.

"No. Cops want her for a witness. Someone shot Digit, you know."

"I do. It's just terrible." She sniffs loudly. I notice her eyes are red.

"Are you crying?"

"Maybe. He's a good kid. Never hurt anyone. Is it true he owed Eddie money?"

I shrug. *Eddie?* Fuck, *I* owe Eddie.

Pamela picks up the knife and goes back to mutilating fruit for a salad that only the Knitter will eat. She's always trying to shove food down our throats.

I lean against the kitchen counter like it's a ballet bar. I point my sneakers and lift my knobby legs up high.

"Feet down when I'm working." She swats my foot.

That's when I swipe the baking soda from the top shelf under the counter. I tuck it in the front of my red shorts, smooth my long shirt over top.

I yawn, and she pops a piece of something awful in my mouth.

"Don't spit it out," she says. "It's papaya. Good for digestion."

The rubbery lump sits uninvited on my tongue.

"What and when was your last meal?"

"Uh ..." I can't remember. I'm chewing and swallowing the fruit, but it might just fly right back up and out of me.

"Here." She shoves a bottle of orange juice at me. "Scurvy's not just for pirates anymore. Argggh."

I roll my eyes. Pamela is so embarrassing. Good thing none of the hot boys are here. I take a bottle of water instead. I can use it with soda to cook the crack.

"May I use the harm reduction closet?"

Pamela's face twitches. "I wish you would eat something first."

"Ah, mama, I ain't hungry." I bat my lashes at her.

She sighs. "There's no one in there right now. Do you need help with anything?" Her voice goes up thin and squeaky at the end. That's how I know she is not really down with the whole shooting up or smoking crack in the "safe" room thing. It was definitely *not* her idea to get it going, but she wants us to like her so bad she goes along with it.

"Fresh pipes, screens, and lip balm are all in the basket," she says. "Needles, too."

That's good, I think. Because once I finish off all my charity cocaine—I'll have a snort while I gear up, then shake and bake so I can free-base some of that beautiful stuff—I'm back to firing rocks in a pipe like usual.

"Don't forget to put the exhaust fan on this time. And take some condoms for later, okay?"

I take the water and stuff a few sugar cookies in my shirt

pocket. Then I make a beeline for High Heaven, which is what *we* call the closet.

"Thanks for the ride." I blow him a kiss. "I had a great time. Call me."

The King glares. He spits out his open window. Then he guns it, exhaust blowing out the back of the cop car.

I sashay down the alley, toward Kiddie Porn Park. It's a bit early, but soon the boys and hos will slink out with the alley cats. Pros and dealers chase the day walkers, with their strollers and lattes and dogs on leashes, their rollerblades. Day walkers go home for pork chops and prime-time TV while we work the trade all night long. So it goes.

I'm itching to bang some more of that lottery blow; now I'm convinced snorting is a waste of good drugs. The needles and crack kits didn't fit in my shirt pocket, so Pamela gave me a fanny pack for my gear. It's around my waist, tucked inside my tight red shorts, hidden by my shirt layers. *More junk in my trunk.*

I jump on the merry-go-round, and one of the straggling mothers gives me a dirty look. I hiss, Goth style. I pump with one foot in the sand, speeding the thing up and hang on as it twirls around and around, fast. I laugh out loud. Especially when she grabs her kid from the sandbox and stuffs him, crying, into a stroller and pushes him away.

"Bye bye," I yell after her. I lie down, flat on my back, look up at the spinning sky until the thing slows down.

"Yo, Darcy. What up, man? Where you been?"

I can't see him, but I know the voice: it's Lil' Brat. Two brown hands grab the merry-go-round rail. He runs, pulling the thing around fast again. Sand sprays up from the ground, into my open mouth. Lil' Brat yells and dives on top of me. He shrieks again, right in my ear. "Get off—" I start coughing. I can't breathe.

"I'm a pussy-pop yo face," he says.

He bounces on top of me, humping my red shorts while we spin around and around. "How much to let me fuck your tight ass, blue veiner?"

I shriek.

Another mother stomps past with twins. She shakes her massive diaper bag at us.

I'm laughing and coughing and wheezing.

"You know I want to get my ting right up you," he says, loud enough for the lady to hear. She walks faster and he yells, "Oh yeah, baby."

Lil' Brat rolls off me. I feel for the fanny pack; it's still there. I shake my sneakers. The foil packages rattle.

When the merry-go-round stops completely, Lil' Brat climbs up and sits in the centre. He's wearing a skin-tight pink shirt, cropped above the nipples. You can see his tight abs, toned belly, sharp hip bones. His tight white shorts show off his booty stack. He's wearing rhinestone-studded pink flats, and his hair is braided with beads. He rubs his own titties and strikes a pose. "So, where you been?"

When I catch my breath I say, "Who cares? Let's bang," and he says, "Alright."

We crawl inside the miniature plastic castle on the playground, and I cook it up fast in my new kit. I offer him a needle, still in the plastic, but he says, "Don't waste it," so we share one instead. We jam it, one after the other.

This shit is good—Lil' Brat smiles and nods. We lean back against the plastic walls and chill.

I'm thinking about the rest of what I got. *Should I shoot it or snort it or shake and bake that shit?* I never had so much all at once.

"Me and Sly got a place," I say, after a while. "Over in the gaybourhood. In some dude's house while he's away."

"You married or what?" Lil' Brat laughs.

"No way. Just stepped out for a bit. All that shit going down. You got picked up, right?"

"Hell, yeah. Threatened to send me back to Africville if I don't get my shit together. So I sucked his dick and he let me go."

"Who, the King? No way." I can't believe he'd pick Lil' Brat over me.

"Naw, that guy is messed. I mean the blond. Anderson." Lil' Brat's white teeth shine in the gloom. "He likes a brown girl."

"Huh." Usually I can tell right away if I can sex my way out of a jam. With these pigs, it never got me out of anything, just back in deeper. "What do you think of the King?"

"Creep show."

"I think he's handsome in that Bad Daddy kind of way. Like an old movie."

"Maybe an old *scary* movie."

"I think he likes me."

Lil' Brat laughs. "Shit."

"You think I'm joking?"

"You watch yourself, Darcy. Pigs hate kids. And the King hates us even worse."

"Maybe, maybe not. Imagine the King driving me all over town, getting me fries in the drive-through, Slurpies at 7-Eleven. Picking up little presents at work and slipping them under my pillow at night." I had a trick that did that all the time. I told him it was lame, but now I think it's kind of nice.

"You *must* be high," he says, laughing.

"Don't be tripping just because I'm in love and important now—"

Lil' Brat waves his hand in my face. "Love, hah. Speaking of important, I saw Ray-Ray this morning. That boy is a *mess*. Can't find his man. Says Eddie's locked up."

"Yeah. He shot Digit."

"What? Eddie don't pack. He's wild, but he's not all that."

"That's the word. Ferret, she seen it, and cops want her for a witness. You know where she's at?"

"What? She's at Ray-Ray's, freaking out *with* him."

"Okay." I smile. Things are falling into place. I figure we can dose some more, chill. I can find the King when I'm good and ready. I can take him right over there, right to Ferret *and* Ray-Ray. He'll be so impressed. *You came through for us, Darcy.* I remember his velvet voice booming around the Factory, filling the huge space. *Just like Elvis Presley.* Then the hit—he sure can pack one.

"I got to go talk to her in a bit."

"Yeah. Bust that out again, Darcy. That's some good shit you got."

I smile. It sure is.

Big House

"You're in the Big House now, young man. C North, number eighteen." Screw opens the cell door for me.

Men's voices echo off the grey walls, grey floors, grey bars. TVs hang from the ceiling in the middle of the hallway, all of them blaring different channels. Doors slam, buzzers blast through tinny speakers, engines rumble. Underneath all that is the whirl of electrical systems, the hum of fluorescent lights. My heels dig into the floor, all on their own.

Screw pushes me. He slams the door. "Play nice, Leroy," he says to the lump in the top bunk.

The lump grunts.

Screw whistles as he walks all the way back to the range doors next to the elevators. Back to his chair and his dog-eared magazine and his half-eaten bag of chips.

The lump waves a tattooed arm in the air. "That's right. You in the Big House now."

I never been in *real* jail before, but I know this ain't the Big House. We're in the frigging Don Jail, not Penetang. Not Kingston.

Leroy sits up. "You best hit the showers. I be smelling you all the way up here. That ain't right." He wrinkles his nose. He's got three teardrops tattooed beside his right eye. I don't miss his colours, neither.

I lean against the bars, feel the metal press into my back.

I do reek, truth. My stink reaches right up my nose into my brain. But I don't know about the whole prison shower thing. Like, if it's how you see on TV, I'd rather rot. I look around the place. It's small, I'd say eight by eight.

"There be no singing, no whistling, no humming. None of that in here, you feel me? Unless you a bull or a punk."

I shrug.

"Corner man say you the youngest felon on the range. That's why they stick you with just me, not three up like the others." He points across the way. I see two guys in the bunks and one lying on a blue mat on the floor. "Uh huh. Corner man say you waitin' on remand."

Leroy jumps down from the bed. He is older and darker and shorter than me. More solid, lots of muscle packed in tight. Probably got twenty, maybe twenty-five pounds on me. His orange jumpsuit is undone to his waist with the long sleeves tied around his middle. He passes a big hand over his shaved head. "You speak English?"

I nod. Truth is, I don't know what to expect. This cell is smaller than juvie. In Goderich we had units; we had space to move around. Same with all those group homes.

"You want trouble?"

I shake my head.

"Good. You got people?"

I look down at my jail shoes—blue sneakers with flat white soles, no laces. Even a piece of string is a weapon in here. Ma hasn't returned my message, let alone come down.

"You got a suit?"

I clear my throat. "Legal aid." My voice cracks. I haven't used it in a while.

"Ah, shit. What the charge?"

I raise my eyebrow. I'm not exactly sure. Breaking probation, definitely. Public drunkenness, probably. Might have had some dirt on me when they got me—not much, though. Possession, maybe, but not trafficking.

"They put you in here with me; that mean you done somethin' real bad. You ain't going nowhere, no time soon."

"You said they put me here cuz I'm young." I look at him hard. I don't know if he's messing with me.

Leroy points. "Don't dis me. You new, so I cut you some slack. But don't you go dissin' me."

I suck my teeth.

He paces between the bunk beds and the urinal, three steps one way, three steps back. "Maybe corner man put you here cuz he owe me. Maybe he knows I like a young man."

I blink. Don't know if I heard it right.

"Nice ink," he says, nodding at my tats, which peek out at the cuffs and collar. "You know, you good lookin'. 'Cept for those teeth—and that stink." Leroy points to the bunk bed. "I'm on top, case girlfriend didn't notice."

"Don't call me that." I brace myself. The smell of the antiseptic pucks they drop in the urinal mixed with piss and all that bad air—a stable of men, snorting and stamping like horses—it's choking me. The paint-chipped, graffiti-covered walls are closing in. *Rest in Pieces* it says in black marker, right above the bed. My muscles tense.

"Relax. I'm just playin' witchoo, Beige. But I do like me a tall boy." Leroy smiles and pouts his full lips. He looks me up and down. I swallow hard. A guy in the cell across the hall catcalls.

I know how it works in juvie; jail can't be too different. You get or you get got. You slam the first motherfucker who messes with you, else they all be tapping your business and pushing you around. I learned that when I was nine years old in foster, and nothing nobody says will ever change my mind on that.

"My name is fucking Eddie." I feel the burn at the back of my throat, the tightness in my belly.

"Okay. But you askin' for a whole lotta trouble."

I lunge. My fist sends him flying to the wall behind. His head hits, bounces off it. Sounds bad. I'm on him like skin before he recovers, nailing him in the gut and in the kidneys when he twists away from me. He presses his face against the cold wall. I clock another, but he pushes off the wall like a jungle cat. He springs high and catches me hard in the face. I fall back against the metal bunk. He lands a couple to my ribs. I'm stuck. My jumpsuit's caught on the metal bed frame and he bats my head like it's a ball of yarn. The cloth tears free. I pop him right in the face, bang his mouth up good. He spits blood on the floor over by the urinal and laughs. I exhale. I'll fucking stomp him. I throw a couple more hard ones, catch a couple right back. Guys in the next cells bang on the bars and cheer for Leroy. There's no bulls coming to split us up. In juvie, this shit would be done by now. Screws would jump in for sure.

Leroy puts up his hand and shrinks from me. "Hold up. You skinny but you can hit, I get it." He's bending down. Looks like he's folding, which surprises me. We're both breathing hard.

"Aagh," I yell. I want to lay into him again, punch all this hate out of me, but he backs into the corner with the miserable urinal. I can't fight him like that. *Fucking pussy.*

"Okay, tall boy. Eddie. You made your point. I be done teasing you. Peace." He stretches his hand out to shake.

I turn away to the foot end of the bunk bed near the cell door I just came in. I breathe slow, let the rage drain away. Blood stops pounding in my ears; I can hear all the other jail sounds starting up again. Men yell at Leroy for cutting short. Nobody roots for me. It's not a death match. It's about rank. I take small steps, shift my weight from one foot to the other, like I'm walking it off, only I'm not going anywhere. There's no place to go. I lean on the bars and peer down the hall. Bull's still way down there, reading his magazine. I shake out my legs, feel the bruises heat up on me. My head throbs from his hits. Finally, I walk over to Leroy.

"Alright, man." I reach for his large tattooed hand. I don't even see it coming. His kick is lightning. It's deadly, aimed right for my balls. The room spins, I gag, and I go down.

Leroy straddles me while I moan and curse. He's got me pinned good. My hands cup my sac. He's sitting right on top of the whole works. "You got to learn the rules. When I say you stink, that mean you hit the showers. You mind your bizness here, show some respect. You ain't got colours. That mean you ain't got friends. You feel me?" Men's voices roar; men bang the cell bars, all the way down the hall. "I got friends. *That's* how you get by around here, girlfriend."

I say, "What the—"

He slams my head into the cement floor. *Lights out.*

I dream of Ray-Ray. He's standing on the roof of Ma's trailer, looking out at the tobacco fields. The sun's going down fast, like in a sped-up film. Colours change all around. The dark rises up, making his long white hair and the blue of his jeans pop. "Ray-Ray, man, talk to me," I say. But he won't. He's got his back turned. "Please." I'm sad in the dream, all alone. When he finally twists, his green face is rotted out. There are worms in his stinking skin. He's some kind of zombie.

I open my eyes. Leroy's heavy man smell is all over me. I can taste it. I'm tucked into bed. Bottom bunk. My head kills. Like someone took a bat to it. The fluorescent lights stab at my eyes. I raise an arm to shield them. I feel lower with my other hand; my swollen nuts ache real bad, but at least I still got my jumpsuit on. Day one and I'm already sick of this place.

"You feeling okay, girlfriend Eddie?" Leroy is pissing at the urinal. He looks at me over his shoulder. He's got a shiner coming on and his lip is busted.

There's a sad pit in my gut, a dark hole left from that dream. *This* is what you get for wanting someone, for giving a shit, I think. *Fucking Ray-Ray*.

"Watch your aim," I say.

"How's your balls? They still warm?"

"Fuck you."

"Ha ha," he says. "You clocked me good, so don't feel bad. Fucking split this shit up."

"Yeah?"

"Hell, yeah," he says, zipping up and turning around. "Look at me. Look what you did to my pretty face." He smiles. He's got gold caps on a few of his teeth. "Got a

bump on the back of my head bigger than your knob, too."
He laughs. "So come on, tell me how bad your nuts ache."

"Lots." I sit up slowly, clutching my business. I swing my
legs slowly over the side of the bed. "Ugh. You smash my
head around?"

"Hell, yeah. Cops probably did on your way down, too."

"Don't remember. Think I got concussed." It'd explain
the weird dreams, for one.

"It called neuromuscular incapacitation." The big words
roll off his tongue in a sing-song voice.

"Huh?"

"You got tased, Eddie friend. Corner man heard."

"Really?" My mind's a swamp. Pictures come in batches,
but they don't make sense. The party. Cops. Ray-Ray—
pushing him out the window, making sure he'd get away.
Then I was falling, flopping, banging off the floor. *Tased.*

"You didn't say you was in for murder."

I look at him. "What?" My mouth dries out.

"No wonder you here with me. You best get cozy. And
you best get a more expensive suit, else you be locked up
with the Feds 'til you an old man."

"Some kid got shot at the party I was at. I didn't even see
it. Cops took me out." I shake my head. *This does not add up.*

"Well, pigs be saying *you* shot the boy. Little Frenchie
from out east. And the news saying that kid died last night
in the hospital. So now, pigs be saying you a murderer. You
feel me?"

My stomach lurches. I almost heave the grey porridge
from breakfast right up on the cell floor. I lay down on my cot
and cover my face with my hands. Questions ricochet around

my aching head. A picture comes into my head of that wiry little French kid—Digit from New Brunswick—the metal head from the Factory squat. Him, dead? *Impossible*.

I remember sitting in cuffs for so long: the lineup, the strip search, the coveralls. Being brought to this cell and all the bullshit with Leroy. Before that, there was the joke of bail court, my pussy lawyer fucking shit up and getting me sent here for who knows how long. Other lawyers got their kids out with promises from parents or social workers, court dates pending. My guy was not so good. He said, "Complications. You win some, you lose some." *Stupid fuck*.

Before that was the 14-Division tank for a day and a half, me with all the winos and wife beaters, a few crust punks with priors, most of the other party kids having been let go with a warning. The clean sparkly ones got phone calls, got picked up, got grounded. The ones caught holding or who had a record or whatnot, we stayed in the pen all weekend and went to bail court Monday morning. We got slapped over to legal aid.

Gossip about a kid in hospital, about a shooting, about the suspect already in custody; that made the rounds fast enough. A shooting at the squat, now that was news.

The fucking Factory party.

When me and Ray-Ray got there, the place was already packed. I didn't know most of those kids, Ray-Ray neither. We didn't even really want to be there—me cuz I been trying to quit the drugs and Ray-Ray on account of his stutter. We stuck with our own kind, squat kids and crust punks, some from the drop-in. At one point, the clean kids outnumbered the crusts and some minor shit went down—drinks were drunk, drugs and wallets disappeared. The hustle don't ever leave the hustler. There was the cake and the butcher's blade—puny compared to what I use at the slaughterhouse. Digit was laughing, standing beside me, eating chocolate icing right off the knife. I remember seeing those cops and pushing Ray-Ray to the open window, so he'd get out safe. His long white hair got lit up by headlights when he went through. I stared after him: the back of his Iron Maiden shirt, his beautiful ass in those tight jeans, the red of his Converse sneakers on the window ledge before he jumped out. I was thinking, *at least my boy is safe*. I was pretty fucked up. I remember going down hard. That's about it. I sure don't remember no gun.

Who the hell would be packing at the Factory squat?

In the Don, my dreams stay messed up. Ray-Ray is there, soft and sweet in his body. His wet mouth finds me night after night and I wake, the sheet sticking to my belly and chest. Sex finds me even when the rest of the dream goes wrong. One night he smiles and kisses me, but his soft hair falls out in clumps, filling my hands. Another night his face is blank. He wants to tell me something, but I can't hear on account of him having no mouth. I say, "Ray-Ray, speak up, man," but he can't. An invisible wall keeps us apart. I panic. Then he grows a mouth, like it's painted on, and it opens right up. He screams, calls me a no-good, calls me a worthless ugly bitch, a fucking moron. I'm crying, "Don't be that way," but he gets even meaner. I'm like a little kid. I just want him to like me, but he don't.

I wake from that one in a sweat. *Fuck, he sounded like my ma—with her hateful screeching.* I'd probably cry if I knew how. I think on how I used to bug her about my dad, about wanting to meet him. Wanting to know the dark side of me. She'd say, "You'll meet him soon enough at this rate. In Penetang, doing life at Oak Ridge forensics."

The fluorescents buzz, cell doors clang, the intercom bell blasts. I been here over a week—no visitors, not even the lawyer, no calls, no nothing to take my mind off it, neither. I got a bad taste in my mouth and a worse feeling in my gut.

Fuck Ray-Ray. He's out there doing who-knows-what, and I'm in lock up. Still in that bottom bunk.

Leroy's large hand drops down from the top bunk. He pretends to knock. "You feeling bad, Eddie? You need to get high?"

"No." I been more or less clean for four months. Other than beers and a little something extra at that party. Been going to work right on time, paying the rent, meeting the probation officer, eating up whatever Ray-Ray made for supper each night, playing with Big Fat Rat Catcher. Behaving—just like a good man should. Even thinking about doing the effing GED, get my grade twelve after all. *Now what for?*

Leroy swings down to the floor. He leans his face into the bottom bunk. "Eddie," he says, like he's already made up his mind. "I'm gonna set you up like you never been. Take your mind off things. You'll thank me." He drops a small foil package on my chest. "Shit is good," he says. "This shit is real good."

I hold the packet in my hand. I shake it back and forth. When even the pillow over my head can't muffle the constant noise from down the hall, I say, *Fuck it.* And I take a closer look at what Leroy gave me.

"Let's think about your future, Edward."

I cringed.

She really pronounced the "k" in think. That was the social services lady at the youth detention centre in Goderich, the blonde one with the streaks and the bright pink lips. I was getting processed on my last day, getting ready to leave that place for good. You always had to meet with one of those ladies on the way in and on the way out. If they liked you, sometimes one of them would meet you half way through the sentence; sometimes she'd get special clearance to take you down by the lake for a sandwich or fries, leave the joint to go talk about your life plans out at the beach. Maybe they'd put you in a support group or a class or something. I never got that with any of them, especially not this blonde. Man, she hated me. I could smell it on her.

"You won't be coming back to this detention centre again, Edward."

"Eddie," I said.

She blinked. "You'll be too old, for one thing." She smiled and I could see the lipstick smeared on her front teeth. It looked pretty crazy, like a kid scribbled over top of them with a fat pink marker.

"Your life could continue to be a series of bad choices that lead to terrible consequences—no diploma, no job, no money. Drugs, drinking, crime. Boys like you become men like that. They don't usually live long." She smiled tightly, this time no teeth at all. She leaned forward, over the stack of files on her big desk. She had pretty big boobs and they were getting closer to my face.

I sat rigid, arms crossed. I stared her down.

"Or you might start making some smart choices instead. You turn eighteen in a couple of months; your record will be wiped clean in time, if you stay out of trouble. You could finish high school, get a job." She stood up and walked around the cramped office.

Now I could read the Keys for Success poster that was on the wall behind her chair. It had a bunch of keys on a chain and each one had a word written on it.

"You might change things around for yourself. Make your mother proud."

I pushed back, scraping my chair on the scuffed tile floor. "Miss, don't talk about my mother."

"Sore point, I see." She walked back toward her desk so she could look me in the face. "Your mother struggled to do right by you, even when that meant giving you to *other* families so you would have more structure and opportunities than she could give you herself, Edward."

"It's Eddie." I clenched my teeth.

"You know, you've had a lot more chances than many kids get." She crossed her arms, too.

At what? I thought. Sucking foster cock?

"You might leave this self-destructive path you're on and still become a useful member of society." Her words were hopeful but her face and her voice and, most of all, her eyes, were not. "You don't have to turn out like your father."

Right then I wanted to become anyone at all, anyone who would not have to listen to her bullshit, that is. She moved directly behind me, but I refused to twist in my chair. She'd have to preach to the back of my head. I stared at the stupid poster. The keys for success were: Self-esteem, Confidence, Honesty, and Courage.

"What's it going to be, Edward?" She was clicking her pen right behind my head.

As if it was that simple. You wake up and say, *I'm going to be a fireman* or whatever, and fuck this shit of a life you've got dragging you down.

"Well?"

I didn't answer. My thirty minutes were almost up. She got paid whether or not I talked, and there was a long line of kids waiting out there on the range.

She threw the pen on her desk—that surprised me. She stomped back to her chair and tossed my big file at me: pages and pages of shit talk by other people just like her, fosters and shrinks and screws. Some paper fell on the floor around me, some landed in my lap. Words jumped out at me from all over the papers: *defiant, delusional, hyperactive, violent.* There were long science words: *schizo-something, psychotic, paranoid.* You name it, someone said it about me.

"What's 'developmentally delayed'?" I asked. "You mean retarded? Someone thinks I'm retarded?" I sucked my teeth. *As if.*

"When you don't communicate it's really difficult to know what *if anything* is going on in your head, Edward." Her consonants were stinging face slaps.

I sat for another minute or two in silence. Those words

burned the pit of my stomach. They were everywhere. And none of them were mine. Papers spilled off my lap, off the desk. They piled up on the floor around my feet.

She opened her office door. I turned my head and could read the large poster that made her office stand out from all the others in this hallway: "You can't pimp this ride: Say no to gangs." It was a picture of a black hearse with a shiny casket sticking out the back.

"This session is over. Good luck, Edward."

That blonde would love to see me now, not even a year later, snorting H with a macho gang leader, locked in the Don, framed for murder. On the street, gangbangers die young; in jail it's the opposite. Here, you need buddies if you want to get through each day. Leroy tells me what's what: don't reach past a man's food tray, don't let no one eat off your plate, no cutting in line, don't drum your fingers on the table. Watch where you're going, don't *ever* fucking bump into a man. *Politics.* Then there's the shower room, yard time, chores. If you want to use the goddamn pay phone, even, you got to *be* somebody or *know* somebody. I still fuck up, being hyper, being new. Sometimes Leroy smoothes it over for me. Sometimes I get a hauling.

Leroy signals one of his boys down the hall—he wants more dirt. He knows all fifty guys on the range, knows the corner man real good, and he's the one who runs shit. He knows folks on the other ranges, too. Little foil packages make their way, pocket to hand, cell to cell, all the way down to us. Even some of the bulls are in on it. Leroy been keeping me up for days now, says I don't owe. Not yet. He's pretty much bringing me in, but I stall.

"You got yourself a better offer?" he asked the other day, eyebrow up.

"Naw. Just, I'm not from here. I get it, but I never had that kind of thing, right? Colours."

"They not just colours, Eddie. They brothas."

And that made me think on all those other "brothers" I had, houses full of them, boys who hate the new kid, hate the whole world, boys looking to fight, boys looking to fuck. Always watching your back and still never seeing it coming. Thinking you got a buddy but instead you just get messed again. I got real weak, thinking on all that.

Now Leroy's chopping the powder on top of a hard cover Don Jail library book with the crisp edge of his lawyer's card. He's teaching me the trade proper, and also all about the In-Justice system. Way better than a GED diploma.

"Eddie," he says. "Remand mean you here now 'til you good and done with the judge, 'til you either sentenced or you set free, charges dropped. But they courts behind schedule, so we stuck waitin'. Sometimes months just sitting here, not even convicted of nothing. You feel me?" He makes two stubby lines on the book. "Judge give you two years or less, you likely finish it out here. You get more than two years, they probably send you to the Feds. Plus they shorten your time on account of this hole being fucked. One day in the Don equals three regular jail days, feel me?"

Leroy snorts the first line and inhales deeply a few times, shaking his head. "Or like, if that dead kid was special, maybe he got rich parents? Court might bump you up a bit, time-wise. Speaking of bump, here you go."

I snuffle the other line. It blazes up my sinus cavity and hits the back of my throat. I sniff, rub my nose, and swallow the chemical drip. I feel the rush immediately.

"Probably, though, you here for the long haul," he says.

That depresses the hell right out of me.

"See, if they gots the murder weapon, if they gots evidence, then that's something. Or an eyeball, a witness, what seen the deed. But if all they gots is bitches *hypothisaying* shit, then that don't mean fuck-all."

I nod. It makes sense. Mostly, it just makes me feel better.

"That's what you need this fag suit for. He may be homo, but he good in court. This fagmother *hate* the pigs. I say you call *him*. We work it out after, what the bill cost, feel me? You pull some jobs, work my crew, you be out even sooner than you know." He taps the book cover with the card again.

I slump back on my mattress and let the drugs course through. The lights and noise dim; it's like a giant spider spins a downy web and I'm tucked safely inside. Lately it's harder to remember Ray-Ray unless I'm high. He comes to me quick on the H; I can hear him, I can smell his skin and feel the tickly ends of his hair brush against my face when we kiss.

Leroy mutters something. He does another line or two and eventually swings up onto his own mattress above. The springs creak and pop as he settles. Then there's just the now-familiar lump of his body in the saggy bed, inches above me.

I think back to the night of the party again, to the moment of seeing that cop, the King, coming right at me through the crowd. Being tall is good and bad. Good, cuz I see far; bad, cuz everyone sees me too. I remember my head swinging around, scanning exits, checking the cops making their way through the joint, kids oblivious: Oreo DJing, Ferret dancing at the edge of the crowd. *Ferret!* She saw me, before it all went fuzzy. *Maybe that's important*, I think, *maybe she saw something*. And then I drift right off to that lush land of dreams.

My turn. I spread. They pat me down all over. I'm clean. There's at least ten of us down here, but only six places for visitors. The guy ahead of me gets a nod. He walks down the last bit of hallway toward the metal doors at the end. I follow him, but the bull puts his arm up right in front of me.

"Wait." He chews gum and smirks at me, his hairy arm like a toll bridge right in front of my neck, his beefy hand planted on the wall beside me.

"No way, man," I say. You only get forty minutes for a visit and this asshole took his own sweet time to bring me down. It's half wasted already.

"Afraid so. There's always tomorrow." He checks his flip chart and laughs. "Oh yeah, this is your second visit this week. No tomorrow for you."

"It's my *first*. First ever, since I been in here."

"Nope. Your little friend came Monday—guess you didn't hear your name. Still counts as a visit." He shrugs and taps the edge of the clipboard with his pen.

"Fuck." I clench and unclench my fists.

There's a sharp whistle from the line behind me. One of Leroy's friends. The screw looks up. He frowns. He swears, too. Leroy's buddy shakes his fingers, some signal I haven't learned yet, and nods at me. I nod back.

My screw yells at the bull down by the metal doors. That bull grabs the collar of the man ahead of me, just going through to the visiting room. Brother gets yanked back. I'm pushed forward.

"Your lucky day, punk," says my screw.

I look in his eyes and see so much. *Surprise, anger, a little fear.* Colours do mean something around here, it never fails.

"Exactly," I say. And I strut past the other growling brother.

The visiting room is painted puke yellow, the first colour I've seen in days, other than our orange coveralls. I get pointed to the last empty chair. There's a bullet-proof glass in the middle that separates the inmates from the visitors. On the other side there's women with their kids, there's a whole family, a couple lawyers. And Ray-Ray.

I sit down and stare through the glass. It's pretty smeary, so that fucks with being able to see him proper. He picks up a phone and holds it to the side of his head. It's on a short wire, so he has to lean close to the cubicle wall. His mouth moves, but I can't hear what he's saying. *Like that dream*, I think. He waves his phone in the air and points to my side of the table.

"Shit."

I pick up the phone on my side and there it is, the tinny echo, the click of some screw listening, and the small sound of Ray-Ray's breath.

"H-hi, Eddie." He blinks. He smiles, but he's unsettled. He jumps at every blast of the intercom. He looks nervously at the other inmates and their visitors, at the bulls pacing back and forth behind me.

"Hey." I slide my chair as close as I can. I hunch over my side of the table, closer to the glass. His eyelids roll down part way. His nostrils flare. He looks away.

I push back in my chair and clear my throat. *I stink.*

"It's sh-sh-sure loud." He smiles sadly.

"You get used to it." Actually, I was thinking how it's way quieter than on the range where we're locked in our cells all day.

"I thought w-w-we'd b-be alone."

"Oh." I swallow. I stare at his hands, his long fingers, slender wrists, and bare forearms. I can taste the salt from his skin, right at the base of his throat, if I try hard enough.

"M-miss you." He looks miserable.

I nod. I bite my lip hard against the rush of emotion that burns my throat, threatening to escape and out me in front of the other men. I bury my face in my hands and press down on my eyelids. I can't. *Not here.* I feel eyes on me, eyes of the dude sitting to my right.

"Eddie?" He leans as close as he can.

His voice whispers from the speaker part of the phone. Like it's a million miles away. I spread my fingers wide and stare at him through the slats; I memorize his face. The small freckle beside his top lip. The pale skin stretched under his eyes, light purple, the tiny folds in his delicate eyelids, the long thick lashes brushing his cheek. The white fuzz that covers his skin. It hurts to not be able to feel the soft fluff of it and then to tease him. *My little man peach.*

My breath stops up in my chest.

"Eddie."

I drop one hand to the table top and hold the phone proper. I clear my throat.

"They say you killed Digit. Shot him."

I snort. "With what? How'd I shoot someone without a gun?"

"I know you d-didn't." He looks hurt.

"So?" I hear the hardness in my voice.

"S-s-so it looks bad." He coughs. "Th-they're saying he owed you money."

I suck my teeth. "He ain't owed me. Even *if*, I don't pack."

"The-they say you grabbed a cop gun, right off the man."

"I'm no killer." Like I have to defend myself to him.

"I'm j-just s-s-saying, is all." Ray-Ray folds into himself a bit.

"Who's this 'they'? *Our* friends? Who's saying shit about me?" I grip the edge of the table. I'm shouting.

Screw smacks the edge of my table with his stick.

"Sorry, sir." I exhale. I get my shit together and he walks away.

"In the p-p-paper. The n-news. Say you were f-f-fucked up on d-dust and f-f-freaked out, like." Ray-Ray is shrinking away from me; he looks tiny in that plastic chair.

My eyes burn. *Me, in the paper?* My knuckles turn white. I'm still gripping the table top. There's a balloon inside me, getting bigger, straining to pop my chest wide open. The thud of blood rushing through my temples is all I hear.

"Did I?" My voice squeaks. All those typed words fly at me, piles of social-work papers filled with long words I don't understand. *Am I a murderer too?*

"No! I m-mean, I don't think so. Y-you were messed up b-but—" Ray-Ray's eyes shift one way, then the next. "It's just, it d-d-don't look so g-good, Eddie. And you know, the k-k-King. He's hard."

My mouth runs dry.

Ray-Ray won't look at me. He lowers the phone.

"What's that fat fuck doing? Huh? What he doing?" *I sound like Leroy.*

Ray-Ray's head stays down. I look at his part; it goes straight most of the way to the centre of his head, just a small detour where the hair grows up in circular pattern. A tiny cyclone of white. His hair is greasy, I notice, hanging limply from the scalp. I see one splat of a tear on his side of the table.

Shit.

He lifts the receiver again. "The k-King is the one t-t-talking. Said it was *his* g-gun."

No shit, I think. And the picture starts to fall into place for me. I think about Leroy's lawyer. About owing favours.

"Listen, Ray-Ray. I think I got some help in here, but I don't know how long it'll take. You know, to straighten all this out. I don't want to be worrying about you, too."

All this time I been feeling sorry for me, but I never thought how it could be on Ray-Ray. He's soft. He couldn't do a day inside, and maybe he can't do it out in the city on his own, either.

"I hate that you're alone. How's Big Fat Rat Cat? I miss our place."

Ray-Ray looks up, his eyes rimmed red. He sniffs loudly.

"I ain't there, Eddie. I d-d-didn't have r-rent. Your b-boss called to say you're f-f-fired, and the landlady k-kicked me out. F-f-fat Ratty's gone. I lost him c-c-crossing t-town." He inhales sharply, a terrible sound squeezing from his throat.

My stomach cramps hard and tight. *No job, no place, no stuff even? Big Fat Rat Catcher—gone?* All the air rushes out of me, all of it gone at once.

When I can talk, I say, "Where you staying? Shit, Ray-Ray."

He shrugs again. Now I notice the small things; pale bruises at the top of his forearms, where the sleeves of his Iron Maiden shirt end. The grimy white parts. The almost golden colour of his skin. It looks good on him, but it's the sick coming up. He probably smells different, not that I'd notice, given the company I been keeping.

"You hustling?"

He nods, miserably.

"Ray-Ray, listen to me, man." I swallow hard, to keep the bile down where it belongs. "You get out of this town. Go home. Go to my ma's, go wherever. Stay with Old Red if my ma's too fucked. You listening? You got to get out of here."

I can hardly see him now, through the red flaring in my brain, through the water in my eyes. "Get out of town. I'll come find you soon as I can."

The intercom blasts louder, longer. Bulls hit the tables, yelling at all us sad sacks to get up, up, line up, back to the wing, chaos breaking out all over with chairs scraping back and last-minute goodbyes getting louder across the room.

Ferret!

"Hey," I'm yelling loud enough to be heard. "Find Ferret!" Screw grabs my shoulder, yanks me out of the chair in front of Ray-Ray's surprised face. I'm still holding the phone. "She's my eyeball. My witness."

Ray-Ray shakes his head. "She's g-gone, Eddie."

The guard grabs the phone from me and hangs it up.

Ray-Ray's mouth drops open, like some terrible thought has just occurred to him. "What?" I yell, through the glass partition.

But I'm dragged into line with a thump on the shoulder blade, I'm shoved along with the others, and Ray-Ray's white hair, his tiny pale self grows smaller in my side vision until I duck past the metal door frame, and he disappears completely.

That night I pace the cell until Leroy yells at me. "Chill, motherfuck."

I punch the air a few times, kick the cement wall beside the urinal.

"Eddie. You got to settle yourself. A man needs quiet in here. You got to respect that."

I need out of this shit hole is what I think. Need to get out where I can breathe and think and fix things, but that is not going to happen. I feel the weight of this place, the metal and concrete and the stink of it, the hate of it, the constant watching and listening, and it tears me right up inside.

Leroy passes me two tablets.

I pop them in my mouth. I don't even ask what they are.

"Talk," he says, his big arms crossed.

"I want your suit."

Leroy smiles wide. "Good choice, Eddie." He chuckles and the low rumble of that makes the hair on the back of my neck stand up. "That mean you ready to play?"

I nod, but don't even look when I hear the zipper on his jumpsuit come all the way down, and the sound of the fabric as it drops in a pile to the cement floor.

Piggy Goes to Market

"How're we supposed to get any money for you? State you're in." An old hard-faced woman barks at me. She holds a basin in her wrinkly hands. When she leans forward, I hear the sloosh, sloosh of water. She sets the basin on the cement floor.

We're in a cellar. There are no windows. Three lit bulbs hang from sockets around the room. Cobwebs waft from rafters. The floor and walls are cold. There's a staircase, narrow and mean, that goes upstairs. On the other side is a metal door, which I now know is bolted from the outside. I have no idea what time of day it is, not even what day it might be.

The Factory birthday party, the last day of my real life, was so long ago.

The woman wrings out a puffy sponge, and the falling water sounds like skin ripping. Her hands are old, big-knuckled. Like they've wrung out a lot of hot cloths, wiped up a lot of mess over the years. The loose skin under her arms shakes when she cleans me. The yellowed pit of her arm shows through the faded housedress she's wearing. It stinks a sharp, sour warmth into my face when she moves closer to remove my scraps of clothes.

I can't talk, not that I want to. My jaw is popped; my mouth hangs open, and saliva pools and spills in long trails, down to my lap. Sometimes it goes on her cloth, her arm.

She wipes it away, annoyed. She soaps and rinses me, but the parts she touches don't belong to me anymore. She pushes my head back and I start to choke on my own spit. I can't swallow or spit, can't get my lips to work. My mouth feels broken. Ugly sounds choke out until she finally sets me back right. Even she's disgusted.

"You must-a seen something. Done something. You're not like the others, not one bit." She stands over me, hands on her wide hips, head cocked to one side. Then she shuffles over to the stairs and heaves herself onto the bottom step. "Earl? What the hell am I s'posed to do with this sack a shit? You leaving her down here or what?"

There are bellows from above, thunder. *Like Elvis but louder.*

My leg shakes. I whimper. Hot piss runs down my thighs.

She shuffles back and sees my new mess. "Now look what you done."

She carries the basin to the centre of the room where there's a drain. She dumps the dirty water down and then refills it from the tap of an old sink. It takes the woman a long time and lots of fresh basins to clean me, but she keeps trucking over to dump out the old, pour in the new. As much as she tries, she can't get the stink of his body, his bad breath, off me. It's inside my head permanently: his animal scent, that boozy sweat, his piss-stinking uniform.

She grunts with effort and mutters while she works. "Can't take you upstairs like this. Turn their stomachs, you will." Twice more she heaves herself back onto the bottom step to holler up to him, the King, the man she calls Earl.

Creak, creak. Yell, yell.

"Not like you can go anyplace, state you're in. Might as well let you rot."

I hover above my lump of a body. I fly around, see dust float in the air, see the mouse turds trailed along the floorboards, spiders spinning. I see myself—a bloated, bruised monster.

If only I'd been arrested with the others. If only I was in jail. If only I was with Oreo.

I see Oreo's face, the King's stick landing on her temple, her eyes twitching shut, her body slumping to the ground, me crawling and fighting my way through the mob to get to her, too late. None of this would've happened if I'd been right by her side, like I wanted to be. If we hadn't had the stupid party. Since the first night I met Oreo, nothing truly bad had happened to me, nobody had messed around with me. Not until the King.

"Locked your Indian butch up tight. She's a fighter," he'd said the night he picked me up, and his deep laugh had filled the cop car.

The old woman grabs hold of my dreadlocks and yanks me back to reality. *Here and now, the cellar.* "Probably got the bugs. Dirty." She clucks her tongue.

Shame warms my cheeks. I see a glint of silver in her hand and gasp.

"Quiet." She pulls a few dreads, then saws at them, down near my scalp.

She's cutting my hair!

I squeal. I lean away but she pulls harder, making my eyes water. *She's strong for an old broad.*

"What kind of hair is this, anyway? Blue!" She drops a

handful onto the floor. It looks like a small dead animal. She grabs a new section and pulls, working the scissors near the roots. "Them others was pretty, not you." More dreads fall. "Them others got us good money. You're nothing but a punch bag whore."

I cry. It hurts so much to know this horrible woman is cutting the punk right out of me, taking the very last bit of me away from myself.

"What's wrong? Cat got your tongue?"

I hiccup.

She shakes her gnarled hands about my head, sends the loose hairs fluttering. My ears are naked. The back of my neck itches.

"Now you're more like a boy. Hmmph." She stands back to look at her work. Her flat, Chinatown slippers trample the pile of my hair.

I hate you, I want to hiss.

She shakes her head, shuffles to the stairs again, and shuffles back with a pile of clothes. She drops them beside the dreads. "I ain't dressing you. The clothes is here, so put 'em on. You won't sell, bare like that. Too skinny. Likely wait a day or two. Get your bruise up. So they know what to do with you." She exhales when she bends to pick up the basin. She grunts when she stands back up. Dumping the last of the water down the drain, the old woman slams the basin onto the cement floor, tosses the sponge inside it.

I don't move.

"You ain't broke all your bones. Get dressed! I want those towels."

I still don't move. I wish I were dead.

"Suit yourself, mule. Sleep with the rags, all I care. Sleep without your soup, too." She stomps heavily up the old stairs, one arthritic step at a time. "Earl, take me home," she hollers. "I had enough of this place."

Creak, creak. Creak, creak. Slam. Click. Bolt.

There's thunder again from above. The King sounds drunk and sloppy and something else. *Why doesn't he come back down?* The voices are ugly loud, his low rumbling and her higher screech, call and response, like some warped hymn from the church orphanage when I was a kid. I think I hear an engine outside, a car starting up. After that it's quiet for a long time. No floorboards squeak, no voices rumble. I drift in and out, not sleeping, not awake.

A door slams someplace above me. I open my eyes. It feels later, but I can't say for sure. The light bulbs glare just as they did when I was first hauled into this dank cell, when the King carried me in blindfolded and dropped me on the floor.

I remember the hood lifting, the heavy fabric being pulled off roughly, some of my dreads caught with it. I was sitting, broken, staring at his shiny cop boots on the grey cement, not saying a word. He was impatient. "Should've got rid of you by now." I looked him in the eyes, in those flat soulless pits, and silently dared him. He had a strange look on his face—not sure what. But he left, locking and bolting the metal door behind him.

Other noises gradually start up—distant footsteps, doors, the thrum of electrical systems, power being gener-ated. Vibrations tremble their way through the wood and steel and glass. A thumping bass shakes the rafters; muffled dance music. Sometimes I hear car engines, motors revving faintly outside. Sometimes the floorboards creak above, but nobody comes when I scream. Mostly there's just the rhythmic throb of dance hits shaking the foundations of the building. It might be Britney.

So they want to sell me off. That means the King can't beat me anymore, not if they want to make any money. *Will he rape me again?* Would he still want the same pile of half-broken bones? If he's human, even partly, he won't come back down. He won't want to see what he's done to me.

Unless he means to kill me.

I blink.

I slowly stretch out, flat on my back. My bones clack into place. I breathe as deeply as I can. My mouth tilts to one side to let the spit pool out. I start at my toes and move them slowly, identifying the hurts, the stiffness. I work my way up my body doing a pain inventory while the bass lines thump above me. *That's AC/DC*, I think. *And Nine Inch Nails.* My thighs are hot with bruises, my hips feel torn. I try not to think about my crotch. It is swollen, mashed beyond recognition. Like it belongs to someone else. It burns *inside*, like that pig branded my soft pink tissue. Like he pounded his name into me, scarring me, taking that pretty place of mine away from me forever.

A sob burns right up from my belly. If I let myself remember the weight of him crushing me, the stink of his breath on my face, the sick pull and slap, the animal mechanics of it, then I will only ever want to die.

I skip up higher on my body, away from those throbbing, mutilated parts. I touch my ribs lightly with one hand. Probably cracked, they're so tender; even when I breathe, it hurts. I can still feel his large hands on my neck, just like how he wrapped them around Oreo's throat that day in the Junction. It's swollen, probably will be marked for days, just like hers. The inside part, my throat, is screamed raw. Not that anyone heard, not in the deserted parking lot where they drove me, him and his blond schizoid partner. It was an old routine they'd worked out long ago, like some married couple going to Sunday dinner.

"Cherry Beach?" asked the blond.

"Naw, Rogers Road," said the King. "I'll drop you home on my way to the club."

The horror settled into my bones when they turned off the ignition in that industrial wasteland, that ghost-filled decrepit lot.

I exhale and try to lift the lower part of my aching jaw so it'll click back into place. I feel little pops under my fingertips when I open my mouth wider and close it gently. The King forced it open. He nearly killed me then, stuffing my throat, choking me from the inside and out. I gag thinking about it. My eyes and nose run. I cover my face with sore hands, bruised from fighting back, from blocking their hits, from trying to cover myself. The blond didn't rape me— not because he's nicer, he just couldn't get it up. Not even when the King laughed at him.

"Not my fault she's too ugly."

I begged him to help me, to end it, but he just turned away. That blond stood lookout while I was pulverized into nothing.

Above me, beyond the floorboards, I hear the tell-tale drum line, the insistent retro guitar riffs, the hair-shaking, head-banging chorus: "Pour some sugar on me!" I catch myself singing along. I'd know Def Leppard anywhere, even as a battered hostage locked in a dirty cellar.

That's what I get for hiding a radio under my pillow every night of my pre-teen life, earphones tangled in my regulation long hair. Radio rock lulled me to sleep, American commercials filled my dreams. Until Sister Anne, the mean one with the hairy face mole, discovered my secret and confiscated the goods. My lemon-yellow radio, my only friend, gone forever!

I curl onto my side, fetal. I gently touch my head. Hair tufts unevenly. I'm cold without my dreads. There they sit, painted the colours of the ocean: purples and blues with murky green tips, my beautiful hair staring back at me from that hateful pile. It's right next to the clothes she brought, which I refuse to consider. I roll away and stare at the opposite grey wall.

"That's the King."

The kid, a pretty hustler boy, nodded his chin slightly when the cop car cruised past our spot at the Spadina-Lake Shore underpass for the third time that morning. No dirty fingers pointing, no rude gestures, no swearing. The kid kept his head down. He stayed in the middle of our group. When he paced in tiny circles, his baggy pants dragged through the long grass of the island that separates east- and west-bound traffic. Each time cops drove by, we had to hide our buckets and squeegees; the City had passed some bylaw about traffic interference. Some days, pigs would be cracking down all over Toronto; other days they didn't give a shit. On that particular morning I didn't know what the cop wanted. That kid did, though, and he fretted. I remember his voice, the one who first warned us. *What was his name?* I had thought he was a girl for the longest time, with that mussy hair and delicate skin. Pretty.

He'd said, "Yep, that's the King. And if he wants you, he'll take you to market."

It was the first I'd heard of the King, although I'd seen him in his car circling like a shark.

Jake. His name was Jake.

About a year before I met Oreo and moved into the Factory, I used to camp down at that underpass with some other kids, like red-headed Darcy. We cleaned windshields at the lights and made pretty good money some days. Jake had been there a while before me but not long after. He just disappeared. Someone said he went back home, back to that small town that puked him up in the first place. Someone else said, "No way, man. He'd never go back there."

That was also the summer I met Cricket. He was out of high school, graduated, though nobody knew it. He was slumming downtown with the punks, pretending to be homeless. As it turns out, he would sneak home to Rosedale some nights, living his double life. Cricket was bummed when Jake went missing. He thought Jake had *revolutionary potential.* I think Cricket just wanted to do it with him. Cricket wanted to start a squat like Andy Warhol's Factory. He tried to convince Jake to join his arts collective, but Jake was more interested in smoking crack and flirting Cricket's money out of his wallet. Cricket never got more than a grope or two, maybe some kisses, but he funded one hell of a habit for the boy. Back then, Cricket was always rattling on about the Paris Commune and Bolsheviks and crap like that. Jake said he'd *been* to Paris and never seen any commies. "Paris, France?" asked Cricket and Jake had blushed, "No—Paris, Ontario."

Next we heard Jake got trapped and rescued by some hard-nosed social workers, fostered out to some suburban family. He was cute, sure, and not old enough to get his own welfare and apartment, but nobody really believed that story. I figured he'd turn up sometime, but no.

That day at the underpass, the last time any of us ever saw Jake, Cricket was shaking his squeegee in the burning noon sun, cursing "the bougie pigs." He was ranting about our rights, trying to get us agitated *and* organized. Jake shrank back from the curb, chewed his nails and flitted nervously; he was bugging people for money, but he already owed most of us and we were totally broke, so that went nowhere. Jake was freaking out. He grabbed my arm—it was a cold, hard grip in spite of the hot day. "He'll take you to market," he'd said again to me, in a panicked voice.

I thought, *this kid is tweaked*, and shook him off.

I called the next set of lights, ran up with my dripping squeegee. I smiled and cleaned the glass. It was a dad driving a frowning wife and some kids who were trapped in the back, looking miserable. The dad gave me a toonie and stared at my tits. *Ugh*. When I hopped back onto the curb, Jake was already gone, who knows where.

To market. Although I never thought he meant it literally.

My stomach growls: *I'm hungry*. I'd forgotten all about food, being in this cellar. In that parking lot, that car. On the street for a couple days before that. I hadn't eaten much then, either.

And I'm something else: *angry*.

Darcy's skittish face comes to me—sketched out at the party. Right before the raid. And again at Ray-Ray's place, right before the King busted down the door. Darcy, phony as fuck and just as high, tripping like some delusional princess. He couldn't even look at me, the traitor.

Darcy, I think, did you know what they would do to me? Did you know I'd rather die than be torn apart by those pigs?

I lick my swollen lip. *So thirsty*. My muscles seize up in the damp cellar, my joints stiffen on the cold floor. I sit up slowly. My jaw clicks when I move my mouth, but it hurts less. I can swallow. I can spit. I'm not dead yet. And I do not want to be touched, not ever again.

Upstairs music pumps away, loud as ever. *It must be a bar or a dance club*. That means there are people up there, lots of them, probably, and that's a good thing.

I look at what she left me to wear: white spandex shorts, long striped socks, a baby doll cotton dress, white pinafore, and shiny black buckled shoes. *Raggedy Porno Ann*. I have nothing else to put on, so what the hell. It takes a long time to fit my limbs into the proper holes. It hurts most to raise my left arm—those ribs must be cracked. When I pull the shorts on, I don't even look down. Don't want to see my battered girl parts. I'd give anything for an ice pack to press *down there*. The shoes are a full size too big, slightly scuffed.

Who wore them before me? Next, I check the metal door. It's definitely bolted. I jiggle the doorknob, slam against the door with all my weight. Nothing but the rattle of the heavy bolt. I remember the sound of it sliding into place, just like the one at the top of the stairs. Oreo could charm this open with her tools and her steady hand and her way with things. My throat burns when I think of her, my insides ache all the more. *Shh, shh*, I tell myself. The cold metal feels good against my swollen face.

I limp to the stairs and sit on the bottom step. The music sounds louder here. *Creak*. I lean against the second step. *Crack*. An old board breaks loose—the wood comes free when I tug hard at one end. *Nice*. Now I have a weapon: a spider-infested two-by-four with rusty nails at either end. I rinse the thing off in the sink, wash the sticky white nests down the drain. I notice daddy longlegs crawling up the underside of the board, elaborate webs trailing from the wood. I chuck it. *Fuck*. Silky tendrils cling to me. I grunt, swiping at myself frantically. Panic bubbles up and I gasp.

Like a spider can hurt me now.

Oreo would laugh. She would cup her big hands around one of them and let it creep over her fingers or hang from a fine thread or hold one dangling from a twitching leg. She would croon, call it *grandmother*.

But Oreo is not here.

I drink from the tap. I rinse my face with cold water. I go get the piece of wood. The last little monster makes a getaway across the grey floor, a mangled leg hanging uselessly, trailing behind. *Poor thing*. She looks like me. Using the basin, I tap three long, rusty nails out of the board. I put them in my pinafore pocket. The last nail is already bent pretty good. It's too hard to remove. I hit it a few more times to make sure it'll stay at a ninety-degree angle. It's my rusty basement bayonet, and I practice waving it around with my good arm. I crawl up the stairs and press my ear against that door. The music is loudest here. The techno bass line vibrates the whole door. The knob shines at me. I turn the deadbolt handle, and the whole door gives slightly. I exhale for what feels like the first time since climbing the stairs. The King locked this door with his key from the outside, and I've undone it. But there's still a bolt on the other side, maybe even a second lock.

I jiggle the handle, bang against the door. I scream. I slam that door with the full weight of my body. I slam my aching shoulder into it over and over. My voice goes hoarse. My shoulder throbs. I slide down to sit on the top step and breathe heavily. Sweat trickles along my hairline, down my back. Blood thumps in my chest, my ears roar. I lick my sore lips. I'm dizzy and have to grab the wall so I don't fall down the stairs.

Hannah fucking Montana? Unbelievable. This shit music might kill me before the cops can! When I get out of here, Oreo will find this part of the story so funny. I can hear her laughing, see those gorgeous teeth shining between full lips, her long braid swinging. *You slay me, Ferret.* If I try hard enough, I can imagine the smell of her skin.

I never had that kind of thing before—love. Suddenly there was Oreo, standing right beside me, protecting me. Making everything come to life, like magic. I was so scared to believe it. What if she freaked and took off? Cricket always said, "Lesbians are delusional and co-dependent. Ferret, you're a blind monogamist!" But I didn't care. I only wanted to be with her, safe and happy, and not afraid of the whole world anymore.

I feel vibrations through the flooring under my butt before I hear the heavy footsteps approaching on the other side of the door. I leap up and bang into the wood, my voice too hoarse to make sounds.

The steps stop right on the other side. I rattle the handle.

There's a knock on the door. "Earl? That you?" A low voice, a man out there.

He thinks I'm the King.

I rattle the doorknob again and knock back.

"You fucking lock yourself in there again? Christ." I hear the faint jingle of keys. The voice is nattering on.

I brace myself against the far wall and hold the wooden board up high. The bolt slides across. Music blares through the tiny crack in the door.

"—only got a ten-minute break, you know—"

I hurl myself against the door, sending the man backward onto the floor.

"What the—?"

I'm on top of him, smashing the board over his bald head. The rusty nail scrapes angry lines across his red face. I pound that broken board into his face until it sticks. The man screams. The nail has sunk in, it's in his face somewhere near his eye, and he bats at it blindly. Blood comes out. My stomach heaves. He pulls at his black shirt uselessly. It says Fillies on the pocket. He rolls partway onto his stomach and sends me flying off him with jabs of his hard knees. His shirt says Security in big white letters on the back. I have no strength left, am gulping for air, every bit of me throbs in pain, I have no weapon. The big man crawls away from me, wood still hanging from his bloody face. His broad shoulders heave with each grunt. He holds the board in place with one hand and uses the other to get to his feet. He staggers toward the open door. I lurch to my feet. I push as hard as I can, and the big bald man falls down, down the stairs, crashing and bellowing. There's a terrible thud when he lands. The white letters on the back of his shirt glow from the darkness of the cellar floor. He's dead quiet. I slam the door and take the keys, still hanging from the lock. I slide the bolt over. My shaking hands put the keys in my apron pocket.

What have I done?

My eyes dart around the space, my brain tries to make sense of it. It's well lit but not very clean. There's a stool with a crossword puzzle folded on top. A paper plate with a piece of pizza on the table beside it. I stuff that into my apron, greasy napkin and all. Music pounds from the other side of a solid door.

Fillies. A strip club. Any second someone could come barrelling through and find me. There are two more doors at the other end; one is plain black, the other a metal door marked with an exit sign. I push that one open.

I'm outside. It's nighttime. The air is warm and there is a breeze. It's a half-empty lot; there's a car and a shiny motorcycle parked out back. Further back is a large dumpster. Beyond that is an alleyway. I don't see anybody. I shut the door behind me, creep alongside the car and make a run for the dumpster. I crouch beside it. My breath comes ragged, shallow. All those sore ribs bang away at my insides, making it hard to think. The longer I stay put, the more I notice the dumpster's stink, garbage stewing in the summer heat. Scattered at my feet are chip bags, broken vials, used condoms. Just down the alley, maybe a few feet away, cars drive past. They honk and squeal tires and blare music. Their engines rev, voices spill from them, laughing, hooting. The city is still here, pulsing its beat of regular nighttime madness, existing all this time without me.

I hear the grinding gears of a city bus, hear the ding of its door opening, the churning motor when it stands at the curb letting people on, letting people off. *My chariot awaits*. And I know right where I'm going. Where else but back to the Factory squat? Back to the hot stink of the slaughterhouse, the itch of the grassy field, the rotting dump: home.

Come and get me, Pig. I double dare you.

Ferret Hunt: A Three-Act Play

ACT ONE: SAFE HOUSE

Cricket waves goodbye to the sleazebag landlord and shuts the door to our very own filthy, east-end rooming house. I can hardly breathe. The place stinks of dead mice and piss-soaked old men. He opens the reeking bar fridge on the other side of the small room, slams it shut. There's an electric hotplate on top. In a closet with a broken door is a leaky toilet and rusting sink. Cricket paid one hundred dollars cash for a week—money his parents gave him to buy textbooks for next semester, which starts in a few days.

Cricket pulls a cobweb from the tip of his blue mohawk. "Ew. We have our safe house, now we just need to find our girl."

"Great." My voice cracks. Lately I'm either raging or weeping, sometimes both at the same time. I lean out the dirty window ledge so he won't notice my eyes getting wet. I dab gently with a corner of my shirt. First, my face is still sore from the King's beat-down, and second, I don't want to smear the mascara and eye shadow Cricket piled on earlier, using samples at the mall. "I just can't believe no one's seen her," I say for the hundredth time. "It's been over a week since the raid."

A hot breeze gusts in, bringing shouts and traffic sounds

from Gerrard Street below. Bollywood music erupts from the downstairs restaurant when customers open the front door. I smell deep fryer and curry. My stomach gurgles. I slump onto the cracked linoleum floor with my back to the wall.

"Don't worry, Oreo, you'll be great as an undercover stripper. Pretend you're on a rerun episode of *Charlie's Angels*." Cricket squeezes my shoulder. His body heat closes in on me in the stuffy room. "Soon we'll all be together again."

Except for Digit. I stare at Cricket until he looks away. The unsaid words hang heavy in the gloom.

I jiggle the CD player we found in the trash. I want to crush it between my strong hands, destroy it, burn this rage out of me so I can snap back to my old useful self.

All we know is while we were getting our asses ridden at 14 Division, Ferret somehow escaped from the Factory squat party raid and eventually hid out with Ray-Ray. Ray-Ray and Darcy say cops picked her up a couple days later. Not just *any* cops—the King himself was hunting her. He knew her real name and everything. By the time they let me out of bail court, Ferret was long gone. Her name didn't turn up anywhere in the system when the drop-in worker started digging.

"We should tell Ray-Ray and Darcy where we are. Ferret might hook up with them again. What do you think, Oreo? I mean, where else would she go?"

"I don't know. Drop-in is off limits, shelters too." We heard the King's harassing all the kids downtown, even more than usual. "She doesn't have family."

"Seriously. Ray-Ray's our best bet."

But I wonder. How far will I go to save Ferret? *All the way, whatever it takes.* "With Eddie in jail, maybe Ray-Ray's ratting. He'd do anything to help his boyfriend. Wouldn't you?"

"Hmmph," says Cricket. "I'd do anything to spring myself, since I don't *have* a boyfriend."

"Well, you already did that." I blow into the CD player's dusty parts.

"Pure luck," he says, smiling.

Pure rich white luck, I think.

"I can't wait to see you in drag, Oreo." Cricket unzips his backpack and dumps everything onto the floor. He sorts it all: the makeup, lingerie, and hooker shoes we shoplifted from Gerrard Square mall. A bottle of vodka stolen from his mother. He empties his pockets—a handful of change, an unopened condom, the clean square card with his dad's big-time lawyer name on it.

"On second thought, you keep this." He hands the card to me. "I know the number. If anything goes down again, just remember to say, 'Officer, am I free to go?' And, 'I would like to call my lawyer.'"

Like it's a game with different rules for each player.

"That judge owed your dad some kind of favour, huh?"

Cricket blushes. "The pigs, too. I'm lucky the charges got reduced. Trespassing and drinking in public? Please, that's nothing."

Cricket's older, so he didn't get the extra $125 for being underage.

He says, "I pay a fine and do some community service,

whatever. I wonder if volunteering with my revolutionary arts collective counts."

I shake my head.

"Well, if I go to jail, it better be for political reasons, not for getting down at a house party."

I laugh. "Honey, you'll never do hard time. You'll be out on bail eating take-out and watching *America's Next Top Model* before you can zip those prison pants."

Meanwhile Eddie and boys like him—mixed-race, tattooed, buck-toothed boys raised by the system—they rot on remand. That stokes the angry fire that burns inside me.

"Whatever, girlfriend." Cricket waves his hand at me. "*You* didn't do too bad either, Oreo. Possession of one joint? Please."

"I got beat up. My face is still a mess. I already had a record, so now I'm on probation." I shake my head. "It's bullshit."

"Still, could've been way worse."

"The squat is shut down permanently, all our stuff is destroyed. My girlfriend got kidnapped by a psycho cop, and Digit is—"

"Don't say it."

"—and Eddie's in jail. Does it need to get worse?" I bang my head on the window sill once, twice.

"Take it easy, Oreo." He looks worried.

Okay. I breathe deeply. Don't want to completely lose it.

"You know, getting arrested was not fun in *my* condition—the Ecstasy-Viagra combo, euphoric with a rock-hard dick for hours. Awkward! I would have totally gotten laid by my bike courier if we hadn't got busted." He sighs loudly. "And I had to toss my amazing stash. It was selling like hotcakes."

"Wish I had my tools here," I say. Making something, fixing something, anything at all, would make me feel better. *Large and in charge.*

"Maybe I would've got a boyfriend in jail," he says wistfully.

A sudden memory from the party slams into my brain. I was spinning, headphones on, didn't hear the cops, the yelling. I was zoned. Then I looked up to see Ferret's terrified face, right as that cop's stick cracked my head. I remember coming to as he dragged me outside. The King threw me against his car to cuff me; my knees buckled. Then, with the bracelets on nice and tight, he sucker-punched me in the face. "Squaw dyke," he said in that sinister low voice. I lay on the ground outside the Factory in all that chaos, blood dripping out of my nose, him leering above me, light bouncing off his silver belt buckle.

Cricket waves a hand in front of my face. "Should we talk about Digit now?"

"No." I jump up and pace back and forth from the window to the fridge. I still can't believe he got shot. *Who brings a gun to a vegan dance party?*

"Couldn't even say goodbye with all those cops parked in front of his hospital room. Ray-Ray heard his folks came all the way from New Brunswick. He was hooked up to machines." He sniffs loudly.

When I picture Digit leaving the hospital, it's on the back of some leather daddy's motorcycle. It's on his mud-covered ATV, or a skateboard he made out of found objects, not in a wheelchair. Not in a wooden box.

I swear and punch the stained wall.

"Easy, Oreo."

One night this summer, me and Digit and Ferret were lying in the field outside the Factory, shooting the shit about where we grew up. I told them about Manitoulin Island, where I'm from, Wikwemikong unceded territory. I wanted to take Ferret home. Wanted her to meet Phoebe, my Auntie's woman who helped raise me. I wanted to take her to the powwow. So she could see that part of me that's always getting watered down around white people. She could hear the drums and singers, smudge with burning sage, and watch the dancers in their beautiful regalia; Hoop Dancing, Men's Fancy, Iron Man and Iron Woman. She could start to know those proud parts of me, who I really am.

Digit wanted to come, too. "Some tings remind me of Neguac, my village," he said. "We catch oysters dere, you know. Each day, every day. I'm supposed to stay wit da oysters and find some girl who's not my cousin to make babies." Digit's accent got thicker the longer he talked about home. He loved it as much as he hated it: ripping around on four-wheelers, chucking dirt bombs at the *école criss*, *tabarnak*, sneaking beers from his drunk uncle's broken barn fridge. Lighting blue angels to impress a girl. "Hi burn my hass so bad, you know, but still she don't like me. She go out wit my friend hinstead!" Ferret and I shrieked when he re-enacted it, dropping his pants and lighting a fart as it reverberated from his bare backside. *Digit*.

Cricket wipes at his eyes with a pair of pink panties from the pile of things. He's blabbing still, going on about Digit.

"We can't do anything for Digit. Let's find Ferret." My knuckles are warm from denting the drywall. "I wish none of this ever happened."

"Yeah," says Cricket. "That party was a stupid idea."

"Fuck you." The party was *my* idea for Ferret's birthday, and *I'm* the one who talked her into having it. "I didn't invite all those university bitches. I didn't post it on Facebook. How do you think the cops found out?"

He clears his throat. "I'm not the enemy, Oreo."

"You sure?" I feel mean. I imagine ripping his throat wide open with my bare hands. "You came out of this pretty clean."

Cricket says, "Do you want me here or not? I should leave. If my parents find out I'm not at Frosh week they'll cut me off. I can't afford tuition. Maybe that doesn't matter to you. But I'd be completely on my own."

Like the rest of us have been for years. "Boo fucking hoo."

Cricket's mouth pops open, but he doesn't argue.

I spin away from him. I march over and yank the window as high as it'll go.

"This place is a dump." Cricket is making nervous small talk.

I say, "It's so un-bougie. I thought you'd love it."

"Very funny. There's a difference between un-bougie and downright ugly. Speaking of which, are you ready to get in drag?"

I grunt. "I don't know about this plan." I kick off my boots, drop my combat pants, ripped T-shirt, boxers, and dirty socks into a pile. I sniff my pits—they are pretty ripe.

I try to wash them in the crap sink with a sliver of dried old soap. I let them dry by the window. The breeze feels good on my bare skin. I shove on the push-up bra with its stiff little hooks, the lace panties, the strange belt with the tiny snaps. It takes a while to get everything in the right place. Finally, I roll the matching stockings over my strong legs. I struggle with the metal clips dangling from the belt. "This is harder than it looks."

"I'll help with the garters." Cricket kneels at my feet. He looks up—the bra is working, I can tell by the shock on his face. "You know, Oreo, if I was even remotely bisexual …"

"Ugh." I stuff my fishnetted feet into second-hand stilettos. I stumble. "Ugh. How am I supposed to dance if I can't even walk?"

Cricket presses his hand on my back lightly. "Shoulders back. Spread your feet wider. You have to find your new centre of balance."

I lurch forward. My left foot slides and I wipe out, land right on my lace-covered ass. "Shit. I can pop the panel from an ignition tumbler and hotwire a car in three minutes, but I can't cross the room in a pair of heels."

"I'd be there in a heartbeat if they'd hire *me*. Sadly, this patriarchal establishment does not pimp my gender." He stares at me down on the floor and says, "Hmmm."

"What?"

He pours two glasses of vodka. "I'm thinking."

I say, "I wish you could come with me." And suddenly I do. I mean it just as much as I wished him away earlier.

"Honey, I'd blow your cover like nine inches at the bathhouse. Here, drink."

I take a swig, cough. "Do you really think Ferret's at this peeler bar?"

He sits on top of the bar fridge and the hot plate. They creak a warning. "I hope so. I mean I do and I don't. Ray-Ray saw the King take her. He did something with her, took her somewhere, and it's not the detention centre."

My stomach twists at the thought. I know what can happen to homeless girls, working girls, Native girls. All over the country our betrayed bodies get swallowed by lakes, by the ocean, and sometimes spat back up on the sand, some dog walker or early-morning jogger finding our parts.

"Darcy heard she might be in the upper lounge at the strip club. I guess it pays to have shady roommates after all, huh? Darcy says that's where the King dumps all his fresh meat for the international buyers. Dopes them up, whores them out."

My mouth waters with sick. What would be worse— death or forced prostitution?

"Sorry," he says. "I know this is hard."

"I still don't get why he'd do that to Ferret. She never hurt anyone. Why would he even bother?"

"Maybe because he can."

"What's that supposed to mean?"

"He's a schizoid power tripper. She's an orphan, a street punk. Queer. Who the hell is going to stop him?"

"I'll kill that fucking pig myself." I'm grinding my teeth, squeezing my fists. I want to destroy something, kick the shit out of somebody, anything to let loose this rage. I wonder why it's not *me* who's missing in action, a statistic waiting to happen. *I didn't protect her. My girlfriend is gone, and it's my fault*. I want to howl, want to rip out my hair and beat my chest.

"Chill, Oreo."

"How would you feel if it was *your* lover?" Heat rises in my cheeks. I remember the sound of the King's voice, the things he said to me that day on the sidewalk. Things he's probably doing to Ferret.

"She's my friend, too." Cricket looks hurt, but that fuels me. "I wish you'd let me talk to my dad. He might know someone …"

"Your dad might get favours at the cop shop or in court. Tell him to help Eddie. But Ferret doesn't need a lawyer. She needs a bounty hunter. Does your dad have a gun?"

Cricket's eyes widen.

"I'm serious. I don't want to fuck with the King and run. He'll find us. He pulls strings all over, nobody knows how far. He runs this town. If I'm facing off, I'm taking him right out." Panic rises in my chest.

"Don't joke, Oreo."

"Who's joking? Nobody else is gonna help. Nobody else gives a shit about us." My voice shakes. I'm yelling, and Cricket shrinks into himself. He moves farther away from me. I want to scream, *you sheltered little bitch*. I want to hit him, slap some meanness out of me and some sense into him.

"I don't want anything bad to happen to her either," he says quietly.

"Bad shit has been happening our whole lives," I yell. "The squat wasn't just a cool hangout. It was her home. We're her family. We have to do something!"

I picture Ferret hurt, scared, feeling like I do, but all alone. *My girl.* I choke back a sob that has been lodged inside, ever since the party raid. When I find her, I'll take her north. Get out of this ugly city for good. I lean out the open window, take deep breaths. Stuff is happening outside—families going for dinner, couples holding hands—and none of it matters. I tell myself that Ferret is still alive.

But Digit isn't. Why should Ferret be?

"What if it's too late?" My voice sounds small. Not mine at all.

"It's not. But we need to get cracking. Darcy says the club has security cameras. Maybe we can get the tapes, get the place busted."

"Busted by who? Cops took her, cops sell the girls, and cops own the fucking club!"

"They can't *all* be in on it," says Cricket.

"Oh yeah? Those blue brothers only protect each other."

"Oh." He looks down at his fair trade sneakers.

I can feel the King's big hands closing around my throat, stopping my air, the way they did on the sidewalk right in front of Ferret. The way everything closed in on me while he hissed into my ear, "I'm gonna rip you apart. You don't even know pain yet. I'm your worst nightmare, you hear me?"

"Oreo. You listening?"

I shake my head. It's so hard to pay attention to the sounds coming out of other people's mouths these days.

"I was saying, make sure you don't do anything dumb tonight. Case the joint, but don't be obvious. If you can send Ferret a message, that's a total bonus, but don't go all He-Man."

I blink a few times.

"No crying, Oreo. It took twenty minutes just to cover your black eye. I didn't steal enough shadow, so don't mess them up. If you see the King, get the hell out. Promise?" He swipes at my face with some powder from the pile of stuff on the table. He waves a lip gloss at me. "For later."

"Shit." I finish my drink. I stand up. I don't know what I'd do if I saw the King face-to-face right now. I might surprise everyone and bawl.

"We still got to do your hair."

I slump on the floor at Cricket's feet. He combs my hair out of the long braid I always wear.

"Ferret needs us. So get in there, get some dancer cred. This is an official undercover operation, Oreo. You make your brotha-from-anotha-motha proud! Chin down, honey. Work it like you own it, like you rentin' all night long."

Cricket snaps his painted fingers and moves like liquid across the tiled floor. He makes it look so easy.

ACT TWO: STRIP CLUB

Hours later, I'm at Fillies in the dark reddish glow. Lights flash on the bar and the stage. Mirrors reflect my angry face from all angles. I gasp. With all the makeup, with my waist-length hair hanging loose, I look like my dead mother. Dance hits pound through the space, through my chest. I'd do anything to slip the DJ a decent playlist. The manager is a creep show wearing a stinky Hawaiian shirt and bad toupée, right out of a cartoon. He points me to the dressing room—a decrepit hole with a couple of toilets, rusted sinks, bad lighting. It smells like dirty crotch and a side order of bourbon.

"Carly, give her the tour," he says. He waits for me to take off my jacket. He frowns at the bear clan tattoo that covers one shoulder. I stick my chest out further. He grunts, gives a slight nod, and leaves.

The other girls ignore me. They're different degrees of naked, white and skinny, black and skinny, lots of brown girls, too. They wear thongs, leather, and lace. They do their makeup, drink, and gossip.

"Come on, hon," says an older blonde woman. *Carly*. "Let's get you settled."

Her voice reminds me of Auntie Tam: gravel and whiskey. She smiles a wide, white set of teeth with a frosted pink frame. When she strolls down the dingy hall in her fringed cowboy boots, I watch the sway of her womanly hips. She points out the important stuff—the stage, the regulars, the private booths where you make the real coin. She tells me to sit and watch the experienced dancers. I ask her what's upstairs, and her face shuts tight, a garage door closing. She leaves. One after the other, girls attack the stage like it's a pommel horse in gym class. They pull fancy tricks, slide into splits; they hump the pole and bounce their dimpled bums in customers' faces.

I'm not playing that game, I decide. I wouldn't even know how.

Around midnight I lurch on stage for my very first solo. I wobble in the stolen shoes. A third drink loosens my limbs, but Cricket's pill gives me the courage to get up in front of everyone. Bottles and glasses clink through the din of voices. My music doesn't start; the strung-out DJ misses another cue. My legs shake. I flick my long hair and inhale deeply. Catcalls from the audience knot my stomach.

I'm dancing for Ferret, I tell myself.

Finally, my song starts. The droney doom metal matches my oxy groove. I close my eyes and let the music tell me how to move. Slowly, I snake my arm above my head. I roll my neck and my long hair tickles my bare shoulders. My body undulates. I roll my shoulder and peer over it toward the crowd, lashes lowered. It's impossible to see anything past the row of bright lights. There are shadows at the edge of the stage, but that's all. I picture Ferret out there in the club, watching. Each step brings me closer to my memories: Ferret smiling and twirling at the Factory dance party, Ferret's soft skin, Ferret writhing beneath me. I'm on stage and at the same time, I'm far away from this terrible place. I'm back at the Factory, before the raid, curled in our nest.

The song ends. I'm lying on the stage touching myself. I roll over and notice the money on the stage. The floor feels cool on my skin. Part of me wants to sink into it, just melt through it and disappear. The other part wants to count money and buy another drink.

A white man leans forward with a fifty dollar bill in his outstretched hand. *Half a week at the rooming house.* I crouch, both hands filled. I am an animal on the road, a car bearing down upon me, sad eyes for headlights, soft hands for a grill. The next dancer, an athletic blonde, is already cleaning the pole with anti-bacterial wipes. I grab the bill and the rest of the money. I stomp down the rickety stairs to the change room.

"Song's too long, Pocahontas," says the manager.

I imagine stabbing his fat gut as I towel off. Instead I check my makeup in the mirror above the sink.

"And don't get weird on stage. This ain't no art bar."

I ignore him and apply more lip gloss, something I haven't worn since I was a closeted fourteen-year-old, back on the Rez.

It's after one a.m. I'm alone in a dark corner. No sign of the King, no sign of Ferret. The dancers won't talk. There's nothing but rat shit and empties in the basement—and a locked furnace room. Another backstage locked door might lead upstairs. One big bouncer reamed me out when he found me fiddling with it. If I had my tools, I'd pop both open in a heartbeat. Meanwhile, I'm terrible at this other job: flirting with men, crawling on their laps to get them hard. All I want is to beat the crap out of them.

"Hey, kiddo." It's Carly, sidling up with two drinks. "How you doing?"

"My feet hurt and I want to go home."

She smiles and hands me a glass.

"No thanks," I say. "I'm trying to not get wasted."

"Relax, it's water. That bozo over there thinks he bought us gin tonics." Carly raises a glass and blows a kiss to the bald lump of a man who pumps his arm feverishly in return. "I get tap water and split the difference with the waitress."

"Smart. Thanks." We sip while a girl twirls around the pole to Bon Jovi. *Wanted dead or alive.*

"Bozo would like a lap dance with you after," she says.

"I'd rather give him a vasectomy."

Carly laughs, a scratchy cackle. "Don't mean to pry. Lord knows we all have our reasons, but this doesn't seem like your kind of place."

I look at her: fake tan, streaked hair, boob job, glow-in-the-dark booty shorts. I see manicured hands with a couple of age spots. Foundation caked in tiny crow's feet at the edge of mascara-framed eyes. She's been around the block. I decide to tell her the truth. "I'm not really a dancer."

"No shit."

"I'm looking for my girlfriend. I think she's upstairs."

Carly moves in closer. "This a joke?"

"No." I stare her down. I wonder if she'll rat me out to the fat jerk manager. "She's shorter than me, white, got blue dreads. She's pretty. Punk pretty."

Carly shakes her head. "I don't know half of what goes on up there, but none of it's good."

"The locked door backstage goes upstairs, right?"

"That's one way." She scans the bar carefully. "This is serious, kiddo."

"No shit."

She nods her chin. "There's a camera's right there. Not sure if there's actual tape running. Be hard to get up there without that big goon noticing. He's not friendly. But he's not the worst."

The stage light follows a girl doing flips. She lands in a bridge with her legs spread wide, front and centre.

"Do you know the King?" I say it straight up, no emotion.

Her eyes narrow. "A girl would be smart to stay the hell away from him."

"My girlfriend never had a choice."

She doesn't take her eyes off mine. She could be protecting him, or warning me, I can't tell. Carly leans against the bar ledge. She looks away. I wonder if this conversation is over.

"I don't want to get you in any trouble. Sorry."

She looks at me again. "Sure about this? No good will come of it."

I nod.

"A real James Dean, aren't you?" She gives me a sad smile. Carly finishes her water. "I'd try tomorrow. Earl—the King—doesn't usually come in on weekends." She points a manicured finger to the main bar. "Wait staff are busier, and security spends more time circulating. They'll be distracted. I'll do some pussy shots by the DJ booth at the end of my first routine, draw the light. Not sure how you'll get through without a key. You better hustle. Manager finds out, you're done for. And I don't mean fired."

"Thanks, Carly."

"You be careful. I mean it." There's a frown line on her brow that isn't good for business. She squeezes my forearm. "Hell, I'm gonna worry about you, now. I'm gonna need a real drink after all."

It's four a.m. when the cab Carly called stops in front of the rooming house. The driver jots something down as I get out. He peels away, leaving me in the street wearing lingerie and a jacket Carly lent me. My regular clothes and boots disappeared from the locker room. Carly says one of the dancers stole them, like a hazing ritual. My key gets stuck in the lock. I yank on the doorknob. Someone gallops down the stairs. The door rips open, almost from its hinges.

"Ohmygodyou'refinallyhome."

I follow Cricket upstairs in the dark. The hall light is burned out, so we feel our way along the disgusting walls. Cricket is wired. "You know, there are a lot of freaks living here. They've been bugging me for smokes. One guy tried to give me mouldy salami." He shudders. "He stuck slices under the door!"

Inside our ugly room I unbuckle the hated shoes and drop them: *One, two.*

"Plus I was getting worried about you."

"Yeah?"

"I *was*. I was worried you'd meet some hot guy and decide to go straight and make babies instead of come back and pay for this luxury room with your stripper tips." He smiles charmingly.

"No worries there." I think of the blobby, faceless men from the club: jocks, gangsters, pervs. They're not even real people. Just lonely creeps.

Cricket counts my money while I rub my swollen feet.

"Wow. You're rich."

"This girly stuff is hard work. I don't even know how to lap dance, by the way. I actually fell off a chair trying."

"Really?"

"I couldn't take his money, it was that bad. I ended up shaking hands with the dude." I comb my hair with my fingers and quickly braid it back the way I normally wear it.

Cricket snorts. "We can practice, Butch-tard. Did you make any friends?"

"As if," I say, yawning. "Those broads are not stripping for the sisterhood. One was nice." Carly's face and her sugar-rough voice come back to me. She's hot, in a not-my-type kind of way.

Cricket folds a few bills into his own pocket. "Choreographer's fee," he says sweetly. "Still got to pay for the stash I dropped." He puts the rest in a pile at my feet. "You're going make lots of money if you get this right."

"I'm going to find Ferret if I get it right."

"Did you see the King?"

I shake my head. I tell him what little I got from Carly.

"Well, that's a start. Maybe tomorrow we'll get upstairs."

The thought of going back to that place makes me nauseous. "I didn't learn anything. We don't even know if Ferret's there. My feet are killing me, I got molested all night by gross dudes, and probably got a fucking STD from the furniture."

"Not if you wore a condom," jokes Cricket.

"Jackass."

Another night without Ferret. She could be anywhere. The enormity sinks into my bones. How could Ferret be held in the same evil place I'd been all night, with the sleazy manager and those mean girls? Wouldn't I sense her? I gag and choke down the bile. I punch the wall as hard as I can. The drywall buckles into a hole slightly larger than my fist. My hand throbs. Someone bangs back from the other side.

"Easy, girl."

I lie on the dirty floor and press my ragged knuckles into my eye sockets. The familiar rage burns my veins, eating me inside out.

Cricket says, "Shh. I promise we'll find her. Tomorrow."
But what happens to her tonight?

ACT THREE: BREAK AND ENTER

Light fills our curtainless room. Dust floats in the sunshine, whirling about, going nowhere. It makes me think about my life in a depressing way, like I'm following the broken footsteps of so many women in my family. It's like we just keep falling into the same shitty circumstances, like nothing will ever change for us.

A brown spider spins a web inches from my face. *Hello, Grandmother.* Her legs keep working on the fine thread, and that makes me feel better.

"Morning, sunshine," says Cricket. We're lying side by side on a pile of dirty clothes.

I groan. "Already?" I had been dreaming of long-ago happy times in Phoebe's kitchen up north: Phoebe and Aunt Sue, Auntie Tam, me, and my mom were making fry bread, whitefish, wild rice. In the dream, they were trying to tell me something. *But what?* The words are gone.

Cricket says, "Maybe some punk rock will help."

"Ow." I'm sore from sleeping on the floor, everything hurts from wearing those killer heels all night, from dancing—if you can call it that. I'm dry-mouthed and achy from the painkillers, the vodka. I roll over carefully. "We don't have music."

"Oh, yes we do!" Cricket shakes a CD. "You fixed that box, whatever you did. Last night, while you were at the club, I went back to the squat. I got so excited about the money I forgot to tell you. Cop tape is all over the place, shit's trashed. A pipe broke, there's water everywhere. But I found some clothes and music. Isn't that awesome? No drugs, though." He presses play and the anarcho-punk Dirt CD fills the ugly space. Cricket shouts the chorus to "Deaf, dumb, and male!"

I shut it off. "Did anyone see you?" I can't believe his stupid grinning face.

"Naw. The cop out front was reading porn. Never even noticed."

"You brought back music?"

"You love this CD!"

"Why didn't you get my fucking tool kit? My picks, my cutters? Fuck, Cricket. That's the shit we need if we want to rescue Ferret. I can't pass as a stripper—I'm not fooling anyone." I want to punch his lights out.

Cricket ejects the CD. "I found your pants. I brought them for you." His voice is pinched and clipped, like an uptight little jerk, like he might cry womanly tears all over me. He tosses a bag beside me.

Fucking baby.

"At least you got that right. I can't be walking around Gerrard Street in this." I pull at the stupid lingerie I'm still wearing.

"You can have my other sneakers," he says, setting them on the floor near me. "Or just a buy a new pair with all your money."

"We'll need that money to get out of town or get settled, asshole." He has *two* pairs of designer shoes from our wreck of a home, and nothing that we actually need. *Food. Tools. Supplies.*

"You don't have to be such a bitch." He's crying, as predicted. "I'm going dumpstering," he blubbers, and slams the door behind him.

I lie there fuming. *Stupid spoiled Cricket can bloody well go home if he wants.* It's not like *I* have a rich family to bail me out, or a beautiful house to run to. My mom and Aunt Sue are dead. *Bam.* Both killed on New Year's Eve. A two-car collision, two dead women; one drunk asshole walks away from the wreck. Tam took it even harder than me. Our family cabin couldn't hold us with all that grief. Last I heard, she was living rough in Winnipeg, trying to forget. She ran west and I came south, leaving Sue's girlfriend Phoebe to deal with it all.

I breathe deeply. I'm more alone than I like to admit. Suddenly, the thought that Cricket might leave is scary. And that I might somehow deserve it, for how I'm treating him.

Inside the bag are my pants, an old black pair, covered in patches, comfortable and familiar. *Mine.* Another thing stares back at me. *Ferret's favourite hoodie.* It's covered in band patches, pins, and buttons; it's customized with metal accessories and spikes along the edge of the hood. She worked so hard to make it perfect, her most prized possession. I clutch it and inhale her scent from the fabric: a hint of patchouli, something like oranges and vanilla mixed together, and there—*there!* Her earthy, tangy skin smell underneath it all: *Ferret.*

I let loose for the first time since the party. Hot tears roll down my face. Snot drips. I weep, holding the hoodie to my face. Smelling her is a shovel hit on the head. I hear her low voice, see her beautiful face with its sharp cheekbones, those big brown eyes, full lips—gone. I bawl until there's nothing left. Then I pull the sleeves over my hands, the hood on my head, and zip it all the way up. I pretend she's right with me, spooning.

The next time I open my eyes, Cricket is eating naan bread. "That cute cook saw me in the dumpster and instead of getting mad he gave me all this free food. I think he likes me." Cricket sounds as flamboyant as ever. He opens the containers: curried vegetables, channa, chutney, and spicy pickles. Good smells make their way to my corner. I sit up at last. I stick a dirty finger into one bowl.

"Mmm." I can't remember my last meal. Spices make my nose run. Salty sweet tickles my mouth. My stomach twists.

"Yum," he says, scooping curry with a piece of naan.

"Thanks, Cricket."

"It's nothing," he says. But he won't look me in the eye, so I know he's still hurt.

Just like a girl.

"I mean it. For everything." I can't talk about the hoodie yet, but he sees me wearing it, plain as day. "Sorry about before." He must know I'm trying, at least.

He shrugs. He eats.

We plough through the containers. We lick each one clean, and the plastic spoons too. I wipe my face on Ferret's sleeve. Cricket burps and finally smiles. Food gives us hope. *Maybe things aren't quite so bad.*

Cricket's grey eyes are a bit watery. His face is still tight.

I get it; deep down all he wants is approval. He—the braggy soapboxer, the one lecturing us with his politics and visions and boring rules—right now, he just wants me to like him.

"Let's go to the club. We'll pick up some tools on the way. We can totally break in before all the security dudes show up for work." I'm like a bloodhound with a fresh scent for the trail, rested and fed and single-minded. "I just need a screwdriver and a paperclip. Some pliers would be awesome."

He looks like a little kid. Like he knows I can turn on a dime and beat him, but is desperately hoping I won't.

"Honest, Cricket," I say, swallowing that awful guilt. "We'll be okay."

In morning light, the club looks pathetic. It sits on some expensive real estate, the busy corner of an east-end intersection. The sign, not lit up, not blinking in neon ecstasy, is benign. Alleys run on either side of the building. We each follow one; they meet at the back where there's a dumpster and space for the manager to park. Staff use the back door; ash piles and cigarette butts mark their smoke breaks. Small square windows with crappy blinds line the top of the building. Cricket knocks the two security cameras out of commission with his slingshot and some rocks from the laneway. That gives him a swagger.

"Oreo, check it out." Cricket points to a door without a handle or lock. Around the edges there are smudges and imprints in the dust; people use it regularly. "Someone lets them in." The weeds have been cleared by the entrance. When I stand in the main alley, the dumpster blocks Cricket and the door from my view.

Clever.

"Think anyone's inside?" says Cricket.

"Maybe a cleaner. Maybe not. We got to hurry. The day shift starts at noon."

The sound of an engine fills the back alley. Cricket and I dive behind the dumpster. The car drives slowly toward us; it stops. Exhaust billows up from the other side of the dumpster. There's a crackle of static, a digital bleep. Cricket's eyes widen. He mouths the word "pig." I'm too scared to actually peek, but it sounds like a radio dispatcher. A taxi. *Or a cop.* The car crawls forward the rest of the way past us, down the gravel lane. It doesn't stop again, and no one gets out.

"Whew," he says.

My legs shake when I stand.

"That's the dressing room." I point to a basement window. We creep closer. The curtain is pushed to one side so we can see the line of sinks and lockers. "The hall on the right leads to the kegs and the empties. I checked last night. The furnace is on the left. There could be other hidden rooms, though."

"She has to be down there," says Cricket. "Or up there," pointing to the row of small windows. There's no movement or light coming from any of them.

"Fuck it. I'm going in." I'm a dog with a bone, and no one can take it from me. "Better now, before the staff show up."

"Wait, Oreo—"

"Keep six."

I take the thin-tipped flathead screwdriver we just ripped

off from the hardware store down the street and tap it hard on the window pane. It cracks; lines ripple outward. One more tap. Glass falls into the basement. I reach in carefully and turn the lock. Then I slip the screwdriver under the wooden frame at the bottom and lift it up a notch. I raise the window smoothly. Cricket holds it up for me while I ease myself into the basement. I land on my feet. Cricket lowers the window and stays outside. I give him thumbs up.

I move through the shitty dressing room into the hallway. Stairs leading up to the club are in front of me. On the right is the beer and empties room. On the left is a padlocked door with a sign: "Keep Out. Furnace."

Fuck you, I think.

The tiny screwdriver fits inside the lower part of the keyhole. Then I take the paperclip from my back pocket. I'd already straightened it out using needle-nose pliers at the hardware store, then bent the end ninety degrees, making a little hook. I slip the modified paperclip into the top of the keyhole. It's hard to see, but you usually don't get to look at much when you're picking. It's all in the feel, in the clicks you hear, the subtle difference in pressure as you pick with the paperclip and torque with the driver. My hands make the tools tango; I keep an even pressure on the bottom with the screwdriver and, at the same time, tap and push the individual pins up and out of the way with the pick, clearing the cylinder one pin set at a time. I work it lightly at first, testing the spring of the internal pins and pushing each set out of the way with a click. Padlocks usually have three or four sets. This one has three, by the feel of things. It takes a couple of minutes but finally, the thing pops.

I open the door. The smell of dead mice fills my nose. I leave the lock hanging in the metal clasp and step forward. It's darker in this room. *Should've grabbed a flashlight.* I walk with one hand out front, one to the side, using the clammy wall as a guide. My eyes gradually adjust. I see a furnace, big and squat. Large pipes run to and from it. The floor and walls are cold cement. There's a dirty window on the far wall—that's the main street out front. Feet and legs walk past every now and then, making sounds that stop me from inching forward, clipping steps getting louder, smaller feet pattering quickly. Voices boom and fade. There is a scrape, a creak, closer and louder than the outside noises. I freeze. I hold my breath, waiting to hear more. *Nothing.*

In front of me, one panel of wall is darker than the rest. I move toward it. It's a steel door, colder than the cement walls. I run my fingertips back and forth across it. There's a heavy bolt, which I draw back and set in place. I find the knob, the raised circle of a deadbolt keyhole.

Can I do this?

There's a soft thud behind me. *Clink.* I drop the screwdriver. *Fuck.* I grip the paperclip tightly between the fingers of my left hand. I bend down and feel the gritty floor with the other. Stuff sticks to my fingers. Something brushes them—a centipede? I feel the whoosh of many legs, like Ferret's eyelashes on my cheek. The thing stretches along the flesh of my hand. I fling it away in the dark. I jump and my shoe hits the damn screwdriver.

Got it.

Sweat trickles down my back. My pits are wet. I exhale, nice and slow. I feel this new lock and imagine how it looks;

the outer circle, the inner small circle with the keyhole and, hidden inside, the cylinder with the pin sets I need to tap into place. Slipping the screwdriver tip into the bottom of the keyhole is pretty easy. I gently twist the screwdriver until I feel that whole inner circle move to the right; I hold it there. Fitting the paperclip in neatly above it is harder. I feel it catch inside—this time, I rake across the pin sets, push the paperclip in and out to scramble them. Then I start with the pin set farthest back from the opening. There's five pin sets in this deadbolt and it takes several minutes for me to tap each one out of the way. Finally, the lock springs. The heavy door swings open toward me. *I'm fucking Houdini Helen Keller. I rock!* I can't wait to brag off on this stunt.

It smells worse in here, worse than the rest of the basement: like urine and sweat and stale air, like shit. Like other bad things. I cover my mouth and nose with my sleeve. I step inside. It's a small room without windows. Three lit bulbs hang from the cobwebby ceiling. There's an old wooden staircase on the far side. The cement floor slopes down in the middle toward one large drain. It's a cell, like an animal's pen. There's an old sink with a drippy faucet, a basin and sponge, a raggedy towel. I walk into the centre of the awful room and that's when I see them.

Ferret's coloured dreads, cut off and piled by the floor drain.

"What the—" I pick one up, touch it softly with my finger. Blue with a touch of purple, greenish on the ends where the colour washed out. *They're hers, alright.*

Behind me the door creaks. I look up in time to see him

grin. It's the King looking strange without his uniform. Hair greased as usual, but like someone's dad might look, pants belted, a clean shirt buttoned right up.

"Well, looky who's here," he says in his full voice. "My newest dancer. Carly told me all about you. How's your face?"

In a flash it comes back to me—my talk with Carly, my disappeared clothes, the cab driver who brought me right to my door, as she insisted.

"I can always count on you kids to make my job easier. You're stupid, predictable, you rat each other out. And you believe anything a junkie whore tells you." The King's mean laugh fills the cellar.

I'm a cement pillar. There's his voice and white noise, static all around me.

The King is so tall he has to duck to avoid hitting his head on the rafters when he steps closer. He's so wide he blocks the whole door, frame to frame. "Your skinny bitch is gone. But have I got a surprise for you." He slams the heavy door shut.

Ledge

I didn't set out to kill no one. Probably don't look that way. But I can't even squash a spider. Hardly swat a fly, myself. I never could. Ask Eddie, he'll tell you.

Standing in the slaughterhouse and watching that dirty cop, the man they call the King, come after her like that, it was hard. Made me think of all the people who had come after me, all the times they had their way and I went along with it, you know. I guess you'd say I snapped. Just seemed natural to do something, make it stop.

Anyways, truth is I really had nothing left to lose.

I went back to the slaughterhouse from habit, from when I'd visit Eddie on break and bring over his supper. We used to sit on the brick ledge that jutted out from the side of the building, me watching him eat, then we'd smoke a cigarette, and then we'd have a nice long goodbye kiss, and he'd go back to work. He'd go, "Ray-Ray, that was one kick-ass sandwich." And I'd feel good about it. Fried tofu and mayonnaise or cheese slices and mustard or peanut butter with lots of drippy strawberry jam, just the way Eddie liked.

With Eddie in jail now and Ferret disappeared, I was pretty much on my own. I'd still go over to sit on the ledge when I was fucked up or scared and had nowhere else to be. Ever since the squat next door got raided, ever since the shooting, the slaughterhouse had run on reduced hours due to all the traffic coming round: cops, politicians, the news. There'd been layoffs and talk of closing the place for good. Sometimes there'd be guys on short shift; some I recognized, some I didn't. Other times it'd be empty. Either way, I'd sit in our old spot. If no one else was around, I'd talk to Eddie out loud, as if he was right there with me and not locked up in the Don waiting on remand. Funny, I hardly stuttered then, neither.

I'd say, "Eddie, you'll be out soon. You'll be back with me, like you should. We'll find a new place, you'll get a new job. We'll start over."

Of course he wasn't there in person, so he didn't answer.

Then I'd think about Big Fat Rat Catcher, how he escaped out of that box and took off like a furry shot into the street, and that'd shut me right up for a while. I couldn't do anything right without Eddie, not even look after his damn cat. If I could at least find Fat Ratty, running wild in some alley, then maybe our luck might change. That's what I'd think.

Sometimes it was hard to picture Eddie the way he used to look. Instead, I'd see him in that terrible orange jail jumpsuit they wear. Him on the other side of the visitors' glass holding that phone, trying not to look me in the eye. I'd shake it right outta my head and remember further back, before things went really rotten, to our hometown and the trailer park, our shitty school. Eddie shooting spitballs off the end of his ruler, sticking gum in girls' hair. Him goofing off and getting yelled at, getting kicked down to the office or suspended. He'd dribble imaginary basketballs down the hallway; shoot them at teachers' heads, score! Drill the edge of his desk with two pencils like a black-metal drummer. Eddie always got on other people's nerves, half on purpose, half accidental. Loud and rough, I knew he was meant for me, long before he ever did.

Sitting on the slaughterhouse ledge, I'd smoke a joint and remember how weed chilled Eddie out. He'd sit still longer, talk slower, bullshit about what we might do—start a band, steal a car, run away. He'd talk about us having money and luck and people giving a shit.

Sometimes I'd even believe him.

Getting high with Eddie back in our school days also meant sometimes we'd make out. Which was magic, those first few times, but then he'd avoid me for days. He'd even join in when the jocks made fun of me. *W-w-what's w-wrong, R-Ray R-Ray?* Once he punched me in the face, right after he came. *Fucking faggot.* His hate for this thing that flared up between us, making our dicks hard—it nearly killed us both. He'd go on rampages, smashing store windows, shitting in front of the mayor's office, stealing stuff. Social workers would swoop in and give him a stint in some boys' home or in juvie, depending.

Those were awful times for me—lonely, dead-end days. I had no friends. I lived with my aunt. Her boyfriend drove a big rig and was on the road most of the time, thank Christ. Otherwise he'd sit in the trailer drinking Pabst Blue Ribbon, eating BBQ chips, and staring at my cousin Lena's tits. Lena was white blonde, like me, but older. She wanted to be a tattoo artist and get the hell out of that stupid town. She practiced on squash from our pathetic roadside garden, which pissed off my aunt, since no one would pay for them covered in blue demons with bony wings and bare-breasted women, horns sprouting from their foreheads. Once Lena tattooed her own knuckles with a math compass and had to be taken to Emergency when they got so infected she couldn't hold a pencil for all the green pus. My aunt drove us in a rainstorm, me riding shotgun, half hanging out the window, reaching to clean the windshield with a rag since her wipers were broke, and Lena stuck between us, cursing and straddling the gear shift.

Lena was the first person who really gave Eddie the time of day, other than me. After the whole knuckle incident, no one else would let her practice. When he got sprung from Goderich one summer, he hung around our place pretty much every day, and she went to work on him. He didn't care what she did or where she did it, just wanted his whole body covered eventually. "Be a giant jigsaw puzzle," he'd said.

He'd haul off his shirt, his jeans, and lay down. His dark skin was nice, scarred, but he was lean, not filled out yet. Just peeking at him would get me heated up. Lena would tie back her long pale hair and scratch away at his skin, leaving ink blobs and outlines, scabs to heal. I wondered if she was *into* him the way I was, and if they'd start messing around too. I wondered if I would die, or just wither. I couldn't stand having him around all the time and not being *with* him. I'd lie in the tobacco fields and imagine myself disintegrating, all my dust blowing away, bit by bit. I didn't know what would happen to me if I didn't leave that town.

"If I was a girl, this would be normal," I'd said to him

one night after doing it on his ma's roof. "You wouldn't hate on me the way you do."

"If you was a girl, I'd fuck you and be done with it. I wouldn't give a shit about you." Then he looked me in the eye and asked if it was true. *Was I really going to pack a bag and leave him?*

"Not you. I'm leaving everything." I was crying and not bothering to hide it, for once.

That's when he kissed me for the first time. Not hard, not fighting or wanting something off me. Just him kissing me as I'd imagined he might all those years, minus my snotty nose.

"Do what you gotta, man," he said.

I hiccupped loudly. My lips burned.

"Think I'll go with you, though."

And he kissed me again, just the same way. It was the start of something totally new between us, and nothing can ever take that away. Not the King, not the Don fucking Jail, not some shit-talking lawyer. And not the men who take turns with me now and throw down some coin.

Lena read our cards before we left. She wanted to have the tarot as a back up in case tattooing didn't work out, and she was getting pretty good. Eddie shuffled the deck. He picked cards and lay them on the back porch table. She flipped them over, one by one. Grinning demons, nude goddesses smirked at us. In the centre was the Hanged Man, a terrifying skeleton in a noose. My stomach lurched.

"Something's ending," she said quickly. "Well, you're moving, so that makes sense. Don't fret, it ain't all bad."

He said, "I guess not."

"You got a lot of water coming your way," she said, pointing to some whirling blue-black cards. "Cups. That's emotion, you know." She frowned.

Later my aunt said, "That boy was born under a bad sign. Don't need to read tea leaves to see that plain as day."

Which is kind of true. Eddie never did have any luck at all, other than me. And what good was I?

So you see. That night, sitting outside, smoking my lonely joint, I heard some awful crying. I followed the sounds into the slaughterhouse through the open side door, right to the killing room. It was dark in there, pretty empty. Just the silver ceiling tracks with their chains hanging down, their shining hooks on the ends. There she was, like a ghost in the shadows—long socks, shorts, and some kind of skirt glowing white in the back corner, a darker shape moving around her. I flicked on the big overhead lights. It was the King, his black hair greased into a pompadour like usual. He blinked against the bright light. He wasn't wearing his uniform and that made him seem softer than usual, older, maybe. He could have been any of the men cruising us on the corner. And behind him, half under him, it was Ferret, alright. Whatever was left of her. When I seen him crouched over her like that, I had to do something.

"You better run, cuz you're next," he yelled, still holding her down.

I wasn't even scared. He'd already taken everything from me.

I just punched the red "safety," the way Eddie always

did after his break, and pulled the long, black lever, hard as I could. Those machines start up pretty quick. One huge hanging chain on a pulley moved down its ceiling track, swinging close behind him. The hook at the end gleamed. He didn't see it coming, he was staring me down from across the room. The chain kept moving forward and the hook swung heavily back again. It struck him. He looked surprised. Ferret grabbed onto the King's sweater sleeve to pull herself up. He shook his arm violently but she clung to it; she was like a rag doll flopping. I ramped up the speed and the chain jerked again, smacking into his broad back. Ferret slammed against his chest with her whole weight then slid to the ground. The King stumbled backward onto the hook. His mouth dropped open. It must have pierced into his back. Air whooshed out of him with a funny sound. I pulled another lever; the machinery almost ground to a halt, then shook back to high hear. The chain and the hook with the King attached to it began shortening as it retracted toward the ceiling. The hook lifted him right up. His body dangled, legs kicking like a giant puppet. Then there was another gear grinding, a jolt, and his weight shifted. He screamed when that big hook pierced all the way through, his middle settling around it. His hands clutched for the hook tip, and I'll never forget his ugly face opening up like that, his throat screaming itself raw with the pain.

The chain jerked again, bringing the King down the track, closer to me. My hand was still on the lever. I remember the feel of it frozen there. My legs were slow and woozy like syrup. I thought I might puke.

"Let me down, you fucking cunt."

Eddie would laugh at that. *Couldn't be nice to save his own life.* The King was a couple feet away. Blood pumped steadily out of him, soaking the front of his clothes, pouring over his hands, dripping onto the already stained cement floor. I looked into his red eyes, his veiny face, his Elvis hair, and I wasn't sorry. Not one bit.

Normally the pigs would be stunned by this point, from electroshock or a bolt pistol to the back of the head. They'd be hanging upside down by the back legs, and this was when Eddie would do his thing, knifing the carotid artery and the jugular vein, bleeding them to death.

I could've left him there.

Meanwhile, Ferret had got up. I squinted. She looked different. Her dreads were all cut off. She was wearing some crazy get-up, all skin and bones. She'd been missing for quite a while already. Nobody knew what happened after the King came and took her from my old place. Mine and Eddie's. After Darcy ratted us out. Kids put bets that we'd never see her again. But here she was. Ferret was hurt bad. She was bruised and swollen in the face, dead in the eyes. She limped carefully around the machinery. She avoided the King flailing. She seen him up there, couldn't believe it probably.

She stood beside me. We looked up at him, and he swore. He squirmed and kicked and screamed. I was thinking how could we try and get him to admit what he'd done—killed Digit and framed Eddie for murder. Who knows what else?

"You fucking diseased shits, let me down."

Ferret and I looked at each other. We looked back at the King. He was pretty pale. He was losing a lot of blood.

"If you sp-spring Eddie yu-yu-you can live."

His eyes lost focus for a sec. Then he stared hard at me. "Screw you, faggot."

I gulped.

"I fucked your gold star butch," he growled at Ferret. "She was even tighter than you."

I felt her body tense, saw her hands ball into fists.

"No." Ferret said this loudly. "*No*," she shouted. Her body shook. She repeated that word, screaming and spitting with a hate that scared me.

Then Ferret reached behind me and took a long rubber apron off Eddie's old shelf. She draped it over herself the way he used to. It was too big for her and dragged on the floor. She tied it loose around her small waist, then picked up a knife, just like the one Eddie used every day on shift. It was big for her, too. She wasn't used to hauling it around the way he was. She had to use both hands just to lift it.

The King muttered some more. Told us what he'd do when he got down from there. What he'd do to us, to all of us.

Ferret goes, "Shut up, Earl."

That must have been his real name, I guess. I still couldn't move. I couldn't say a word. I just watched. It took a long time. We'd all seen Eddie at work. Mostly you'd wish you hadn't. Those aren't pictures you can erase from your mind easy. Ferret had the general idea but was not used to doing this sort of thing, obviously. Even after his head came off—not cleanly, either, that took a lot of work—the rest of him kicked and twitched. Blood sprayed, it hit us in the face, it coated the walls. It was gruesome. The smell was awful. Let's just say she finally finished him off and dumped him where the rest of the meat was kept, in the freezing cold storage, where it got boxed and sent out to be eaten. I might have helped carrying stuff, I don't even remember.

After all that, we hosed down the floor, the walls, the hooks, the apron. The slippery knife. Our shoes. We didn't know what to do about his clothes, his belt, but there was a separate place for all the terrible pig parts nobody could sell—and that's where we dumped them in the end. We put everything else back where it belonged. And then we went outside to sit on the ledge.

We sat there a long time not talking. We'd have smoked, but we didn't have any. Our feet matched up, side by side, leaving prints in the soft ground. I was looking down at them and at the arc of cigarette butts flicked all around. This ledge was where all the men used to take their break, Eddie included. There were hundreds of pinched filters stubbed out in the ground. Each one marked a long shift, ten to twelve hours cut up into manageable parts, just like the meat inside.

"W-we make a good p-p-pair," I said at last.

That's when she started to cry, and me, too.

"None of this was supposed to happen," she sobbed.

"C-course n-not." I was supposed to be with my Eddie, Ferret with Oreo. All of us, all us reject kids, should've been left alone to make our own way in this fucked-up world, the best we could.

I leaned closer to Ferret. Her shoulder pressed against me. Her hands were messed up, splintered something bad. I held them gently. There was blood around her nails still.

My own fingers were filthy, the skin chewed, hangnails angry red.

It was that special bold sky time, just before dawn. Dark blues burst out of black, clouds of colour brooding around the city. I tried not to look at the Factory anymore, cop tape flapping in the breeze, orange construction flags posted here and there. The city was going to demolish it. They'd taken the roof off with a wrecking ball already. It was so wrong. Like a half-dead thing, still crawling. The slaughterhouse would be closed for good, too. The soil would be treated, and then they'd start building. A drawing of the condos stood at the end of the gravel road, next to the little information office the company put up the other day.

If you bought in now, you could save a bundle off your new luxury home.

Bush

"So now you're up here hanging with the Rezbians. How's that for ya?" Phoebe cracks open a Blue Light for Ferret. Before Ferret can answer, Phoebe says, "Sorry about the beer. Doc says I got to watch my calories. I says, 'You want to love a little less of *all this*?' and he goes, 'That's what I'm telling ya, Phoebe Marie. You got to shave a few pounds off your lovely behind.'" Phoebe chuckles, and the mountain that is her, glorious her, shakes in her Moose FM T-shirt. Her laugh turns to a cough that sounds like an outboard motor turning over in her big bosom.

"It's good to see you, Phoebes," I say. Phoebe is older and heavier and more tired since I left two years ago. Her feet bother her so much she's using a cane now. But her smile still lights up the room and her hugs, those warm, strong arms of hers, still squeeze the badness right out of me. I've got a goofy smile plastered on my face in spite of the shit we've waded through just to be here, now.

Ferret sips her beer. I squeeze her hand. I can tell by her worried face that she doesn't know what to make of things. She keeps looking sideways to the front door where our backpacks sit in a mud-sprayed lump, all we have left on this earth.

Phoebe runs a hand through her greying hair. "Now don't be polite, Oreo; be yourself. Sure yous aren't hungry?"

Ferret shakes her head. Food smells fill the little house, but there is nothing vegan about them. I nudge her with my pointy chin. She doesn't budge. It's been over a day since we ate anything other than extra-strength Wake-Ups. My stomach is sour and tight from them, and can't take food yet. The pills kept us up for the whole trek north from Toronto. Hitching can be fun, but not when you're tired and beat up and broken-hearted, not with every cop in the province hunting your ass. You got to be alert, and then some.

Afternoon sun pours in the big window of Phoebe's front room, onto the back of my head, making me dozy. Chemicals twitch in random parts of my body, but the tension I've been carrying in my shoulders, my back, starts to unwind. My feet throb now that I've kicked off my rank boots. Me and Ferret are wedged between a dozen hand-made cushions on Phoebe's dog couch, covered in the bristly fur of her old mutt, Jack Daniels. Jack Daniels is lying on the front porch, keeping six.

For sure I thought we'd never make it.

Phoebe sits across from us in her favourite chair, an old La-Z Boy recliner that faces the big window so she can see everyone going up and down the main paved road that cuts our land in half. She knows when the mail is in, when Andy's General Store has got the fresh meat delivery, and if Alan Fox is late to call the seven o'clock bingo.

"I know if the RCMP are coming almost before they do," she says. "Tribal Police get the heads up, and they'd call me first. I don't know what exactly happened to yous girls, but you're safe here."

I don't know what to say to her, where to start. I pick the

skin around a torn cuticle on my dirty fingers.

"I know what sent you running away from here, Oreo, and that was bad. Whatever chased you back must be way worse."

I nod. I stretch my arm around Ferret's shoulders, and say, "It is, Phoebe. It's messed up. Last thing I want is to get you in trouble, though."

"I figure I can handle my bad self just fine." Phoebe is not smiling, but her voice is. It's warm and rough and in charge. "This is your home, Oreo. Time you come back to it."

She gestures behind her, meaning my mom's house next door. I walked the long way around to Phoebe's bungalow porch, just so I wouldn't have to look at it.

"You okay?"

"Yeah," I say. "Just tired. Long haul, lots of stops."

It started out pretty good. We caught our first truck going north all the way to Owen Sound. We dumpstered bagels from behind an artsy café, and one of the cashiers gave us free coffee. She let us crash in the back corner until they locked the doors late that night. Then Ferret lay low while I panhandled, keeping one eye on news headlines to make sure there was no mention of us and the whole cop-killing thing back in Toronto. I was looking for a drive north and got pointed to a high school teacher—nice, kind of dorky. She promised to pick us up in front of the café at six a.m. and take us to the ferry docks in Tobermory, where we could cross over to the island first thing. She didn't mind giving us a lift at all. I wanted to stuff this act of kindness in my mouth and swallow it, to keep it safe. Instead, I crawled under a park bench with Ferret and nestled my face on the back of her neck, whispering the plan. The hard knot in my stomach loosened just thinking about going home, finally. By the time morning rolled around, of course, things had gone bad for us, as usual.

Doesn't matter, I tell myself. We got here anyways.

I try to forget it all—the drunk boys who found us in the park early that morning and had to be fought off. Someone called the cops. This scared off the assholes, but lost us our ride with the nice teacher. Frigging pigs skulked around uselessly, drinking coffee and shooting the shit for an hour, right in front of the bush we hid behind. Later, we took the first ride we could, even though we ended up going the long way, up 69 north to Sudbury where we sat for half a day at a truck stop, waiting for a ride without a hand-job clause in the fine print. Finally we caught a four-by-four with headbangers who raced to Espanola to pick up weed, smoked it, then drove way below the speed limit to the Island, crossing the swing bridge at Little Current at dawn. *What a shit show.*

I focus on the here and now—Phoebe and her small, familiar house. Ferret—skinny and bruised and scared, her pretty dreads cut off so she looks like a half-starved boy: seriously damaged goods but still alive, at least. Me—holding it together the best I can.

I realize that Phoebe's mouth has been moving and I have no idea what she's saying. She looks at me strangely and moves her mouth some more. "You all right, Oreo? Jeez, you've been gone some time, huh?"

"It's good to be back, Phoebe. Thanks." I kick my feet

up on the coffee table and try to smile, even though I feel wrung out and dry as an old rag.

"Comfortable?" Phoebe playfully swats my feet with her cane. "What kind of manners you learn down south?" Phoebe winks at Ferret. "White folks turned you into a savage, that's what." She laughs, a belly laugh with a thigh slap to go with it that makes me feel even more at home. "Yous going to the arena dance Friday?"

Ferret's fingers tighten their hold on my thigh. Her forehead creases deeply so I know the last thing she wants to do is go to the damn dance.

"We'll see," I say.

Phoebe says, "We don't get your punk bands up here. Dances are pretty much it. If you don't go, you might be bored before you know it."

"It's probably better if no one knows we're here," I say quickly. Sooner or later I'm going to have to tell Phoebe the real truth: that we're not just *in trouble*, as she put it, but seriously on the lam. Possibly even wanted for first-degree murder, for killing a city cop. Which would make her an accessory to the crime, and that doesn't sit right.

I stroke Ferret's almost bald head. Each stroke softens the lines in her forehead, lowers the lids of her eyes. If she were a cat, she'd maybe start to purr.

Phoebe raises an eyebrow. "How else you gonna get the gossip wheels spinning? I can only do so much damage on the Facebook." She points her cane to the computer in the corner.

"What?" My stomach churns.

"Sure enough. I updated my status: 'Long-lost Indian

warrior returns to the Rez, dragging her young wife.' What do you think? That'll get tongues wagging, eh?"

"Ha," I say, weakly. "You didn't use my name, did you?"

"Course not." Phoebe says to Ferret, "I bet you never got to hear any embarrassing stories about Oreo. Never had anyone to tell them, huh?"

"Uh, no," Ferret says quietly. Her eyes are huge right now, dark and shining.

"That's too bad. I'm the only one around who knows." She tries to say it lightly, but it's not. It's hard and sad and leaves an angry echo bouncing around the room. I guess I never thought much about how she felt, being left alone up here with the memories, with all our ghosts.

I walk to the front door and look out the window, press my forehead against the glass. No one is driving, no one is walking. There's just the main road with tall grass on either side. There are houses at intervals all the way down, as far as you can see. As a kid, it was great. You could run wild, play where you wanted. But at twelve, thirteen, it was boring and claustrophobic. I hated how you knew everything about everyone else, and they knew everything about you, too. I'd watch MuchMusic, wear tons of eyeliner, and dream about moving south to start a band, dream about meeting lots of other gays and eventually getting a girlfriend. Once Aunt Tam said, "So go there. Go find out like everyone else that the city is a burial ground, nothing but a place to go and die alone."

A sudden lump sits in my throat like a clogged drain. Of course I didn't listen to Tam, who probably knew a thing or two about living rough in the city. Who might be doing more of the same right now, wherever she is, out west. Summers were fun at first—meeting other punks and partying, hooking up with girls. In the city, nobody gave a shit what we did, as long as we didn't do it on or near their property. Later, it was more work. Fighting for a place to sleep, for food, to not get raped or fucked with, running from cops and thugs and jocks. Always fighting, always running. That gets harder to take.

"Oreo, go get my glasses from the bedroom," says Phoebe brightly. "Now Ferret," she says, "did Oreo ever tell you how she got her name?"

I groan.

Ferret kisses my cheek. She says in a sing-song voice, "She's dry and crusty on the outside and gooey sweet inside?"

"That's right. Now what you don't know about Oreo is ..."

Phoebe's kitchen is smaller than I remember. The little gas stove is busy as ever. There's the culprit, a large pot simmering on the back burner. I lift the hot lid. *Moose stew.* The smell hits me hard. One thing, I haven't been around cooked meat in a long time, especially not wild game. But mostly those smells remind me of my mom and the aunties. They'd have it bubbling, be baking scones or bannock, sometimes have wild rice in another small pot. Good times happened in this kitchen and in ours. Fights got worked out, jokes told over and over again, marriages were arranged, repaired, and dissolved around these Formica tables with Phoebe and my mom, with my aunties holding court, the swag lamps collecting all of our secrets in their dusty bulbs.

Phoebe's voice fills the small house as I walk through it, touching stuff, noticing all her special things crammed into every imaginable space, including her Red Rose Tea company figurine collectibles. Even if I can't hear exactly what she's saying, there's the ebb and flow of her throaty laugh, the rumble of her imitating someone; there's the timid murmur of Ferret answering a question.

Phoebe's bedroom smells like Vicks VapoRub and sweet-grass. Her dresser is cluttered with photographs, some new ones of people I don't even know—like her life kept going after the accident. Right in the centre, though, there used to be a big, framed picture of them all: Phoebe and Aunt Sue front and centre, Aunt Tam, my mom, and even Jack Daniels. In Toronto, whenever I thought about my family, I'd remember this blown-up photo of them laughing together. But it's not here. For some reason that makes me mad. I can almost remember holding the camera, my chubby kid fingers lining up the zoom box on the bunch of them, and clicking the button. Sometimes I just *think* I remember it because I've heard the story so many times—that I grabbed Tam's camera and hollered while they horsed around on Phoebe's front porch. "Nobody move a muscle!"

Other than the photos and piles of loose change on the dresser, there are a bunch of pill bottles. I pick them up and shake them, but I don't know what the long words mean, other than Oxycontin and the Perc family—Cet and Dan—which would be great for making quick cash on the street. Great for blanking out, for coping. I set the bottles back down. Phoebe's got the diabetes. She's got heartache, too, and no matter how many pills her young doctor gives her, they can't cure that.

Phoebe's glasses are nowhere to be found. I walk back to the kitchen, check the ledge behind the old yellow curtains that hang in the window above the sink. There's her same table with the three and a half chairs around it, the broken one being the thing that saved Aunt Sue from an enraged black bear that came up onto the front porch one spring, years ago. Auntie Sue, her lover, had moved in by then. My mom, Tam, and I were at our place next door having supper when we heard Sue scream. My mom came out with the rifle but never had to use it, since Phoebe was waving the kitchen chair in the muzzle of this huge animal up on its hind legs, roaring into Sue's terrified face.

"Ith Phoebe a thuperhero?" Phoebe exaggerates my little-kid high-octave voice.

"*Aaniin*, I'm right here," I call into the front room. "I can hear what you're saying, you know."

Ferret giggles when I peek around the corner.

"Shush, I'm telling my story," Phoebe says. "Where's my glasses?"

"I have no idea."

"Oh shit, they're around my neck." Phoebe pulls the silver chain she's wearing and out from the neck of her T-shirt comes a pair of eyeglasses. "And so you see, Ferret, from the time Oreo was a wee toothless critter, she's always known the truth—that I have magical powers and can talk to the bears. I said to that sonuvabitch, 'You get the hell away from my woman! If anyone's eating her tonight, it's me!'"

Ferret laughs for real, and so do I, even though I've

heard that story a hundred times.

"We're Bear Clan. Oreo ever tell you that?"

"Yes," she says. "It's on her tattoo."

"First thing I got inked when I was in Toronto. So I wouldn't forget where I came from." I stretch the neck of my T-shirt over my shoulder to show Phoebe.

Phoebe puts on her glasses and blinks a few times while she adjusts to the prescription lenses. She shakes her cane toward me and says, "Oreo, Hon, that's real nice. But you don't need a tattoo to know who you are. That runs all through you, day and night, in your blood. No one can take it away from you, not if you don't let them."

Phoebe leans forward and grunts as she puts her weight onto the cane and slowly stands up. She looks real tired. "I was gonna get out the big book, but that can wait." She waves at a stack of phonebooks and newspapers in one corner, but I know she means *our* big book, the family album, which is probably on the bottom of that pile. If just *thinking* about one photo can mess me up, I can't imagine flipping through a lifetime.

"Make yourselves at home while I have a rest. Oreo, if you want to go next door, the key is in my cupboard like always." Phoebe shuffles toward the kitchen. Eventually I hear the springs of her bed creak when she sits on the mattress.

Ferret exhales loudly and slumps back onto the couch. "What should we do, Oreo?"

But I'm already tapping on the keyboard, scrolling down the computer screen to check exactly what Phoebe posted. I delete her status update. No one has commented on it yet.

Ferret rocks back and forth on the couch. Her breathing is shallow. She's working up from serious anxiety toward a full-on panic attack. Not pretty.

The thing about Ferret, she's not hard—she's tough enough, she's got heart and she's wily—but she's got no meanness whatsoever. Ray-Ray even less. That boy is a Popsicle. So wasting that rapist, that psycho cop, it's weighing heavy on them both.

"Ferret, listen to me."

I wait for her to slow her breathing a bit and to stop rocking frenetically.

"First, I want to find out who knows we're here." It wouldn't take much. A do-gooder social worker, a kid with a grudge, even a friend who said something to the wrong person could fuck us up.

"Who even knows where you're from?"

Digit, but he's dead.

"Cricket knows I'm Native, but he never remembers anything else. He says it's too complicated."

"Ray-Ray actually listens to people." Ferret exhales slowly.

"Yeah, I'm not worried about Ray-Ray anymore. I even told him to come up here if he needs a place."

"What about the drop-in worker, Pamela?"

I press my fists against my closed eyes. *Pamela.* I remember hearing her talk about coming to Wiky for the annual powwow. And how proud I was to tell her that I was *from* here, that my family *came* from these parts, and how she'd never forget that, seeing as she'd been here. "Shit."

"She'll talk, all right."

My foot taps restlessly while I keep surfing. "I told Pamela I hadn't been here in years and might never come back."

"Really?"

"Yeah. I thought I wouldn't. Not 'til all that shit went down and you were gone. All I wanted was to bring you here so we could be safe." My voice cracks.

Ferret climbs onto my lap and kisses my ear, my throat. She squishes her face against mine. "We'll never be safe, will we?"

"Actually, we could never be safer, now that *he's* dead." My voice wavers. Ferret told me everything that happened, everything the King did. And what he was planning to do, if she hadn't escaped. Every time I think about it, I choke back vomit. I have to breathe deeply and keep moving, so the hate doesn't stop up my veins and cripple me forever.

On the CBC website is a photo of the King, "a brave law officer, a hero gone missing." *Not dead, at least.* Beside the article are the words, in a large bold font, Police Search for Persons of Interest. It's a photo of Ferret and me in front of the Factory squat, our arms around each other, smiling defiantly into the camera.

"Shit." I bite my bottom lip.

"Anyone with information is asked to contact police. Crime Stoppers offers up to $2,000 for anonymous tips leading to the capture and arrest of wanted criminals," reads Ferret out loud. "That's a lot of money."

Our friends, our neighbours, they all hate being poor. But luckily for us, I think they hate cops more.

"Does that mean they don't know what happened to him yet?" Ferret looks sick.

We can't tear our eyes away from that picture of the King. I hate his stupid face, his leering mouth, and his Elvis hair. I can smell the pomade, his boozy, tainted breath. I still feel his fists pounding me, his hands choking me, his belt buckle scraping my soft skin, the metal parts slapping onto the hard floor.

"Oreo?"

The room spins. Ferret shakes my shoulders gently. I open my eyes wide.

"So they haven't found any ... parts yet." Ferret looks wigged out.

"Babe," I say, trying to get my shit together. The last thing Ferret needs now is to have to take care of me. "They might never find out. So you got to figure out how to carry this thing. I wish it was me that did it; you have no idea how much. It wouldn't wreck me the way it might you—if you let it."

In fact, sometimes all I can think about is how much I wish *my* hands had pulled the lever that severed his limbs and let him bleed out, that *I* had cut his dead body down from the slaughterhouse chains myself. Maybe then I would believe he was truly gone, and his bloated face would stop jumping out at me from shadows, like in some cheesy horror movie. Maybe then I could purge this poison from me, this thing that is shrinking me from the inside out.

Ferret sits up taller. "You're right. Maybe they never will find out the truth." She clenches her jaw. "Lots of people knew what he was into. Think of all those women he trafficked. Anyone could have wanted revenge. Lots of people wanted him dead."

I nod.

I scroll down slowly, so the picture of him gradually disappears. Ferret slumps against me when the last of him is gone. Hot tears roll down her face, trickle onto my skin. They run down my neck, into my T-shirt. Saliva pools in her mouth and drips out when she cries louder. Her shoulders shake. She gasps, and there is another sound, an ugly hacking sound. It is me crying, too, which is a total shock.

"I'm s-sick from all the things he did to me," I say. Sick of not owning my girl body, my boy body. Sick with his DNA all over me, inside me. "Nothing belongs to me anymore."

Ferret knows what I am trying to say. She smoothes my long hair, re-braids it, and pets my heaving shoulders. She says, "We are still alive, Oreo, you and me. That pig is dead, and he deserved it. And it almost was a different end to this story. So now we got to keep moving, we got to keep living, and make the most of it, whatever happens next."

I wipe my face and blow my nose.

Ferret is pulling it together, but this is my land. I need to step up. An image of our summer camp comes to me, though I haven't been there since I was a kid, foraging for berries and roots and edible plants, fishing in the cold lake, sleeping under the stars and in rough shelters.

"Alright then, Ferret. We're going bush side."

While Ferret showers and changes her clothes, I take Phoebe's key and go next door. Just looking at the neglected house makes my chest burn, my breath come fast and shallow. Peeling paint hangs in strips; the porch screen has been ripped open by an animal. The wooden steps creak under my feet. The key fits in the lock, turns, but the door sticks. I heave my shoulder against it once, twice. It scrapes open, and the musty smell explodes. Curtains are drawn on every window. I step inside, right through an elaborate spider web hanging in the dark. *Sorry, Grandmother.*

Bed sheets drape the furniture like Halloween ghosts. The front room feels damp; the rug is rotting. My mom's bedroom is bare—stripped bed, dresser cleared, nothing on the walls. The drawers and closet are empty except for her bush jacket, her work gloves, and boots, which I put in my knapsack. The room I shared with the aunties is a trip—half closed down and half preserved like some teenage museum. Band posters are still plastered around the room near my old bed. It's a punk shrine: Siouxie Sioux, Motörhead, Nina Hagen, Amebix. A couple of Sue's childhood toys—a dolly, a plastic piggy bank—perch on top of the dresser. Her adult life had been next door with Phoebe, so who knows what happened to all those things? Tam's stuff is packed in boxes, labelled with her name. Another stack of boxes glare at me, my name scrawled across them in black marker. *Phoebe had to deal with that, alone.*

The kitchen is the hardest part. I shut my eyes, but can still see their faces, hear them laughing, shouting, gossiping. The missing framed photo smiles into me from the middle of the round table. A close-up of Phoebe and Aunt Sue, slim and brown and laughing, their arms around each other, their hair loose and beautiful. They look like teenagers, like me and Ferret, but were probably into their twenties. My mom and Aunt Tam are in the background, also laughing. Tam is holding Jack Daniels—he's just a pup, his tongue lapping at her chin. They're on Phoebe's front porch, but the shot is crooked and the proportions are wonky; the big camera slipped in my hands and aimed at the sky above them, just higher than the porch roof. Looking at it now, the picture seems to have been a warning or some kind of prophecy. The focus is on the up and away, the sky, the place where spirits roam.

I find the rest of the things I need in the pantry and hall closet: matches, hunting knife, compass, our old tent, a sleeping bag, a medium-sized pot and pan. There are dry soup mixes, cans of beans, an opener. Each thing I wipe and pack reminds me of something else we'll need: rope, a small axe, duct tape. The Browning BPS Hunter is still there, all twenty-eight inches of its walnut finish, an extra loaded clip, and the gun-cleaning kit, too. I lift it and look down the sights. I aim out the back window at the nowhere road. I remember learning to shoot with my mom, the pull and release, the smell of a shot fired.

This is all the stuff we'll need while we wait it out into the fall. We'll leave at dawn, the best time to start a new plan, a new life. Phoebe will know where we're headed, no doubt about it. We have no place else to be and nowhere else to go. I figure we'll be okay as long as I can remember all those things my mom and the aunties taught me. Time is different when you're living with the land, different than in the city where you fight against it just to survive. Once we get there, we'll be in no rush, Ferret and me. We'll be in no rush at all.

Kristyn Dunnion is a self-professed "Lady punk warrior" and the author of the novels *Big Big Sky*, *Missing Matthew*, and *Mosh Pit* (all Red Deer Press). She studied English Literature and Theatre at McGill University and earned a Masters Degree in English at the University of Guelph. She performs creeptastic art as Miss Kitty Galore, and is also the bass player for dykemetal heartthrobs, Heavy Filth. She lives in Toronto.